CHANNEL FEAR

LISA RICHARDSON

A MESSAGE FROM CHICKEN HOUSE

There's a point in Lisa's chilling new horror classic when the characters feel lost, out of control, out of love . . . and out of chances. Will they recover from all that – or will the haunted house, the disappearances and the false hopes break their resolve? Honestly, how can I ever watch a ghost hunter channel again, when I've witnessed the unfolding terror of this story?! Brilliant!

BARRY CUNNINGHAM
Publisher
Chicken House

CHANNEL FEAR

LISA RICHARDSON

Chicken House

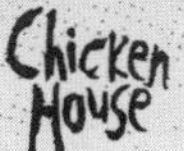

2 PALMER STREET, FROME,
SOMERSET BA11 1DS

First published in Great Britain in 2023
Chicken House
2 Palmer Street
Frome, Somerset BA11 1DS
United Kingdom
www.chickenhousebooks.com

Chicken House/Scholastic Ireland, 89E Lagan Road, Dublin Industrial Estate, Glasnevin, Dublin D11 HP5F, Republic of Ireland

Cover and interior design by Andrew Davis
Cover photograph by Lyn Randle/Trevillion Images
Typeset by Dorchester Typesetting Group Ltd
Printed in Great Britain by Clays, Elcograf S.p.A

1 3 5 7 9 10 8 6 4 2

British Library Cataloguing in Publication data available.

PB ISBN 978-1-915026-12-5
eISBN 978-1-915026-84-2

For Tom and Dexter

PROLOGUE

'HAVE YOU HIT that subscribe button yet? If not, why not?' Zach mock-scowls from my laptop screen, his blue eyes locking on to mine, even though he has no idea that I even exist. Or maybe he does . . . I like to think that he and Lucas have watched our channel. God knows I've put the link in their comments enough times.

> Hey Zach and Lucas, love your vids. Check out our ghost hunt channel here!
>
> Hey guys! We're a group of three friends with one of the hottest up-and-coming supernatural investigation channels. Check out our videos on the following link! A shout-out would be great!
>
> Hi there, we just want to say that we're massive fans. You're our biggest inspiration. Check out our paranormal exploration videos on Channel Fear!

'You need to make that right, right now, people, and hit us up. Come on, guys,' says a smiling Lucas. He good-naturedly jostles Zach for centre stage, while Zach continues to mock-scowl into the camera, a smile just tweaking at the edges of his perfect mouth. Unable to hold it in any longer, Zach breaks into a grin and swipes a long lock of dark-blonde hair from his eyes; hair that is just on the right side of unclean and mussy, and that makes him look like he's just too cool to care: like Kurt Cobain's even cuter younger brother.

Correction: made.

Made him look like he was too cool to care.

'What happened to you?' I say to myself, as I touch the screen, my fingertips brushing over the bright young faces of Zach and Lucas: two of the most successful paranormal vloggers in the UK, with just over three million subscribers.

'Those of you wonderful, wonderful people who follow our channel will know that we bring you the very best ghost hunt videos,' continues Zach.

'*The* best videos out there right now,' adds Lucas, his cheek piercings accentuating his dimples as he smiles.

'And that we're constantly striving to go . . .'

'. . . where no other ghost hunters dare.' Lucas narrows his dark eyes for effect as he holds a look to camera, face mock-stern.

'So, we wanted to share with you folks that we've got something a Little. Bit. Extra. Special. for our next series. A location so *haunted*,' Zach pauses to emphasize the word 'haunted', his beautiful eyes wide and stormy, 'that we – me and my man Lucas here – are truly terrified.'

'Yeah, we're not even joking, guys,' Lucas cuts in. 'There are some seriously creepy stories about this place.'

'And we're pretty psyched about filming there.'

'And scared, too, man.'

'Scared [bleep]-less.'

'But we're doing this for YOU lot, because we're dedicated to bringing you guys the best . . .'

'. . . the most terrifying . . .'

'. . . and the most epic videos on the internet.'

Zach mouths 'Subscribe' over Lucas's shoulder, while Lucas does a shoulder-rolling dance move to non-existing music.

'But to be serious for just a minute,' says Zach as he shifts closer to the camera, his messily made bed and laptop visible in the background. 'This place is dark, guys. From what we've uncovered, it's next level [bleep], and not to be messed with, OK?'

'Yeah, no joke, man,' says Lucas.

'And we know that some of you like to go to the places we visit and make your own videos.' My cheeks flush at this, as they have each and every time I've watched – studied – this last uploaded video. 'And we don't want any of you guys getting hurt or putting yourselves in danger of any kind. OK?'

'It's just not worth it, kids,' says Lucas in a children's TV presenter voice, while pointing at the camera with a black-painted fingernail; each finger is adorned with a wide silver ring. His usually gentle features are stern.

'We're doing this so you don't have to.'

'Because we're the professionals,' adds Lucas.

'And listen up, if you guys get us up to fifty thousand likes for this teaser video in the next twenty-four hours, before we go, we'll stay the WHOLE weekend at our secret location.'

'So just hit that "like" button, and we'll do it.'

'Anyway, that just about wraps it up for now. Make sure to keep an eye out for the new videos, coming your way, right here on the Zach and Lucas channel.'

'And remember to grab our merch. Link in the description,' says Lucas, pointing down with his two index fingers to where *LINK IN THE DESCRIPTION!* in bold white lettering has appeared along the bottom of the screen.

'And hit us up with a subscribe, dudes.'

'Do it. You know you want to.'

'And we will see you on the other side, people.'

'Peace out.'

I sigh as the screen fades and *The Next Chapter. Coming Soon!!!* flashes up in white gothic lettering against black, teasing a series that never came. Dramatic music starts playing over clips of Zach and Lucas from previous ghost hunts: a shot of them on location in a Scottish castle, gasping and freaking out as a candle flickers, seemingly in response to the question, 'Is there anyone in the room with us? Make yourself known.' Now in an abandoned rectory, Zach trying to find Lucas in the dark twisting corridors, while Lucas's panicked shouts can be heard from somewhere deeper in the building. Next, the two of them running through a dark forest, just the sound of their breath and the whoosh of their legs tearing through the undergrowth, flashes of trees and bushes lit by a torch as they flee from some unseen horror.

I pause the video, and I glance at the date it was uploaded: 29 October last year. Two days later, Zach Cooper and Lucas Yeun disappeared. They didn't tell anyone where they were going. The police search turned up nothing. Tips led to dead ends.

They just vanished off the face of the earth. Breaking my heart.

I had tickets to their meet-and-greet event that November. Now I'll never get to meet them. To meet *him*.

Zach.

I sigh, heavy and hard, and I shift my laptop off my crossed legs and on to the rumpled sheets beside me. Immediately, I miss the heat of it. A heat I didn't even register until it was gone. I flop back, my curls – pineappled on top of my head in a high, loose ponytail, ready for bed – making soft slaps as I land on a pile of printouts of haunted locations in the UK. Reference books, more printouts and notebooks are sprawled all over my bed. Using the printouts as a makeshift pillow, my sandblasted eyes find the map stuck to a corkboard on the wall next to my bed. Pins mark any legitimate-sounding sightings of Zach and Lucas, gleaned from comments on social media sites. String connects the sighting to any abandoned and 'haunted' locations in the vicinity.

I notice how dark it's got, with only my bedside lamp and the laptop screen lighting the room. It's silent. Early morning silent. I follow criss-crossing lines of red, which lead to the places we've already tried – lines that fade into the gloom.

This is hard.

Harder than I thought it would be.

I let my eyes stray around my bedroom to relax them. Other than the sprawling mess of research materials on my bed, the room is trademark neat: white walls, white furniture. Clean. Fresh. Everything in its place. A contrast to the chaotic but cosy craziness that awaits outside my bedroom door, and throughout the rest of the house. My weary eyes settle on my bedside table, where a paperback copy of *The Shining* lies beside a framed photo of me, Byron and Molly. It was taken at a party that Molly talked me and By into going to. Byron and I hate parties. And we hated that party. But I love that photo. Byron is in the middle, and Molly has one arm slung around his shoulder. The camera caught the exact moment after Byron made some dry remark in my ear. I forget what exactly, something about how lame the party was, and his body is leaning in towards me, and our faces are turned to each other and I'm laughing, my face lit up, head thrown back a little, eyes closed, and Byron is gazing right at me, his face all glowing grin. While Molly is face on, smiling her cute smile to the camera, almost as if she's posing in a different line-up altogether. Next to that is a snap of me and Byron, taken at Chessington World of Adventures. I'm six, he'd just turned seven. We're standing in front of the big wheel, and we both have huge beaming grins, faces sticky with candy floss, eyes wide and sparkling with sugar and wonder. I smile at the memory of that day: the free, innocent and uncomplicated fun of little kids. Before hormones got in the way.

I curl on to my side, so that I'm looking at the grainy image of Zach's back, caught at an angle in Lucas's camera as they run from something in the woods. I place my palm against the screen. Maybe they found a long-abandoned house so beautiful that they couldn't leave, and they started new lives there. And, when I find them, Zach's eyes will meet mine and he'll fall so in love with me that he'll ask me to stay, too.

'Where are you? Just let me know. Somehow. Anyhow. Give me a sign.'

After a beat, I sigh and click on to our channel. With its seventy-eight subscribers. Our latest video, *Hunting for Zach and Lucas: The Series. Overnight in Lonslow Castle. (GONE WRONG!)* has only 356 views. More than the twenty or thirty or so we used to get, before the *Hunting for Zach and Lucas* series. But still . . . not what I was hoping for when I came up with the idea. And the comments . . .

You suck.

Boooooooring!

Losers.

Yet another video of a bunch of idiots running around in the dark and getting freaked out over nothing. Grow up.

Have u got nothing better to do with ur time? This is morbid. They're missing people. Get a life.

What a surprise, they're not there! Again.

I ended the video with a promise that I'd do a lone vigil for one hour at the next location if the video gets a hundred likes. It has nineteen.

I sit up, push the curls that flop forwards from the pineapple out of my eyes and, cross-legged, take a deep, resolute breath.

'This *is* going to pay off,' I say out loud, just to give the words more power.

'I *will* find you.'

1

SHOVING MY BACKPACK into the boot of the car, I turn to find my Canon G7 X right up in my face.

'Jesus, Byron,' I say, using a hand, palm out in front of me, trying to get him to back up a bit, while I head round to the passenger side. 'Give me the camera, dude.'

'So, what makes you so sure this is the one?' he says a little provocatively, ignoring my request and following me too closely with the camera. He gets like this sometimes: metaphorically pulling my pigtails, to get my attention.

I stop, one arm leaning on the open passenger door. The metal is hot on my bare skin. 'Byron, just give—'

'No, come on, Iris,' he persists, as he comes round in front of me. 'What makes you think that this is the one, over the fifty wasted journeys—'

'It's not fifty. It's twelve. Stop exaggerating. Twelve locations,' I say, exasperated. I'm squinting into the sun.

I'm hot and sticky in my T-shirt and jeans, but it's the best outfit for ghost hunting. Shorts result in scraped shins and splinters and scratches.

'And to be fair, they weren't wasted journeys. Not really,' says Molly, from behind me, more because she's really into this ghost stuff than necessarily as a show of solidarity with me. 'We did get some really good stuff at Briarburn Manor,' she adds, as she tries to ram her sleeping bag and cooler in the remaining space in the boot. 'The orbs we caught on camera, remember?'

'Dust particles,' says Byron. The hint of a mischievous smile plays at the corner of his lips, as he keeps his eyes and the camera on me, enjoying both the debunk and annoying me.

'And the taps during the seance.'

'Wooden joists cooling down at night.'

'*Byron*,' Molly scolds him in her super-sweet way, which no one could ever feel chastised by. 'What about Lonslow Castle, eh? And that creepy voice we all heard.'

'We don't know what we heard,' says Byron, glancing at her briefly. 'The camera didn't pick it up, so we couldn't analyse it. And, anyway, that's not what we went for, was it, huh, Iris?'

I glance between Molly and Byron as they both stare at me, and I let out a sigh.

'So, why this one, Iris?'

'Because,' I begin, looking at Byron, rather than at the camera, right into his eyeliner-darkened eyes, 'I have a feeling.'

'A *feeling*?'

'Yes. A *feeling*.'

'Great. We're going to end up fodder for the trolls for the sake of a *feeling*.'

'OK. Look, this will be the last one, I promise,' I say, my hands clasped in front of me as if I'm praying, my eyes wide and imploring, a pretty-please smile on my lips, as though I'm afraid he's going to say, *That's it, I've had enough. I'm going home.*

'You said that last time.'

'I know,' I say, realizing that he's seen right through me. 'But I mean it this time. I promise. I *double* promise that if we don't find anything, we'll go back to the regular exploration videos. No more Zach and Lucas. Done. Over. It'll be just for us.'

'But you can't help yourself.'

'Byron . . .'

'Look, Iris, I don't—'

'This is the *One*,' I say, cutting him off, before he can say anything that I don't want to hear. It's like he got out of bed on the wrong side this morning. I mean, he can be a bit of a grump, which is sort of his thing and which he usually pulls off rather endearingly, but, come on. So, I smile sweetly in a way that I hope is utterly appealing, and add, 'Trust me, By. Hmm?'

I imagine Molly rolling her eyes behind me. Or maybe I'm just projecting.

Byron takes a deep breath in and lets it out.

When he doesn't speak, I say, 'Look, By, this is all

going to pay off. I promise. We're going to blow up the internet when we find out where Zach and Lucas went. You just need to believe in me.'

His eyes find mine: years of teasing and play-fights and crushes and secrets and promises and hopes and disappointments and wants and denials and comfort and laughter and awkwardness passing between us – a whole lot of history that Molly wasn't a party to and so couldn't possibly understand.

'Look, Iris, I wasn't going to say anything until we got back, but—'

'No. No no no,' I say, in anticipation of what's coming.

He sighs. 'I've decided this is going to be my last video. Like, completely.'

My heart doesn't so much sink as hit the floor, cracking like an egg. 'What? Byron. No. *Completely?* No. You can't . . . *Completely* completely?' I know he's been getting tired of the *Hunting for Zach and Lucas* series. He's uncomfortable with the increasingly negative comments. While all I see is that the views and subscriptions are also increasing. So the news doesn't come as a total shock, but I didn't expect him to quit *completely*. I'm thrown for a moment, the wind knocked out of me. 'I don't . . . I . . . Uh . . . Molly, tell him,' I say, turning to her.

She grimaces – she already knows. Something inside me clenches, knowing that he discussed it with her before me. 'I tried,' she says heavily, and she puts her hands up palms out, as if to say, *Been there, done that.* I know that she loves the explorations, but I can't help wondering if she'll leave too – I mean, it'll be a bit awkward just the two of us. Where will that leave me and the channel?

Where will it leave me and Byron?

Still in disbelief, I turn back to him. 'But you can't leave,' I say. 'I need you. Like totally and utterly need you. Dude. Don't leave me!'

I lean in and give his chin a playful squeeze, attempting to show that I'm only half serious; when, really, it's more like ninety per cent serious. OK, one hundred percent. I *do* need him. I hold him there, my eyes on his. Hoping he'll see through the act and just stay. But when Molly makes the subtlest, softest, politest throat-clearing sound from the back of the car, I'm suddenly self-conscious, and no longer sure how I'm supposed to act and whether this sort of thing is OK. I back up a bit, while Byron's cheeks flush a little and his eyes flick over my shoulder, offering Molly a sheepish smile.

Handing me the Canon, Byron says, 'Look, we'll talk about it when we get back.'

'So, there's room for discussion . . .'

He won't leave.

Will he?

Oh god. He can't.

Byron shakes his head, sighs and, breaking into a wry smile, he says, 'Just get in the bloody car, idiot.' And he boops me on the nose, like he does when he's trying to cheer me up.

'But . . .'

'Car.'

Leaving me to swallow down my frustration and disappointment, Byron strides round the front of the car on long, slender legs. He pauses to bend down and kiss Molly on the lips when she comes round to his side of the car. She's a little stiff, after #chingate, but Byron does this little nose to nose thing, which is a bit nauseating but which makes her laugh coyly. And they're OK again. I stand by the passenger side, pretending to do something on my camera, but, really, I'm battling with the *Why would I care? I don't think of him that way. I'm happy for him. For the both of them. Really, I am* thing that strikes me in such situations, and that causes my cheeks to flush. Molly catches my eye and offers me one of her brightest olive-branch smiles across the roof of the car, before climbing into the back seat, behind Byron. And we're OK. She knows we have to be.

I'm the Best Friend.

I've been around since, like, *forever*.

And I always will be.

He was mine first.

I slide into the passenger seat, the fabric hot beneath me. Giving up riding shotgun really smarted when those two started going out with each other. I was displaced. Demoted. No one likes that. But I suggested I take the passenger seat for this trip because it's easier for me to film both inside the car and out of the windscreen. Molly couldn't really argue – not that she ever does, as she's too sweet and worried about hurting people's feelings – without looking like a dick and turning it into a big deal. (If roles were reversed and it were me, I would argue. I don't care about looking like a dick if the outcome is worth it.)

Molly's a people person. I am not. She has a massive, selfless heart. While mine is a bit gristly and sinewy and takes a while, on a low heat, to get tender.

'A *feeling*,' muses Byron from beside me, as he slides the key into the ignition. 'A bloody wild goose chase, more like it,' he grumbles. His lips tighten as I catch his eye, as if he's trying not to smile.

'Byron, there is such a thing as a sixth sense,' says Molly, as she wedges herself between the seats, her elfin chin resting on his shoulder. Looking at him with her big, round eyes, she slides an arm through and gives him a one-armed hug. I grit my teeth. 'Sometimes people just know stuff.'

'It's called coincidence, Moll,' says Byron, glancing back at her. 'Things sometimes connect in unexpected ways,' he continues smugly. 'And most of the time, they do not.'

Molly shakes her head as she shifts back in her seat, but she's smiling, and I know she's thinking sweet, generous thoughts of *Let it go. Just let it go.*

'A *feeling* . . .' Byron mutters.

'By, you're getting boring,' I say. But then, to lighten the mood, and to show that I don't really think he's boring, I playfully pinch his side with my thumb and forefinger (a little harder than necessary as I'm still a little gutted about his announcement). He laughs, though he's trying not to, and flinches, and says, 'Oi!' and flashes me a playful warning look from beneath his dyed-green fringe. I giggle as he sticks his tongue out at me. 'None of that,' he says, feigning seriousness, before turning back to the wheel.

'You guys,' says Molly, mock-chiding us. She's smiling and doe-eyed, but I sense the underlying awkwardness.

Ugh, it's just so natural for me and By to play-fight and be all touchy-feely. We've grown up like that. I keep forgetting to modify my behaviour now that I have to share him with her.

Note to self: must be on best behaviour.

'I'm just pointing out that I'd rather have something a bit stronger than a feeling to go on. You know, like evidence. Facts. Figures,' continues Byron.

'Well, it's a strong feeling,' I offer tentatively.

Byron snorts with reluctant laughter. And he starts the engine.

2

'HEY GUYS!' I say, holding my Canon in front of me, using a mini tripod as a stick. The flip screen is up so that I can see myself while I record. 'Iris here – bringing you another great video. With the lovely Molly . . .' I angle the camera to shoot over my shoulder at Molly, who smiles and waves excitedly from the back seat.

'What's up, guys!' she says, looking so cute that I hate her.

I don't.

I do.

It's hard not to like Molly. And believe me, I have tried over the last four months, since she and Byron started going out with each other. It was just me and Byron doing the exploring before that. Molly jumped at the chance to get involved. My first thought was, *Oh, you don't trust me and By alone, huh*? But I couldn't have been more wrong. Molly is obsessed with the paranormal. She wants to be a parapsychologist. Totally into it.

'. . . and the even lovelier Byron,' I continue, now swinging the camera round to get Byron in shot as he drives. As I watch him, I can't help remembering his words. *This is going to be my last video. Like, completely.* And my stomach feels like it's crumpling into a tiny paper ball.

'Yo,' he says, flicking only the briefest glance at the camera. 'It's us idiots again,' he adds half-jokingly. 'Putting ourselves at risk to explore some freaky-arsed deserted building in the middle of no-flipping-where, so you don't have to.'

'Tell it how it is, Byron,' I say, pushing down my feelings and swinging the camera back on myself. Byron grins but keeps his eyes on the way ahead. 'Welcome, guys, to another *Hunting for Zach and Lucas* video.'

'We're on the road,' says Molly from over my shoulder, and I give a little *whoop!* and Byron adds a deadpan, 'Oh yeah!'

'So, as we hinted in the teaser trailer, which we uploaded for you guys before we left,' I continue to camera, 'we've uncovered a pretty creepy location. A location that we believe is where Zach and Lucas may have been heading when they disappeared last October.'

'This is the one,' says Molly.

'I like that positivity,' I say, turning the camera towards her. She does a peace sign and blows an air kiss.

'Yeah, Iris has a *feeling* this is the one,' says Byron

drily, without taking his eyes off the road, though he's smiling.

I turn the camera back on myself. 'So, By is giving me a bit of hard time over this. But when Byron and I started this series, we knew there'd have to be a bit of trial and error. That's why it's called *Hunting* for Zach and Lucas. I mean, the police can't even find them. And have you any idea how many abandoned locations there are in the UK? It's. A. Lot. So, it may take us a while, so what? We're still bringing you guys some great exploration vids, right?'

'Right,' adds Molly over my shoulder.

'Anyway,' I say, getting back on track, 'you may be wondering where we're going. *Where is this super-haunted location?* I hear you say. Well, we're currently heading . . .' I turn the camera so that it films the road out in front of us. It's pretty quiet, as we're a good few hours ahead of the rush-hour traffic. I turn the camera back on myself . . . 'to a place called Thornhanger House. It's just under a six-hour drive, depending on traffic and whether we stop on the way. And it's in the Middle. Of. No. Freaking. Where.'

'Literally in the middle of nowhere,' adds Byron. 'So, we need to get there before sundown. Or we'll probably never find the place. Oh god, imagine if we get held up and can't find the place in the dark.'

'It'll be fine, By,' says Molly, slipping a hand through the gap between the seats and massaging his left shoulder. 'We've got plenty of time. It's not going to be dark until about nine.'

'Anyway, a bit of history on where we going,' I continue, addressing the camera as we head down the stretch of motorway. 'Built in the early 1800s for Lord Thornhanger and his soon-to-be wife, Emma, who both tragically died in a fire in the ballroom, Thornhanger House became home to the Turner family in the late 1800s. According to local legend, Edward Turner was away on business when his wife, Charlotte Turner, died suddenly, so Edward's sister, Anne, was called in to look after his young daughter, Elizabeth. BUT. And it's a big BUT. Anne totally resented the fact that she had to uproot her life to look after her brother's kid, and she mistreated Elizabeth.'

'The bitch!' says Byron.

'We don't like Anne,' adds Molly.

'Nope, we don't like Anne at all. Especially as she used to lock Elizabeth in a cupboard to punish her over the smallest things. And it's while Elizabeth was locked in the cupboard that Anne had an accident and died in the woods on the Turners' estate. When Edward eventually returned home, he found not only Anne's body in the woods, but Elizabeth's body, too, still trapped in the cupboard. Nails torn to shreds from where she tried to claw her way out.'

'That's dark,' says Byron.

'It gets darker,' I say.

'It always does,' he says drily.

'So, after losing his wife and daughter, and his horrible sister, in such tragic circumstances, Edward took his own life, slitting his throat while staring into the mirror in his bedroom.'

'That's creepy,' says Byron.

'I know, right? And, even creepier, the actual mirror is supposed to still be there today,' I add.

'Oh man,' says Molly, excitedly, and I angle the camera to her. 'A haunted mirror.'

'You think a mirror can be haunted?' I ask her.

'Yeah, definitely. Especially if someone looked into it as they died, trapping their soul. For sure it's haunted.'

'Haunted mirror, my arse,' says Byron.

Molly and I ignore him.

'So, that gives us a few potential spirits to be looking out for,' I say, as I turn the camera back to myself. 'Elizabeth, her mother and father, the wicked aunt, and maybe even Lord Thornhanger and his wife. I think the place was run as a boarding school at some point. And then in the 1980s it was being done up as a hotel, but it was never finished. Work just stopped all of a sudden, I don't know why, other than I think someone died and no one wanted to go back into the place.'

'That is seriously creepy,' says Molly.

'It's all hearsay,' adds Byron. 'But it makes a good story.'

Byron loves all this ghost stuff, really, even if he doesn't believe in it. His parents are pretty strict – a real zero-tolerance household. I mean, he wasn't even allowed any 'baddie' action figures as a kid. He has piano lessons every Monday after school, even though he hates them; he has to study with a private tutor every Tuesday evening; and he's expected to attend church with them every Sunday – morning or evening prayer, if not both. He's counting down the days until he turns eighteen in September, when he won't have to go any more. His parents were furious when he dyed his hair and don't get me started on what they think about him wearing eyeliner. I think the ghost stuff is another act of rebellion. A secret act of rebellion, because they don't know about it.

'Whether ghosts exist or not,' I say, 'you can't deny that a big old creepy place in the middle of nowhere all to ourselves for the entire weekend is going to be fun, fun, fun!'

'OK. OK. It sounds freaking awesome!' And he gives me a wry smile.

When he catches my eye, for a moment it's like two spacecraft docking. I'm safe and secure and not so alone in the endless space of my life. The connection breaks as he looks back to the road, and I turn back to the camera. 'We're doing this for you, our viewers,' I continue, my tone upbeat, using my 'camera voice', as Byron calls it, 'because this is what it is all about – us putting ourselves in scary-arsed situations so that you don't have to. You can just sit back and enjoy this from the comfort of your own homes. While we bring you next-level creepy content.'

'Risking our safety, just for you,' adds Byron, half-jokingly.

'So, keep watching,' I say. 'Hit that "like" button.

Subscribe, and let us know what you think of our videos in the comments.'

I stop recording and lower the camera, cradling it in my lap.

We each settle into the subdued stance of the long-distance traveller. I slip off my Converse and socks – as it's So. Damn. Hot. – balancing my feet on my high-tops, as the mat is too warm and a bit gritty. The air con isn't working, and the heat inside the Volkswagen Polo is draining, making me lethargic. It's Byron's mum's car. She lets him borrow it while he saves up for his own, on condition that he is super *super* careful, which he always is, because he is super *super* sensible and always super *super* reliable.

His mum doesn't know we're going ghost hunting. She would freak – she'd see it as Byron dabbling in the occult. She thinks we're going camping for the weekend (as do all our parents, so they don't slip up with Byron's) – swimming in a lake and sunbathing by day, and toasting marshmallows around the campfire by night. Good wholesome fun (which, btw, always ends up with a psychopath murdering all but the virgins in every teen slasher movie ever made . . . meaning I'd be safe).

It's Molly who breaks the silence after a while, when she says, 'Shall we put some music on?'

Turning in my seat, I'm like, 'Oh, is it OK if we don't? I'd like to think about shots I want to get on the way and I need to concentrate,' when what I really mean is, *No, because you stole the love of my life before I was able to tell him that I finally realized he's the love of my life, despite the fact that he has seen me as the love of his life for, like, his entire life.* Guilt immediately gets the better of me, and I add, 'In a bit though, yeah? Your choice.' She responds with a warm *I'm going to do my very best to understand Iris and her funny ways even if it kills me* smile, and says, 'Sure. No worries. Let me know if I can help with ideas for the video,' and she rests her head against the window, her eyes fixed on the outside world as it whizzes by.

I settle back in my seat and gaze out of my own side window. Ugh, Byron's announcement sucks. I remember the first ever investigation he and I went on. We had no idea what we were doing in terms of vlogging, and, self-conscious in front of the camera, neither of us could keep a straight face. We finally managed an intro piece about the history of the derelict office building where neither of us giggled when Byron smacked straight into a door frame. Like, *Slam.* We laughed so hard we both had tears running down our cheeks. I think about all the cold, hard floors we've slept on, us taking it in turns to tell spooky stories, until we'd fall asleep side by side. The little victories of finding our way inside places – some of which had been boarded up for decades – and feeling each time as if we'd discovered a new world.

And then I think about how many times we've done this: set off wondering if we were going to end the mystery of what happened to Zach and Lucas, only to find nothing but cold, damp, empty rooms, full of dust and cobwebs and disappointment. So maybe I don't blame him. Though, as I slouch down further with the camera pointing out of the windscreen, my stomach starts to fill with bubbles of excitement and fear that maybe – just maybe – I could be right this time.

3

'HI GUYS!' I say into the camera, which is being held by Molly. 'So, we're in the village of Hillthorn. Still twenty miles or so from our destination, but this is, like, one of the *last* bits of civilization before we get to Thornhanger House.'

'It really is in the middle of no-freaking-where,' adds Byron from beside me. He's leaning an elbow casually on my shoulder.

'By, for someone who doesn't believe in ghosts, I've noticed you're always the one who freaks out the most about explorations,' says Molly, from behind the camera.

'Yeah, but not because of ghosts – because They. Are. Not. Real.' He over-emphasizes the last few words. 'It's rotten floorboards and dodgy ceilings and any other accidents waiting to happen that I'm scared of, especially when the hospitals are, like, miles and miles away.'

'*Anyway*,' I say into camera, as Byron starts fiddling with the silver fidget ring on his thumb, 'we're here in Hillthorn, and we've been asking a few locals what they know about Thornhanger House. A surprising number are completely unaware of the place.'

'Or just didn't want to stop to talk to us,' says Byron.

'There's that,' I say. 'Though we just spoke to one old guy, Bert, who didn't want to be filmed but who told us that hikers are known to have gone missing in the area, and he described it as a sort of Bermuda Triangle, which is creepy. Said he'd not go near the place.' I shrug and widen my eyes in a *Can you believe that?* gesture to camera.

'Bert was so sweet,' Molly interjects. 'A real gentleman. If we weren't so far from home, I'd introduce him to my grandmother.' She gives this cute little shoulder-shrug, nose-wrinkle laugh, glancing at us while she continues to record me and By. It is utterly endearing and irresistibly cute. And, annoyingly, I can see what Byron sees in her.

Molly has the biggest, most beautiful eyes, like Bambi, and a bob, cut sharp at her jaw, with a blunt fringe. But her hairstyle is the only severe thing about Molly. She is the sweetest, loveliest, most patient – and I test her patience on a regular basis – person in the world. To a fault, sometimes. She does things like take the smaller slice of cake or pie or sandwich or whatever, so that someone else doesn't have to. And she'll let *everyone* else off the bus ahead of us, as though their time is more important than ours. She's even adorable when she's pissed off. When she's annoyed, it's like she's swallowed a grenade, you can see the blast beneath the surface, but she'd rather suck it up than let it out and risk causing even more damage.

But she's no pushover. If she sees an injustice she will fight to the death. She once went for a guy twice her size because she saw him hit his dog on the nose. I really thought he was going to punch her, until Byron and I rocked up.

I'm distracted by my phone beeping and I pull it out of my pocket to see that I have a text from my sister Amba, written all in caps:

> WHAT U DOING FOR MUMS BDAY SURPRISE??? TELL ME NOW!!!!!!!! NO LAME VIDEOS

Amba is a year older than me. She's a loud, bossy high-achiever, who is pretty much great at everything she tries to do and who can't understand why other people aren't. Which sucks for me. I'm the quiet introvert who, when not with Byron, is usually curled up in my room with a book. I usually end up feeling invisible and surplus to requirements, like a penny that has slipped down the back of a sofa: really not worth the bother to dig out. I shove my phone back into my pocket without replying. What does she want me to say? Compared to my sisters, I have nothing to offer. All I have is the channel – mine and Byron's channel. The one place where I can express myself, and through which I hope my life will become something more one day. That I can be someone. Be noticed.

And now I'm not sure how much longer I'll have that.

We interview a skinny teenager with bleached hair called Justin who tells us how he heard a whole bunch of kids went missing when his mum was little, in the 70s or 80s maybe, and there were rumours it had something to do with the house. Then there was a story about another kid who fell off the roof there more recently. He's always avoided the place. It's all good atmosphere for the video but the info's pretty vague. Then there's an old lady, Vera.

'Thornhanger House, you say? Yes, I've heard of the place, lovey. I've lived here all my life,' she tells us. 'My old mum wasn't the only one around here who used to say, "Now off to bed with you, or the Lady of the House'll get you!" to make their kids go to bed good.' Vera gives a red-lipped smile, just feathering slightly into the wrinkles around her thinning lips. 'I still cross my heart each night before bed and pray that she'll not haunt my dreams. Old habits and all that.'

'Who's the Lady of the House?' I ask. 'Could it be Charlotte . . . Elizabeth's mother?'

'Or Anne,' adds Molly.

'Who, dear?'

'The Turners – the family who owned Thornhanger House.'

'Did they? The place certainly changed hands a few times over the years. If a place can be unlucky . . . It was built by Lord Thornhanger and some say he was murdered there.'

'Murdered . . . by who?'

'I'm not sure, dear. And then it was a school in the 1970s. Did you know it was a school? A boarding school, as far as I know. But there were some deaths and disappearances, and the place was shut down, I believe. Then they were going to develop it into . . . oh . . . into flats, I think. Second homes for people with more money than sense, most likely – these yuppies, or what d'you call them these days . . . hippies. Hamsters. No, hipsters. Hipsters, isn't it? I mean, who'd want to live in the middle of nowhere?' She makes a tutting sound.

'My thoughts exactly, Vera,' Byron cuts in.

'It was a few years back. I forget when,' Vera continues. 'But I think there was some sort of accident and it was never finished.'

I bring up a Google image of Zach and Lucas. 'Have you ever seen these boys?' I ask her, holding my phone screen up for her. 'Like, around here. Did they pass through this way, d'you think? It would have been a few months ago now. Well . . . late last year.'

Vera takes off her metal-framed glasses and squints her rheumy eyes a little as she studies the screen. I hold my breath while I wait. I mean, if she recognizes them, we could really be on to something.

'No, my love,' she says with a shake of her head – her perfectly set silver hair not budging at all with the movement. 'I've never seen them before. But my memory isn't what it was. Lovely looking boys, though, aren't they?'

'Oh, OK,' I say, hardly managing to hide my disappointment. It doesn't mean anything – I mean, what are the chances that Zach and Lucas would have run into the same old lady we did? 'One last thing,' I add. 'Have you ever been there, to Thornhanger House?'

'No, my dear. And I wouldn't. Not on your nelly!'

That's now three people who've said that in the space of about half an hour. As Vera shuffles off, Molly pans the camera to me. But I can't think of anything to say, and I stand there awkwardly, biting a thumbnail, as it sinks in that we're about to spend the whole weekend there.

The place where no one wants to go.

I film through the car window as houses become fewer and further between, scattered like breadcrumbs along the side of the road, until I realize that I haven't seen one in a while, and we're surrounded by nothing but open moorland in all directions. The car winds through country roads that grow narrower with each turn. The bushes and trees that line the roads grow thicker and higher, breaking on occasion to give glimpses of the rocky moors and rolling hills beyond, which are gone again in an instant as we're engulfed once more by the wild, dense verges. As I watch, sunlight breaks through the trees and hits my eyes in a strobe effect. After a while, it becomes hypnotic and lulls me into a dream state. Until the car slows and jolts, as we turn on to a dirt track, the kind where grass grows in tufts down the centre, and where the tyres of any passing vehicles have made tracks either side over the years. Though, as weeds are sprouting and spreading and joining with the grass, it's clearly been a long time since anyone has driven this way regularly.

After what feels like forever, we turn down another overgrown dirt track. A little way up are the remains of a gatehouse. The arch across the track still stands to mark the boundary of the grounds. But the little house to the left is nothing more than a ruin, buried in a tangle of dark, twisted ivy. I hold my breath as Byron drives beneath the arch. I press myself against the passenger-side window and glance up at the aged flint structure, hoping that it doesn't all come tumbling down and crush us. Once we are through, it gets lighter again, as if the world blinked, and the car continues down the uneven track.

Trepidation rumbles inside me, and I feel so far from home as I film our approach to Thornhanger House.

4

'SO, THIS IS it, guys – Thornhanger House.'

The Volkswagen struggles on the grassed-over dirt track, and I rock with every bump and scrape.

'We'rrrrrrre here,' says Byron, in a sinister voice. He stops the car in the shadow of the huge iron gates that guard the inner perimeter of the house from the wider estate we've driven through.

The gates themselves, though dull with rust, look in good shape and are padlocked. The tall, ornate stone posts that they are set into have also stood up well to the test of time, but the lichen-covered flint wall on either side is crumbling in places, where weeds have delved their roots deep inside any cracks.

'Right, let's get out and find a way into our splendid weekend accommodation,' says Byron.

'Oooh, I do hope they leave those little chocolates on

our pillows at night,' I joke, as I raise myself off my seat and crane my neck to get my first look at the house. But I can't see much through the trees on the other side of the gates.

'And I do rather like a turndown service,' says Byron, giving me a wry smile.

'So, are we leaving the gear here for now or taking it all in?' says Molly, as she slides over a bit and leans through the gap between the seats. One of her hands finds one of Byron's.

'Let's just take what we need for now,' I suggest, keen to get inside and start exploring. 'We can check the place out and come back for the gear in a bit.'

'We should aim to get our stuff set up before dark, though,' says Byron. 'Let's find somewhere to use as a base camp.'

'Cool,' I say, with a nod. 'Let's do it.'

As I open the car door and step outside, a chill in the air creeps over me, causing goosebumps to rise on my bare arms. It was stuffy inside the car, and it had been hot and sticky when we stopped in Hillthorn. But now the day is fading, and we're in the shade of the tall trees that line the narrow track. My feet crunch on weed-infested gravel as I edge closer to the gate. I can now just about glimpse the house between the trees and overgrown bushes. Just a flash of age-browned and lichen-greened stone in the distance. Its grime-blackened windows like soulless eyes, glinting in the soft early evening light. Molly draws up beside me.

'Oh boy,' she says in awe.

Byron sidles up beside Molly. He slides a long arm around her waist and bends to kiss the top of her head. She glances up at him. I can't see her face from where I stand, but I can imagine the look of sweet adoration she is giving him, and it makes me bristle. She goes up on her tiptoes to kiss his lips, while he bends down. They do look cute together. And I hate that fact. HATE IT HATE IT HATE IT. It makes my stomach squirm, like someone is going crazy inside it with a can of silly string. I wonder if I'll ever get over it?

They met at a gaming tournament, held every other Sunday in a music venue in town. Byron is a gamer. He's good too, apparently. He's even developing his own role-playing game, called *The Last Season*. It's pretty cool, from what he's shown me. I'm not a gamer, and so I've never gone along to the tournaments. But I knew something was going on when they started waving at each other across the school canteen at lunchtime, and I'm like, *How do you know her?* Waves turned into *Hello*s, and *Hello*s turned into chats in the corridors. Gaming references that went over my head. While my stomach sank lower and lower, as he slipped away from me.

I only have myself to blame.

I was too busy chasing the dream of Zach to admit even to myself how I felt about Byron.

I take a deep breath, hold up the camera, and with forced enthusiasm say to it, 'Oooooh, I just got a shiver, guys.' I use the tripod to raise the camera higher, to get a shot of the house. 'Just look at that place. Gives me the chills.'

'You know, I don't want to put a dampener on anything . . .'

'But . . .' I urge, lowering the camera and looking at Byron.

'No car,' he says, motioning around the area outside the gates with a flick of his head.

I know exactly what he means, as I glance about myself and back down the track, to where his mum's car sits. We've done twelve locations before this one in the *Hunting for Zach and Lucas* series, and each one has started with us not finding their car out front – followed by us not finding any sign of them inside, either. Just to be sure, I even scan between the tall trees either side of the track, in case they pulled off-road to park inside the sparse woods, for some reason. But no car. I make a silent *Ahhh* with my mouth, as my heart sinks: OK, probably not the One, then.

Molly is gazing at me with a sympathetic smile that barely masks her own disappointment.

'It doesn't matter,' I say, with a shake of my head, before anyone else can say it. Because if either of them had been the one to say it, I would have hated them for it. Because it does matter. Byron is looking at me with an *I'm not going to say 'I told you so', because I am truly sorry and I don't want you to be any more upset than you already are* expression. And I want to cry. Just for a moment. *Crap*. I had been so sure. So sure. I swallow back the sting of tears – tears of disappointment and frustration – and I say again, brighter this time, 'It doesn't matter.' And to camera, I say, 'Well, not the best start. Their car isn't here. But so what? Let's just get in and explore. The place looks awesome, guys.'

Molly nods and says, 'It'll still be amazing. Whatever happens. The place looks so spooky.'

I know she's being sweet. And I know she's feeling it too. I'm just glad that she didn't beat me to saying, *It doesn't matter*.

BECAUSE IT DOES.

So, I smile back. It's tight-lipped, weighed down by a heaviness inside my gut, but it's a smile.

'Look. That way,' says Byron, nodding to the left. 'Wall's caved in.'

Molly and I follow him, me filming as I go, to a section of wall that has crumbled and formed a lichen-covered hill. It's easy to scramble over, even one-handed.

'This is so exciting, guys,' I say, using my 'camera voice', with as much oomph and pizzazz as I can muster, once I'm in the house's formal grounds; grounds that are wild from years of neglect. 'Who knows what awaits us inside Thornhanger House.'

'Mmmmmwwwahahahaha,' says Byron, as he passes me, unable to resist giving my side a poke, and quickening his pace so that I can't get him back.

I smile, even though he doesn't look back, but I don't give chase, as I think I'm meant to, as he disappears into the undergrowth; the lingering disappointment at not finding Zach and Lucas's car out the front combined with the news that Byron is leaving the channel has killed my mood. So, I let the others go on ahead of me as I slow down to film the once-grand gardens. The long dirt and gravel driveway continues on up to the house, but it's so overgrown with weeds and mossy grass that you can hardly tell where it ends and the lawns begin. Brown spiky bushes, weeds and grasses tangle with each other, and they smell fresh and earthy in the evening air. Trees loom from the overgrown lawn, having sprung up in random places. They cast ominous shadows. Hedges have run amok. I try to imagine the landscape as it would have been when Elizabeth lived here – perfectly edged lawns, colourful flower beds and elaborate topiary. A croquet set. But it's so ruined that I struggle to hold the image in my mind.

The day has that early-summer-evening stillness to it, like it's just taking the time to cool off before it heads into night-time. I'm appreciating the coolness after the long journey in a stifling car with sweaty knee-pits and a damp patch at the back of my T-shirt. Over the hills, back the way we came, the horizon is streaked with pink and orange, but, as I turn the camera towards the distant house, I see dark, angry clouds of Prussian blue and gunmetal grey creeping in.

'That had better not be an omen,' I say, without turning the camera on myself. 'And it'd better not be rain. God knows how waterproof the old place is.'

Trekking along the remains of the driveway, I stumble

upon an old folly, concealed in the rogue bushes and trees. It's not quite twice my height and circular in shape. Byron, Molly and I might just be able to touch fingertips if we stood around its crumbling, mildewed circumference. Three stone steps lead up to a narrow arched doorway: its insides cold and black. Something about that doorway reminds me of a crocodile's eye, peeking above the water-line. I hurry past, my feet crunching on weeds and gravel, keen to be away from the dark, dark doorway. It sent a shiver up my spine.

The trees thin as I draw closer to the house, and I spot that the large arched door is boarded up. I take in the grand portico, with its detailed stonework. On the side of the house, to the left of the portico – my left as I look at the house – there is a large double-storey bay window, which is easily the width of our whole Victorian terrace back home; elaborate detail is carved into the stone above it, where it forms a balcony for the window on the top floor. I can't see well from where I stand, because of the hedgerows and trees, but towards the back of the house, the structure branches off into two wings. It's so big. And I feel so small.

I can't see the others anywhere, and I assume that they've gone around the back of the house to look for a way in. I raise the camera upwards, trying to catch all of the impressive front aspect: three storeys; tall chimney pots; to my right is a small turret that protrudes from the corner of the top floor; and up to my left, there's a lone window in the pitched roof, topped with a scalloped stone arch, which reveals another storey in the eaves on that side. As I stare at the small, round attic window, I think how, if this were a movie, I would probably catch a momentary glimpse of a pale face, staring down at me.

The building is quite magnificent, even in its sorry, time-forgotten state, and I forget to address the camera for a while. Just lost in the wonder and magic of it all, I stand hugging the camera to my chest, like it's a teddy bear. I let it ground me. Its familiarity is comforting in this strange place. My camera is my prized possession. My baby. It's a Canon PowerShot G7 X Mark II, the same make and model that Zach uses. Used. That Zach *used*. I saved up for it by working holidays in a shoe shop, surrounded by smelly feet and annoying people – people who have the audacity to want things, like shoes – in order to upgrade from the beat-up old Canon EOS 70D my dad gave me for my sixteenth birthday.

I was trying to figure out *my thing*, my talent, my purpose in life, and I mentioned that maybe, possibly, perhaps I might be interested in taking film studies at uni. Dad got all excited and super supportive that maybe, possibly, perhaps I'd finally figured out what I wanted to do with my life. When he gave me the second-hand camera, he said, *Go. Have fun. Create. Make stuff. Experiment.* But I never made any short films. Because I never had any ideas. And instead of becoming the next great auteur, Byron and I eventually reinvented ourselves as paranormal vloggers and urban explorers. That was well over a year ago now. I don't think it was quite what Dad had in mind, but my parents were just happy to support me in doing my thing. Only, it turned out I'm not any good at that, either. Practically no one watches our videos. No matter how much effort we make.

I push that thought out of my mind and concentrate on the monster of a house before me. And I start to feel excitement rise again. Excitement that is threaded with the intrigue of Elizabeth's story. The history of the place. So what if Zach and Lucas were never here? *It doesn't matter.* And this time I even mean it. We'll still make a good exploration video. Remembering myself, I raise the camera and start to talk, 'So this is where Elizabeth and her family would have alighted their carriages and—'

Molly's sharp yell cuts through the middle-of-freaking-nowhere silence. She's shouting my name, and the piercing urgency causes a twisting inside my gut. I turn the camera until I spot her standing at the corner of the building, to my right, motioning furiously at me to come. Come! COME! Her expression is hard to read from this distance: wide-eyed and stunned. I can't see Byron anywhere.

'Iris, come on! COME ON!'

My heart stops. A chill seeps into my bones. 'I think something's wrong, guys,' I say to camera, as I start to move towards the house. Mechanically at first, like my body is trying to catch up with my brain, then I break into a sprint, urged on by Molly's shouts. She waits until she is sure that I'm coming, and then she disappears around the side of the house. I make to follow her. As I round the corner, I see Molly scramble through a window some way down the side of the building.

'Wait!' I call.

She leans out of the window, waiting for me to catch up.

'Hurry,' she says, beckoning. Her eyes have a wildness to them which makes me run faster. 'Come on. Hurry up!'

'I don't like this,' I say for the camera's benefit, though I'm not sure what I'm pointing it at right now. 'Molly! Molly, what's going on?' I call as I run, my feet crunching on cracked, weed-infested stone paving slabs. 'Where's Byron?' I'm shouting myself hoarse. 'MOLLY!' If anything should have happened . . . But she's already ducked her head inside, like a rabbit bobbing into its warren.

'Molly. Wait!'

I reach the window, its glass missing, just in time to see Molly disappear into the gloom. Consumed by the house.

My heart pounds. Worried that something has happened to Byron – fallen through rotten floorboards or the ceiling caved in on him, just like he feared – I grasp the peeling window frame and pull myself up. I know that all the camera will be picking up will be my ragged breath and snatches of wall and windowsill as I climb through, but I don't stop filming. That would only slow me down.

'Molly! Byron!' I call into the dank stillness, as my feet crunch on rubble-strewn floorboards. There are two large doorways off this cavernous room, and I'm not sure which one Molly went through. 'Molly!' The place is eerily quiet and my voice echoes off the cold walls. I smell damp and mould and dust and emptiness. '*Guys?*' I edge through the large, high-ceilinged room, a couple of its walls lined with shelves of dark, dark wood. I imagine it must have been a library in Elizabeth's time, the shelves filled with books, right up to the ceiling. I can still smell the mustiness of old books in the air.

'Guys, if this is some sort of joke . . .'

'Iris, in here!'

Breath held at what I'm about to find, I follow the sound of Molly's voice, through an arched doorway and into an enormous room with a wooden balcony along the left-hand wall and a high, domed ceiling. Not much light penetrates the large grimy windows, despite it being daylight outside. Dust motes swirl. My heart is thudding. I'd been so convinced that something had happened to Byron that as my eyes adjust to the gloom and I can make him out on his haunches in the centre of the room, his back to me, I let out a sigh of relief.

'By?' I say, coming further into the room. When he doesn't move, my chest tightens again. My mouth is dry. Molly is stood next to him, arms wrapped around herself. She's biting her lower lip. 'Guys?' Her wide eyes flick to me for a beat, and then back to whatever it is that she and Byron are both staring at. Something I can't yet see. I'm trembling as I take another step. And another. As I draw closer, I can see that before him is strewn a pile of junk. '*Byron?*' I stop when he turns and holds something up to me, his expression stupefied. Mouth open. I would recognize the thing he's holding anywhere: a Canon PowerShot G7 X Mark II.

Zach's camera.

5

WHAT I THOUGHT was junk is a backpack, contents sprawled across the floor. Byron finds a spare battery among the items and he switches it out for the one inside Zach's Canon, before rising to his feet. He stares down at the camera, turning it around in his hands.

'You think it's . . .'

'It has to be,' I say to him, my own camera hanging forgotten at my side. I can't help a stunned giggle escaping me – I mean, we've found Zach and Lucas's stuff – but it dries up really fast. The enormity of it all. I mean, we've found Zach and Lucas's stuff. But where the hell are *they*?

'They're here,' says Molly in not much more than a rasped whisper, as if she had heard the question that I asked inside my own head. 'You were right, Iris. They're here.'

I can't even revel in the I-told-you-so moment, I'm too

stunned that I was right. Instead, I focus on Molly as she glances about the big, dusty old room, as if she expects to see them crouched in the gloomy corners, waiting to spring out and shout, *BOO! Gotcha! What took you so long? We can all go home now.*

'Molly . . .'

She ignores me.

'Zach . . . Lucas . . . ?' she calls, tentatively at first, then, 'ZACH! LUCAS! ZACH!'

'Molly. Don't.' I place a hand on her forearm, but she shrugs me off and scurries towards one of the room's three large doorways, each like yawning mouths, and she's calling, 'ZACH! LUCAS!' over and over, and I think that she must be in shock and she's not thinking straight. Her voice echoes through the ingrained silence, as if it might shatter it like glass.

'Molly, stop!' I go after her. Grasping her arm, I pull her round to face me. 'For Christ's sake, Moll,' I say. 'They're not just taking high tea in the sunroom. What good's shouting your head off going to do?'

'Yeah, you'll wake the dead, Moll,' says Byron, raising his arms like a zombie and making a *Whoooo* sound.

'Byron, that's not funny,' says Molly, hugging herself.

'I know,' says Byron solemnly. His face drops, and he stares at the camera in his hand. He runs his free hand through his dyed fringe, where it comes to a stop at the shorter, dark brown hair at the back of his head, and he mutters, 'I can't believe it. I just can't believe it.'

I remember the whole point of why we're here. The

video. I raise the camera, which had been filming this whole time, and with a trembling hand, I point it at myself. 'This is it,' I say. I move the Canon to get a shot of the grubby and rumpled clothing littering the floor, before panning it around the room. It really is huge. There is a fireplace at one end so large that all three of us could stand in it. Perfect for a witch's cauldron. Grand chandeliers hang from the three domes in the ceiling. And what looks like partially dismantled scaffolding and plasterboard leans up against one of the walls. I get the feeling that this was a grand ballroom in its day and was in the process of being converted, probably into the hotel's dining room. This must be where Lord Thornhanger and Emma died – were murdered? – in a fire.

As I continue to pan around the room, I have to use my other hand to steady my camera hand. I'm shaking like I'm shut in a deep freeze, like when you see someone get locked in one of those big walk-in freezers in movies and they get colder and colder and start to tremble and shake and turn white with frost. But it's not even all that cold in here. Sure, there's an underlying, deep-rooted chill, but it's not *that* cold. I just can't stop shaking. 'This is actually it, guys. We've found their stuff,' I say from behind the camera, my words rippled with astonishment and excitement and thrill, all kept in check by apprehension. 'We've found proof that Thornhanger House is the last known whereabouts of Zach and Lucas.' I stop the camera on Byron. 'Could you just state for the record what you're holding, By?'

He doesn't move for a moment. Then, as if someone has just fed him a penny, he looks to camera. 'Er . . . yeah . . . We think this is Zach Cooper's camera,' he says, robotically, holding it up. 'We've not looked at any footage yet, but –' he stops to give a little half laugh that is devoid of humour – 'it looks like Zach and Lucas were here and, wherever they are now, and for whatever reason, they've left their stuff. Or at least, Zach has.'

I scan the floor again with my camera. 'I don't know if you can pick this up on-screen,' I say. 'It's pretty gloomy in here and evening is settling in outside. But there's a backpack and clothing and stuff all over the floor.' I go down on to my haunches, reaching out my free hand to lift the sleeve of a hoodie. I wrap my fingers around the fabric, aware that I'm quite possibly touching something that Zach wore. I hold on to this piece of him for a moment, then, knowing how embarrassed I'd be to admit out loud how much this means to me, I let it go and stand up. 'We didn't see a car out the front,' I continue. 'So, it's possible that Zach and Lucas left in a hurry. But if that's the case, what drove them away, and where are they now?' I swing the camera round to me. On the flip screen I can see that my eyes are big and round with the enormity of it all. There's a wild look in them that scares me a little – I look unhinged with morbid wonder. 'But whatever happened to them it began here. At Thornhanger House.'

I stop recording and lower the Canon to my side, needing a moment to catch a breath. 'This is it,' I say after a beat. 'This is big, you guys. We've hit the jackpot! We get to solve the mystery of what—'

'Guys,' Molly says as I start recording again and swing the camera up so that she's in frame. She's shaking her head, and I get a chill in the pit of my stomach, sure I'm not going to like what she's about to say. 'I think we should report this to the police. Like, right away. Now.'

'What?'

'She's got a point. This has just got a bit too real.'

'What?' I say turning to Byron.

'This is bigger than us, Iris,' he says. 'Bigger than some YouTube series.'

'What? I . . . No. What did you think—'

'We need to report this immediately,' he continues, cutting me off. 'We've found the personal belongings of a missing person. Possibly two missing people.'

'Yeah, *aaaand* we need to investigate what happened to them. Try to find out where they are now.'

'Iris. They could still be here.'

'Moll, we've been through—'

'No. Listen. What if they parked somewhere else? Maybe they parked further up the road, rather than turn down the track to the house like we did. Or there could be another entrance somewhere. I mean, there's probably loads of places their car could be. These grounds are massive. Maybe they wanted it hidden in case a security guard came by, or . . . I don't know. What if they never left? And what if something in this house – some entity – harmed them?'

'*Or* they had some sort of accident,' adds Byron.

'Iris, their bodies . . .'

There's a silence while that thought hangs in the dusty, musty air between us for a moment.

'Shit,' I say at last, a lump in my throat. 'I didn't think of that.'

'We need to call the police.'

'She's right, Iris. We have to. Let's not touch anything else. We should leave everything as we found it, in case we disturb any evidence.'

I make a little gasping sound, my breath escaping me, and that's all I can do for a moment. Months and months of work, researching and searching and going over and over every comment on YouTube and the Facebook page and Instagram and trekking more than halfway up the country and now I'm standing next to Zach's stuff – his camera – and . . . 'Whoa. Wait a minute. Let me get this straight. You want to give up on the find of the century – the video that can make our channel—'

'It's not just about the channel, Iris. Zach and Lucas's welfare – *our* welfare – is more important than a sodding video,' says Byron, his eyes darkened to a slate grey by the room's shadows.

'Nothing is more important than the videos!' I hiss. I stop, mouth open, at the sight of Byron and Molly staring at me with wide eyes. The look of horror on their faces makes my cheeks burn.

'Do you really mean that?' asks Molly, her voice small and strained.

'We made a promise to our viewers,' I say, weakly,

trying to justify my previous statement. 'That we would find Zach and Lucas.'

'What viewers?'

I glare at Byron.

'Iris, you can't mean what you said.'

I look back to Molly. 'I . . . uh . . . I don't . . . No. Of course, I don't. I . . . uh . . . Look, we've got a chance here,' I say, scrambling for the right words; knowing that if this ends here, so will the channel. It'll be over. Byron will leave, and he'll drift away from me. There will be nothing stopping him from spending all his time with Molly. And if she leaves too . . . I can't let them go to the police yet. I have to keep the investigation going. 'A chance to find out what happened to Zach and Lucas. To watch their footage. To explore this place. But once the police are involved, that chance goes. They'll be all over this place. It'll be cordoned off. That,' I say, pointing to the camera in Byron's hand, 'will be evidence, along with all their other belongings, and it'll all be taken away. Away!' I say with a sweeping hand gesture for dramatic effect. 'Locked up in an evidence room somewhere. And we won't get to see any of it. No one will. And if something *otherworldly* did happen here . . .' I glance at Molly, hoping to get her hooked; because she must want Byron to stay with the channel as much as I do; surely, she doesn't want the explorations to end. Because they will, without Byron . . . 'do you think that the police will follow that line of enquiry? Do you think that they will believe it? No. No, they won't. It'll end up an unsolved mystery. Dusty and forgotten. And we'll have lost our chance. Our chance for a resolution for Zach and Lucas. A chance for answers for ourselves and for the viewers. For Zach and Lucas's families. So, we owe it to all of them. We owe it to ourselves, to find out what really happened here.'

'Iris . . .'

'We're not leaving. Not until we have answers. We didn't come all this way to give up before we even begin. We're not leaving. We're not!'

'But won't we get into trouble with the police if we—?' Molly doesn't get any further. At the faint, muffled sound of static and screams, we both turn to Byron.

He's staring, wide-eyed, at the flip screen on Zach's camera. 'Guys. I, um, I really think you should see this. It's the last thing Zach recorded.'

I edge towards him, a tight ball in my stomach, wondering if I do want to see what is on that camera and knowing that I want to see it more than anything in the world. I carry on filming, recording everything for evidence.

With me on one side and Molly on the other, he plays the video from the beginning. At first, I struggle to make anything out. The footage is grainy and dark and I see flashes of torchlight and someone's legs as they tear down corridors while carrying the camera. They are not pointing the camera at anything in particular, just holding it while it records. I glimpse doorways and wood panelling. The flash of someone at the end of a corridor. Or was it just a shadow? Walls. Floorboards. There's screaming.

Shouting. But I can't tell if it's one person. Two. More than two? Or even if the screams are coming from the person holding the camera or from somewhere else in the house, because the sound is as distorted as the image is grainy. And it's confusing and disorientating. Down a set of stairs. Whoever it is stops abruptly. I get a flash of a mirror, a bit of wall. Then the camera and torch must drop from the person's hands. There's a thud and distortion. And then I see a flash of someone's booted feet, caught in a beam of light, not moving, before the recording ends. It's over so quick, and I'm left wondering what the hell I saw. I shiver with uncertainty and fear and the uncomfortable feeling you get when you know something is very wrong but you don't know what. And I know I never want to see that video again. Something about it, I just . . .

'What *was* that?'

'That's it, I'm calling the police,' says Byron, a tremble in his voice. He pulls his phone out and . . . 'Crap.'

'What?'

'No service.'

I fumble for my own phone, at the same time as Molly pulls hers out of her pocket.

'Me neither,' she says, her voice breathy. 'What was that? On the video. What did we just watch?'

'Iris?' Byron ignores Molly and looks at me expectantly as I stare at my phone screen.

'Nothing.'

'Shit.'

'What. Was. That?'

'Molly. Calm down,' says Byron, as he turns to her and envelops her in a hug. 'There's got to be some sort of explanation,' he says, stroking her hair. 'They just freaked themselves out, OK? It's easy to do. This is a creepy old house. It just got into their heads. It just . . .'

'Just what, Byron?' says Molly in an uncharacteristically harsh tone as she pulls back from him. 'There is something bad in this house and it got them.'

'Moll, come on. That's ridiculous. It's not possible,' says Byron.

'Where are they, then?'

He shakes his head, a small movement, as if he doesn't want to fully admit that he can't adequately explain in a rational, everyday way what we just saw and where Zach and Lucas are now.

'Come on,' he says, as he turns and strides across the room, his black Converse-clad feet crunching on dust and debris.

'Where are you going?' I call after him.

Without turning around, Byron says, 'You can do what you like, but I'm going to get back into the car and I'm going to drive to—'

'No!'

I can't let Byron leave.

Not this house.

Or the channel.

Or me.

'Iris. He's right. This is a police matter,' says Molly. She gives me a pained smile, before starting after Byron.

'But . . .' I let my words trail off in a gasp as my hand instinctively clamps to the back of my neck. I turn my head sharply to look up in the direction of the balcony. 'Guys!'

Byron halts, swinging round. 'What?'

'I-I just . . . I . . .' I stutter, giving a little shake of my head. 'I felt prickles on the back of my neck, like someone's up there.' I motion towards the balcony with a finger. 'Watching us.' I turn back to the others.

Molly's mouth hangs open as her gaze flits to the balcony and back to me.

'It's just, I think this is the room where Lord Thornhanger and Emma died,' I continue. 'And—'

'And nothing,' says Byron, cutting me off. 'You're just spooking yourself, Iris.' He turns and starts towards the door, quicker than before, while Molly wavers.

'No. Wait. Listen. Both of you.' Byron doesn't stop. He's reached the doorway. 'Byron!'

At the sharpness in my voice, he stops and turns. We lock eyes.

There's a brief pause where no one moves. Then, calmly, he says, 'What, Iris?'

'Look, to know what we saw in that video, we need to watch the rest of the footage on that camera. From the beginning. I know you guys want to bring the police in, and I agree that's what we should do. *But* here's the thing,' I say imploringly. 'Let's take a quick look around to see if we find any . . . bodies.' I say the word quickly, as if it is too heavy a word to hold in my mouth. 'If we do, we head straight back to Hillthorn and we bring MI5 down on this place if we have to. You have my word that's what we'll do. But if we don't . . . then I say we give ourselves a bit of time to watch the footage and explore every bit of this place, everywhere Zach and Lucas went, before reporting anything. And find out *exactly* what happened here. We'll still go to the police, so we won't get into any trouble.' I direct this last bit to Molly. 'But we'll know we did everything we could to solve it first. They'll probably thank us.'

'They definitely won't thank us,' says Byron. 'It's probably obstructing an investigation or something.'

'This stuff has been here for months,' I say, pointing at the belongings on the floor. 'What difference is it going to make if we wait another day or two before reporting it?'

Byron shakes his head at me.

'Molly, come on,' I say, giving up on him and changing tack. 'Something happened here. Possibly something strange – otherworldly, even. You think there's something in this house, right?' I add, appealing to her love of the mysterious and the supernatural, even though I'm not sure whether I believe it myself. I'm not sure what I believe. Molly nods. 'Well, if we leave now, you'll regret giving up the chance to investigate this house. You need this, Molls. You know you do. You. Need. It.'

So do I.

This can't be the end.

'Iris, I don't know.'

'Moll, this could be the place where we prove ghosts are real – would you want to pass up on that?'

She lets out a long breath. She bites her lip. 'OK,' she says after a beat, apprehension in her voice. 'OK. I'll stay. But if we find so much as a drop of blood . . .'

'We drive straight to the police. I get it. Are you in?'

Molly nods.

'Moll . . . Iris . . .' begins Byron, glancing from one of us to the other. Then he dissolves in a sort of resigned groan. Two against one. 'OK, I'm in,' he says reluctantly.

As we trek back to the car for our gear and some torches, the confusing images from Zach's camera replaying in my mind, I get the first pinch of trepidation that maybe, just maybe, Molly and Byron are right and we should leave right now. Just get in the car and drive away from Thornhanger House before it swallows us up.

6

OUTSIDE, THE DARK clouds of earlier have passed, and the sky is ablaze with orange and pink and violet, as the egg-yolk sun dips towards the horizon. But inside, the grimy, creeper-covered downstairs windows let in only a few shards of the dying daylight. They delve into the hazy, shadowy interior like long, bony fingers.

My camera hangs around my neck in its case. I'm not intending to film this initial search, as I'll be hurrying, and I don't want to risk filming, you know . . . *bodies*. My heart lurches at every thought of the word *bodies*. I mean, I know that Zach and Lucas haven't been seen in eight months. And I know that something terrible must have happened to them. But thinking of them in the cold, hard terms of *bodies* makes this all too real. But I want the Canon on me in the event that I find anything interesting for the video.

With no reception, I leave my phone with our backpacks and sleeping bags in the large, L-shaped room that we are using as our base camp. The room is off the huge entrance hall, to the left, and just across from the room with the bookshelves that we're referring to as the 'library', where the broken window is. I imagine our base camp as the former drawing room, with stiff-backed chairs positioned around the grand fireplace, where guests would have been entertained. There's nothing in here now, other than a rusting stepladder leaning against a wall. A massive bay window lets in the grime-filtered light and brings the outside in as much as it's ever going to get. And it feels a bit . . . I don't know . . . a little less spooky than the few other downstairs rooms we've been in so far. But what it's like when the sun goes all the way down remains to be seen.

For three horror movie-obsessed teens, we don't appear to have learnt a thing from our many hours of movie watching – though in Byron's case it's more like watching one-eyed from behind a cushion because, for such a non-believer, he's a big old scaredy-cat when it comes to creepy movies. We're about to commit the worst teen horror movie sin of all time: we've agreed to split up.

Split up.

I mean, Oh. My. God. Right?

Byron was like: 'It's the quickest way, guys.' And Molly and I were like: 'No. No. No.' And Byron was like: 'It's the best way to get this first sweep over with before it gets dark.'

In the end, Molly and I had to agree because we all want this over with as quickly as possible, and before it gets dark, seeing as what we're looking for is . . .

Bodies.

Remains.

Nausea rakes through me. I mean, what would be left of a person after eight months? I shudder at the thought. Am I prepared for what seeing that will do to me . . . to Molly? To Byron.

But it's why we came all the way here. To find out the truth.

It's like when you see a cactus, all spiky and sharp, and you want to touch it. Just to know how it feels. To just poke it with a finger. You know that it'll hurt if you do, but you just – for some strange reason that you can't explain – need to know what those spikes feel like. You can't stop yourself. Well, it's like that, only a millionfold. I don't want to see a dead body; I know it will change me forever. But I just can't stop.

I have too much riding on this.

We agree to each cover as much ground as we can in an hour, before meeting back at the base camp.

Just a quick sweep, I remind myself, as my feet crunch on dusty floorboards through the entrance hall, *and then I'm not going anywhere alone for as long as we're in this creepy-arsed house*. Or maybe ever again. On the plus side, at least it's still just about light outside. I mean, I don't think Molly or I would have agreed to this if it were dark already. Molly firmly believes in what lurks in the darkness. My mind is open, and it opens even wider in the dark. Especially *alone* in the dark.

Leaving the others to check the warren of rooms on the ground and first floors, I set out for the second floor. I pause for a moment at the base of the grand central staircase, taking it in. The dark wood is dull with age, and varnish peels like diseased skin.

It's gloomy in the hall, so I switch on my torch and shine its beam up and along the elaborately carved balustrade, up towards a landing part the way up where the staircase splits to carry on up to the left and right sides of the first floor. I feel the weight of whatever is up there pressing down on me. The empty rooms; the dust and the dank air; the years of memories of the people who once lived here; the years and years of nothing but time passing. The decay. The held breath of a dying house.

It's all up there.

Waiting.

Here we go. I swallow back my trepidation, trying not to think of missing vloggers and vengeful spirits. Of little girls locked in cupboards. I place a foot on the first stair, testing it out. I have enough experience of old abandoned buildings to know that a foot can easily pass right through a rotten floorboard or a stair, soft from years of rainwater getting in or just general disrepair. Ghost hunting can be a dangerous sport. The step creaks, but it feels solid. I climb, pausing for just a moment when I hear a shuffling from somewhere below me. I wait. I listen. But I hear nothing more, and I tell myself that it was Molly or Byron.

Nothing to freak out over.

I'm not the one who thinks every little creak or knock is something ghostly – that's Molly. Molly the Believer. Since she came on board with the videos, just after she and Byron started going out with each other, it's been good having the balance of Believer, Sceptic and Non-believer. Though I do always seem to be in the middle.

The gooseberry.

I continue to edge my way up the staircase, my ears straining and my eyes scouring the shadows. I want to believe. I really do. Not like Byron, who literally lives to debunk everything. Fearless, because there is nothing to be afraid of. Unless we're watching a horror movie, of course. I want to believe; I just need convincing. We've had creepy things happen during our ghost hunts: cold spots; icy breath or a whispered word in your ear when there is no one close; knocks that happen seemingly in response to questions asked; things falling off shelves by themselves. Enough, sometimes, to make me believe, at least in that moment. But nothing that can't be explained or rationalized – usually by Byron – once we're back in the comfort of our own homes. When I need to, I can put most things down to damp, rot, a settling house, cooling pipework, rusty hinges and draughts.

But what do I put Zach and Lucas's disappearance down to – natural causes, like a tragic accident; something supernatural; or something else entirely? I will resist jumping to any conclusions until we watch more of the footage. Until we have some sort of evidence.

With each step up, my hands sweat, and my heart thumps harder and louder, belying my status of sceptic. And I guess, on some level, deep down, I do believe. Or at least I'm willing to accept that just because I don't believe in ghosts, it doesn't make them not real. I mean, if pushed I'd call myself a non-believer, but I would never – NEVER – do a Ouija board in my house. No way. Not in the house I live and sleep in. But Byron, he did a Ouija board in his own bedroom. Twice. Once with us – just because I wouldn't do one in my *own* bedroom, doesn't mean I wouldn't do one in someone else's, if they are game – and once on his own.

On his own!

He says that nothing happened when he did it alone. But the one we did together, me, Molly and Byron, the planchette moved to *Yes*, when we asked if there was anyone there.

I halt when I hear the crunch of a foot on bare floorboards from below me.

Molly or Byron.

Molly or Byron.

With my hand on the banister, I glance down the way I came, but there is no one in the entrance hall that I can see.

'Guys?' I say tentatively. But either there really is no one there, or my words get lost in the large open space – a space that reaches right up to the first-floor ceiling, with a sorry-looking chandelier dangling over the stairs. I wait a beat, but nothing stirs the heavy silence. I continue up.

I think back to the Ouija board. Molly would never cheat. She takes this stuff way too seriously. And Byron? He's the one who is more likely to pull a prank to wind me up. But his sole function in life seems to have become debunking all this ghost stuff over the year and a half that he and I have been doing these videos, so I don't think it was him. And I know *I* didn't move the planchette that night. If it were my room, I'd never sleep again. Byron, however, claims to sleep like a baby, explaining it away as either one of us knowingly moving the planchette to fool the others, or unintentional muscle movements: an ideomotor response, he called it, brought about by a desire for something to happen. In other words, we did it subconsciously.

I keep an open mind.

I shall try to keep an open mind about this place, too.

I stop on the landing part way up the central staircase, where it branches up to the left and right sides of the house, while I consider which way to go. There's likely access to the upper floors from either side, but I want to find the nearest staircase. I sweep the torch and – SHIT! – drop it. It lands with a thud on the bare boards. Snatching it up, I shine it at what had startled me and – Oh my god. Oh sweet Jesus. Oh. Oh – I let out a calming breath. I scared myself silly catching a glimpse of my reflection in a huge mirror, tarnished with age spots and grimy with dust. Oh blimey, that freaked me out. I wonder if this is the mirror that Elizabeth's father slit his throat in front of, and that just freaks me out even more. Another couple of calming breaths and I decide on heading right – because that sounds . . . um, well . . . *right*.

Being that funny sort of sceptic who would never do a Ouija board in their own room or do anything that could potentially annoy any *possible* spirits that could *perhaps*, *maybe*, *possibly* exist, I sometimes find myself doing little precautionary things, like not stepping on cracks, or not walking under ladders and to always, if possible, say *Goodbye* after doing a Ouija board – or risk being *perhaps*, *maybe*, *possibly* haunted forever. Just in case. So, turning to the right sounds like the best direction. Just, you know, because.

I hold on to the ornate banister as I climb, feeling the aged wood, cold and clammy with damp. My ears strain for any sounds and my heart thuds, and I'm fearful of what I might find at any moment.

Human remains.

Shifting shadows.

Things that live in the dark places.

Pull yourself together.

At the very top of the grand staircase, I stop to get my bearings. There is a corridor straight ahead of me, and another that mirrors it on the other side of the stairs. These corridors are long and dark and have doors off either side, and, I can just make out in the gloom, they both appear to branch to the left and right at the end. This place is a labyrinth.

I turn to my right, where a wide walkway runs along the top of the staircase, leading all the way around to the other side, to the stairs that branched left. There is a carved wooden balustrade all the way around it, and you would be able to see down to the entrance hall if you peeked over the edge. On this side, there are three doors coming off the walkway to the left, and further down, but not quite to the far end, I see the foot of a smaller, single set of stairs leading up to the left, which I guess will take me to the second floor. At the very far end of the walkway, the part that bridges the left and right sides of the house, there are three grand square-paned windows that let in enough light that I don't really need my torch.

I hear the shuffling from below again, and, heart thumping, I shine my torch down the stairs, into the gloomy hall, but I can't see anyone. Mouth dry and palms sweating, my stomach fluttering with excitement and dread, I edge along the walkway. Floorboards creak underfoot, my eyes flick to the doors as I pass them, imagining what I'll do if one starts to open – would I scream and run or would I stand and face whatever is inside? Oh my god, I want to run. I want to stay. I want to know. And I don't. Frustrated by the mystery of what happened to Zach and Lucas, there is no question that I am going to stay and see this through.

I pause, needing to hold on to the balustrade. My heart is pounding so hard I think it's going to explode . . . Calm. *Remember your breathing.*

Breathe.

Breathe.

Breathe.

Grounded, I carry on. I focus on how the dying sun filters through the tall windows at the end of the walkway, casting patterns of light and shadow on the walls and floorboards which make me feel a little less isolated. A little more connected to the outside world. As I reach them, I step on the patches of light as if they offer some sort of divine safety. At the foot of the single staircase, I swing the torch beam up to where the beginnings of twilight can't reach. I look up, and I gasp and jump, and a hand instinctively goes to my heart as a shadow shifts, just around the corner.

Don't panic, I tell myself. *You're letting your imagination run away with you. There's nothing up there but shadows and cobwebs and dust.*

Breathe.

I stand and listen for a moment. A shuffling from somewhere down below.

Molly or Byron.

Then silence.

Wanting to get this over with as soon as possible so that I can meet up with the others, I take the stairs two at a time. I slow as I approach the corner, where the steps turn to the left. Jesus Christ, this place is so creepy. I pause and shine the torch around the corner, and up the remaining steps to the next floor. No bodies. No ghosts. No demons. No disorientated, half-starved YouTubers waiting to be found and reminded of who they are.

At the top, I find myself on an L-shaped landing.

Round to the right, the landing ends in a small turret with three narrow, square-paned windows. One of the panes is smashed. I shiver with a chill that I assume is getting in through the broken window. The evening air had still been warm when we fetched our gear from the car, but perhaps the damp of the walls cools the air as it comes in, and that's why the house is cold inside? The thing that really strikes me about the turret, though, is how the twilight doesn't make it through the windows. No pools of light spill on to the floor or walls, as they did on the floor below. Nothing. Only shadow. As if something is blocking the light, making it darker here than it should be. I consider if the turret is on a different side of the building, and therefore catching a different angle of the light. But when I trace my steps back down in my head, I realize that it is definitely on the same side as the windows above the walkway and must be the turret I saw from the outside, when we first arrived. And with the turret having windows on three aspects, if anything, there should be even more light.

Weird.

Maybe it's because these windows are smaller? Or maybe the light has changed in that small space of time it took me to climb the stairs?

I shrug it off and step away. But something in that strange, dead gloom clings to me.

There are two doors off the landing straight ahead of me. Taking a deep breath, I edge towards the closest one. It is open a little way, and I shine the torch through the gap, illuminating the gloom directly ahead.

'Hello,' I say as I pause in the doorway. Though who I'm saying it to, I have no idea. And I certainly don't want an answer. Not now. Not when I'm alone. Heart thumping, stomach turning, and breaths coming much too fast, I step forward and poke my head all the way around the door. Inside the dingy room is a disordered row of metal bed frames, no mattresses. It looks like a small dormitory, just five beds, probably from when the place was briefly a school. There is one window, blocked by the branches of a tree that press against the glass, the way that zombies press against the windows of old houses, groping for a way inside.

I direct the torch's beam into the dark corners, sweeping it over the bare floorboards, while my feet crunch on plaster and bricks where they have crumbled from the walls. As I pass, I touch the rusting foot of a bedframe with my fingertips. A shiver ripples through me from the cold metal. I stop. I thought I heard something: a whine or a sob. It can't have been. It must have been the rubber sole of my Converse scuffing the floor. I pull my hand away from the bed, but halt as a drop of icy water hits the back of it. Like a raindrop. *Or a tear.* I stare at my wet hand a beat, dumbfounded, before glancing up to the ceiling, searching out the source of the drop with my torch, which flickers once, twice, then is fine again. Other than patches of mildew, the ceiling appears dry. Something cold flutters in the pit of my stomach. *Where did the drip come from?* With a frown, I wipe the back of my hand on my jeans, before hastily retreating from the room, casting glances back as I go.

Just a slow leak.

That's all.

Not tears of the dead.

A slow leak.

Breathe.

Back out on the landing, the door to the next room is closed. Bracing myself, I place a hand on the doorknob and . . .

. . . three, two, one . . .

. . . I swing it open as if I'm about to yell *Surprise!* to a room full of long-lost family.

Empty.

Phew.

Down a narrow corridor and up a small set of creaky steps, I duck my head through every doorway I come to. One corridor turns into the next as I tear around the second floor. I find nothing but empty rooms and dusty, forgotten belongings from different eras. I must be almost back to where I started when I stop outside a door. It's open just a crack, and I push it further with my free hand. It is lighter inside than out in the corridor because of a large, grime-coated window, which opens on to a balcony, but I glide the torch beam across the floor and into the shadowy nooks and crannies anyway, hoping I don't see anything that I will never be able to erase from my mind. But I keep looking, the way you do when you see a car crash. Almost like a dare.

The room is large, and it bends around to the right in an L-shape. In front of the window is the skeleton of a rusting bed frame, with a festering mattress, and, next to it, a wooden bedside table. The mattress has a slight dip towards the middle of one side, like the imprint of where someone sat on the edge of the bed over the years, perhaps kissing someone goodnight. Or maybe there is someone sitting there, right now. Silent. Staring.

Stop freaking yourself out.

I wonder whose room this would have been years ago, when the Turners lived here. Family? Staff? There is still one more floor in the eaves, on one side of the building, and I think that servants tended to sleep in attics or the kitchens – and I doubt they got balconies. So, probably not servants' quarters.

Elizabeth's room, maybe?

I crane my neck around the corner, into the L-shape, but I realize that I'm going to have to actually go in if I want to be able to see all the way around. Drawing in a deep breath, I take a step into the room.

I follow the room as it turns to the right and stop – dead. There, at the far end of the L-shape, is an EMF reader – a device used in ghost hunting – and a laptop. A *smashed* laptop. And when I say smashed . . . the screen is shattered in a spiderweb pattern and the keyboard is bent and warped as if it's been through a mangle, its keys loose and scattered across the floor. With a hand over my mouth and a heavy, sick feeling in the pit of my stomach, I take in the sight for a moment: it's one thing to find some abandoned belongings, possibly left by someone fleeing in a hurry. But to see this level of destruction of someone's personal items . . .

I draw one conclusion: something bad happened inside this house.

7

SNAPPING OUT OF my initial shock, I dart across the room and go down on my haunches beside the wrecked laptop. Gently pushing the cracked screen down a little way, I gasp when I see the *Scream* 'Ghostface' decal. It's Zach's. My stomach sinks but it flutters with excitement at the same time, because . . . Oh my god, the evidence. The evidence! I breathe in deep to steady myself.

With trembling fingers, I pull the Canon out of its case and start to film.

'So, this is a crazy development, you guys,' I say from behind camera. 'This is Zach's laptop.' I angle the Canon so that it picks up Ghostface. 'It's in a room on the second floor of Thornhanger House, and it is smashed to pieces, adding to the mystery of what happened to him and Lucas here. I mean, whoever did this, they obviously didn't have good intentions.'

I turn the camera so that my face is in frame and add, 'So, the question is: who smashed Zach's laptop and why?'

Buzzing with adrenaline, I shove the EMF reader into my hoodie pocket and, leaving the laptop where I found it, I head down to find the others. I spot both of them on the walkway at the top of the central staircase, and I immediately press record on the Canon, wanting to capture their reactions to my discovery.

'Guys,' I begin, raising the camera to get Molly and Byron in frame as I approach them. They both halt at the sound of my voice. 'You'll never guess what I found upstairs.'

'Hey. What'd you find?' asks Byron.

'An EMF reader,' I say, pulling the device a little way out of my pocket to show the others. 'And – wait for it – Zach's laptop. Smashed to pieces.'

'Smashed?' says Molly, her eyes widening.

'Yep.' I stop with a hand resting on the balustrade as I draw up to them. 'Smashed. I mean, that confirms something sketchy happened here, right?'

'Yeah. I mean. Wow,' says Molly. 'Poltergeist activity, perhaps?'

'Or human activity,' says Byron. 'There's any number of logical reasons why the laptop could've got smashed: an accident, an argument between Zach and Lucas that got out of hand, or maybe it was vandals not realizing or caring what they'd stumbled upon . . .'

'Oh, and that's not all,' I say, ignoring Byron's scepticism. 'In an old dormitory, I heard what sounded like a sob and then droplets of some sort of clear liquid started dripping on to the back of my hand. I swear. I looked up, thinking there had to be a leak, but there was nothing coming from the ceiling. Totally dry. But there they were – droplets. On my hand. Like . . .' I pause a beat . . . '*tears*?'

Byron snorts and Molly says, 'Oh wow. Did you get it on film? We should all go and check it out. You have to show us, Iris. Blimey. Nothing like that happened to either of us. Though I experienced a couple of cold spots and I felt watched.'

'I found a mobile phone,' says Byron. 'Out of battery so I left it. And useless without knowing the passcode, anyway.'

'Oh. Damn. It would've been good to see if there was anything useful on it,' I say. 'Some footage or messages or something. Some sort of clue.'

With just the attic left to search, we decide to head up there together. It's grown darker in the time since we started the search, and none of us particularly want to be alone in the increasing gloom. And there's something super creepy about attics. I'm not sure why. Maybe because they are more remote, sort of cut off from the domesticity of the main house. We find the way up by taking a narrow, winding staircase that Byron found during his search, with Molly and Byron lighting the way ahead with their torches, while I film from the back.

We walk in silence down a narrow corridor with a

sloping ceiling, Molly and Byron opening doors and poking their heads through doorways, before saying, 'Clear'. Then, suddenly . . .

'Ow!'

The others stop and swing round. 'What? What happened?'

'My back,' I begin. 'It hurts. Like it's burning.' I reach my right hand towards my left shoulder blade to indicate the source of the pain, while holding the Canon in my left hand, still filming. 'Can someone take a look? It really hurts.'

I turn and Molly lifts the back of my T-shirt. 'I don't see— Oh,' she says as she raises the fabric higher to expose my shoulder blade. 'Oh. My. God.'

'What? What is it?' I say.

'Scratch marks,' says Molly, her words breathy. 'Iris, something scratched you.'

'What?' Pulling the back of my T-shirt all the way up, I crane my head to look and, in the torchlight, I can see where four angry red lines stop at the top of my shoulder. Switching the Canon to my right hand, I angle it over my shoulder to get the marks on film and to get a better look. On the flip screen, I can see how the scratches begin about halfway down my shoulder blade and continue up along the inside of where my bra strap sits, to the top of my shoulder. 'Oh my god. Something scratched me?'

Byron moves in for a closer look, one finger gently touching my exposed skin as he stoops down a little.

'Ouch!'

'Sorry. Sorry,' he says, his eyes flicking up to meet mine as I look over my shoulder. So close. Keeping eye contact with me, he says, 'You OK?'

'Yeah. Yeah. I just . . . How the hell did I get scratched?'

'It's not uncommon for people to be scratched during paranormal activity,' says Molly.

Byron and I break apart, him straightening up and shifting back a little as I release the edge of my T-shirt, letting the fabric fall down my back. Though I feel his eyes on me still.

I turn to face the others.

'Did you brush against anything . . . try to squeeze through any narrow gaps . . . ?' asks Byron, ignoring Molly's comment.

'No. I . . . I didn't. I only just felt the pain. Look, there's nothing near me,' I say, indicating the empty corridor.

'Well, you must have done it earlier and only just noticed the pain. Maybe where the scratches have been rubbing against your T-shirt,' he persists.

'Possibly,' I say, and I grimace into the camera in such a way that says I don't believe that at all.

8

'YO, GUYS, WHAT'S up? Zach and Lucas here, with another awesome exploration Vid. E. O.' Lucas spreads his arms wide in front of the manor house, still a little way down the overgrown drive, as Zach points the camera at him.

'We're here at this big-arsed old place, called Thornhanger House,' says Zach, turning the camera on himself, and flashing one of his perfect smiles.

'Yeah, this place is something a little extra special.'

Zach angles the camera up, to get a shot of the huge building.

'Super haunted,' says Zach, as he films himself walking closer to the front of the house. 'Built in the early 1800s, the place has been abandoned for decades, and has seen *way* more than its fair share of tragedy.'

'No lie, this place is creepy as anything,' adds Lucas,

swiping a lock of jet-black hair from his eye.

The boys come to a stop just outside the imposing main door, clearly boarded up.

'Which makes it a sure thing for paranormal activity.'

'Let's hope so, dude,' says Lucas, with a snigger.

'Or not,' says Zach. 'I mean, uh, are we ready for this, man?'

'Yeah, you bet we are. It's what we live for, right dude?'

'OK, let's do this,' Zach says with a nervous laugh, which may or may not be hammed up for the camera's benefit.

The camera follows Lucas as he gives the board at the door a tug. It doesn't budge. Zach must be concentrating on finding a way in, rather than filming, as there's a blur of movement and then a shot of the base of the house, where tall weeds and brown, tangled vines grow up the pale, weather-worn stone. The camera tracks the boys' journey around the elaborate stone arch that frames the door and along the portico, where an arm in a black long-sleeve T-shirt can be seen coming out from behind the camera to try a window. Sealed shut. Along the front wall, they try another window. Shut. Around the corner to the side of the house. Distracted as he tries to find a way in, Zach is not paying attention to where he is pointing the camera, and all that can be seen in frame are flashes of weeds and stone, and one booted foot that goes in and out of shot as he walks. He stops, and the camera moves erratically for a moment, but settles on a shot of the side of the house – cold greying stone. A grunt can be heard, followed by a sharp, hard *snap*. A scuffling, followed by another grunt, then, 'Dude, this way!' and the crunch of feet on stone and the swish of denim through tall grass and dry, prickly weeds can be heard, which must be Lucas, catching up to Zach.

'Dude, be careful,' says Zach as he lifts the camera to show a window, the glass within its frame broken. 'There're some jagged bits. I knocked a big piece out, but it's still a bit dodge.'

Zach films Lucas peering inside, shining a torch. 'You didn't smash it, did you?' Lucas turns to camera.

'Na, man. Course not. Leave as we find, dude.'

'Cool.'

'I just helped it along a bit.'

Zach films Lucas climbing through the window, then passes the camera to him. Lucas scans the camera around a large, high-ceilinged room, its corners gloomy, its walls peeling paint like dried scabs. He captures a glimpse of Zach as he drops down from the window. Lucas continues to sweep the camera around. The room is huge, with floor-to-ceiling bookshelves in dark wood along two walls. There is a big bay window along to the right that lets in a light that is filtered by grime and creepers. The camera moves a bit too fast to take in much detail, but, other than debris that has crumbled from the walls and the ceiling, the room appears to be bare.

Feet crunch on decades worth of dust as the camera tracks their progress across the room, through one of the large doorways, and out into a massive entrance hall. To the right, the grand central staircase sweeps upwards, branching left and right. Above the staircase, the ceiling rises right up to that of the first floor, increasing the sense of space, and as Lucas moves the camera up and down and around, the remains of an old chandelier can be seen.

'Holy shit, this place is huge!' says Lucas from behind the camera.

There is only one small window in the entrance hall, but it's bright outside, one of those crisp autumn days that hold a memory of summer and a promise of winter, and some light spills from the floor above, so there is enough natural light to see. Though Zach shines a torch ahead of him anyway.

'So, this is the inside of Thornhanger House. It. Is. Awesome,' says Zach, and Lucas swings the camera round to frame him as he stops in the centre of the entrance hall.

'So cool, dude.'

Zach pulls something out of his jeans pocket. He unfolds it to reveal sheets of A4 paper, covered in printed and handwritten text, front and back.

'Oooh, he's come prepared,' says Lucas from behind the camera.

'Yep, you better believe it,' says Zach, smiling. 'OK. So, a bit of history about the old place,' he begins. 'Thornhanger House was built in 1827 for Lord Thornhanger and his soon-to-be wife, Emma. However, Lord Thornhanger wasn't quite the upstanding guy everyone thought, and he had a *dalliance* with one of the housemaids: a young girl named Violet.' He glances intermittently at his notes as he speaks. 'Violet bragged to the other maids that she was to become Lady Thornhanger instead of Emma, craving the fame and fortune that the title would bring. But when the marriage went ahead, she felt the ultimate betrayal. In a jealous rage, it's thought that Violet murdered Lord Thornhanger and Emma, just hours after they said their vows, taking her own life in the process.'

'That's wild,' adds Lucas.

'It gets wilder,' says Zach. 'The three bodies were found in the ballroom, still set for the marriage banquet, charred beyond recognition and identifiable only from the few bits of clothing or jewellery that survived. But what's really odd is that the house itself suffered no damage, and rumours spread that Violet called upon dark forces to commit the murders. Some believed that those dark forces never left.'

'Stop it,' says Lucas. 'Dude, that's messed up.'

'I know, right. With locals believing the place was cursed, the house stood empty until the late 1800s, when it was sold to a wealthy lawyer, Edward Turner, who moved in with his wife, Charlotte, and their young daughter, Elizabeth.' He glances at his notes. 'And according to folklore, while Elizabeth's father was away on business, her mother had a riding accident, coming off her horse in the meadow just outside the manor house grounds, breaking her neck. She died instantly.'

'That's dark, man.'

'Yep.' Zach looks down at the crumpled paper in his

hand, and back to camera. 'The story goes that Edward's sister, Anne, was called for to act as Elizabeth's guardian until her father returned home, which wouldn't be for months.'

'Aw, poor kid,' says Lucas. 'Mum dead. Dad away, like, forever . . .'

'Uh-huh, and that's not even the worst of it. You see, Edward's fortune was self-made. He and Anne came from humble beginnings, from which Anne never escaped, having refused her brother's *charity*. Now resident in Thornhanger House, and seeing Elizabeth's privileged upbringing for herself, Anne became envious of the little girl and the opportunities that a life of wealth afforded her. Though she kept that bitter side of herself hidden, she resented having to look after Elizabeth.'

'Great stuff,' adds Lucas, as he follows Zach into the next room: a large L-shaped space with a high ceiling and crumbling ceiling roses. There's a large bay window on the front wall and two more smaller windows on the side, and a grand fireplace. A stepladder rests against a wall.

'According to legend, Anne derived a perverse pleasure from being cruel to Elizabeth, as if each vindictive act were making up for everything that she herself had gone without as a child. From heavily oversalting Elizabeth's food and forcing the young child to eat it, to punishing her over the smallest things by locking her in a cupboard and leaving her in the suffocating pitch-dark for hours on end. All the while, maintaining the pretence of being the doting aunt in her correspondence with Edward.'

'Man, that's horrible,' says Lucas, distaste clear in his voice. 'She's like, the worst auntie ever.'

'I mean, she pretty much sucks,' adds Zach.

The next room is slightly smaller than the last, but with another large bay window, though this one is partially covered by a bush that has grown unimpeded just outside it. Lucas follows Zach with the camera as they weave through tall items of furniture, each covered with a grimy dust sheet, like Halloween ghosts that have seen better days.

'One day, a housemaid . . .' Zach trails off. 'Man, I thought I saw something moving over there.' He pauses to direct his torch beam towards a corner.

'Yeah, dude, I keep thinking there's someone under one of those sheets, just waiting to leap out at us,' says Lucas from behind the camera.

Zach glances back at him, his eyebrows raised. 'Ah, man, why'd you have to put that thought in my head.' He gives a shiver and quickens his pace. 'Anyway. One day, a housemaid let slip that, while foraging for mushrooms in the woods—' Zach's head snaps to the left and he pauses to listen. 'D'you hear that?'

'I don't hear anything, dude,' says Lucas.

'A groan.'

'Nah, man.'

Zach shrugs and carries on, torch flicking left and right. 'So, the housemaid claimed she'd glimpsed the ghost of Elizabeth's mother in the meadow on the other side of the stream, which marks the edge of the property line on one side of the house. Furious that she'd spread such outlandish stories, the aunt sacked the housemaid on the spot.'

'Harsh,' comes Lucas's voice from behind the camera.

'Definitely harsh. Elizabeth was desperate to see her mother again, so she began spending her days in the wood, searching for her dead mother's ghost in the meadow beyond the stream.'

'Ah, this story gives me the chills, man,' says Lucas, following Zach into the next room, much smaller than the previous rooms, and with no windows at all. Zach's torch beam bounces from one wall to the next as he takes in his surroundings. 'Did she find her mum's ghost?'

Zach stops and shines the torch on his notes. 'Well, according to the story, old Anne started to go nuts, shouting at the staff and refusing to eat or wash or change her clothes. At night, she could be heard pacing her bedchamber, and by day she would keep watch out across the wood and the meadow beyond the grounds, the circles beneath her eyes getting darker and darker.' He shifts closer to the camera, holding the torch beneath his chin to create an eerie shadowed effect with his features as he speaks. 'Wild-haired and nothing more than bones,' he says, increasing the drama in his voice, 'she would rant and rave that her dead sister-in-law was searching for a way on to the property to get her.' He pulls a mock-alarmed face to camera. As he carries on with the story, he starts to walk, Lucas following, filming him. 'Rumours spread between the household staff that Anne's fear of

Charlotte's ghost was down to her guilty conscience over her mistreatment of little Elizabeth. She was afraid that Charlotte would make her pay for it.'

'Quite right. Old Anne's a grade-A bitch.'

'That's it, Lucas, piss off Anne's ghost.'

'One way to get some activity.'

The boys are now in a corridor, heading further into the house. It is narrow and gloomy, though they manage with just Zach's torch.

'Anne became reclusive and wouldn't let Elizabeth go outside. She started sacking all the staff, and some left of their own accord, afraid of what she might be capable of doing to them.'

'I don't blame them. Jeez, what a nutter.'

'Oh, you know what, dude,' Zach stops, looks right into the camera, his piercing eyes wide, 'maybe we should do a seance later and try to rile old Anne up a bit.' He grins.

'Like, try to piss her off?'

'Yeah, see if we can get some activity by making her hate us.'

'Are you sure?'

'Yeah,' he says with a shrug. 'Why not?'

'I don't know, dude. I mean, the more of these videos we make, the more seems to happen, and the more I start to believe that supernatural stuff is really happening.'

'Me too, man.'

'It's just . . . ah . . . Anne sounds properly nuts. You know, if her spirit is here, is it such a great idea to annoy her?'

'Who started it, with the name-calling?' says Zach, playfully. 'Besides, what've we got to lose? And we could get some *pretty good footage.*' Zach says the last few words in a sing-song voice.

From behind the camera, Lucas lets out a long breath. 'I don't know, man. Is doing this shit really worth it for a video?'

'Yes.'

Both boys snort with laughter.

'Yeah, all right, you got me,' says Lucas, as Zach moves off again and he follows him with the camera. Lucas films Zach passing through a door and into another corridor and round a corner, where he halts with a shriek, and when the camera catches up with him, a marble statue of a woman with long hair piled on top of her head and a long, billowing dress, tarnished with dirt, can be seen in a recess in the wall. Zach is stood with his hand against the wall, saying, 'Jesus, I thought someone was standing there. Christ, I think I just crapped myself.' Lucas's laughter can be heard off camera, the footage shaking in time to the outburst of giggles. They continue into another room – with a tree sprouting through the floorboards – and out into another corridor, and Zach's tale is punctuated by *Ohhh*s, and *Ahh*s and *Whoa*s as he and Lucas take in their grand but decaying surroundings.

'One day, Anne spots Elizabeth slipping into the woods,' says Zach, pausing to inspect a grandfather clock which has long since stopped, before heading into the next room.

'Oh, I bet she was mad.'

'Oh yeah, she was mad, all right. She chased after Elizabeth, and before the kid could cross the stream, where she believed her mother was waiting for her in the meadow, Anne caught her by the arm and dragged her, kicking and screaming, back to the house.'

'Ah, man, I'm not sure I want to hear the rest of this story,' says Lucas, turning the camera on himself and pulling a worried face.

An old free-standing dresser, cobwebbed and peeling with age, can be seen behind him. As he pans the camera around, a cast iron cooking range, black and thick with dust, still sits within a brick hearth, indicating that this was the former kitchen. This room would once have been filled with steam and delicious smells, and the clang of pots and pans as hearty meals were prepared for former residents. The heart of the house. Though this heart has long stopped beating. The boys wander around the room, opening and closing cupboards and drawers.

'Anne is supposed to have locked Elizabeth in a cupboard before marching back down towards the meadow, yelling curses to her dead sister-in-law as she went, and the one remaining member of staff, a young housemaid, ran away in fear,' Zach continues. 'Just before leaving the grounds, the maid is reported to have heard a short, ear-piercing scream from the direction of the woods. When Elizabeth's father returned, he discovered his sister's body in the wood, down by the stream. Her face was frozen in torment, as though she had died of fright.'

'Oh man. I'm totally picturing that dude from *The Ring*, the one who dies cos he's seen that creepy girl come out of the TV.'

Zach, who is currently inspecting a pile of festering newspapers in the corner of the room, snorts and says, 'Dude, Anne is *so* going to be after you,' before standing and heading for the door to the next room.

'Zach, man, don't say that. What if she attaches herself to me and, like, follows me home?'

'Why would you say that?' says Zach, stopping to glance back at Lucas. 'It's like you want her to go home with you.'

'No way, man. That's creepy.' Lucas turns around so that he is in front of the camera, to show his freaked-out face. Zach can be seen behind him, laughing.

'Anyway,' continues Zach, as Lucas goes back behind the camera, 'unable to find his daughter or any staff, the dad conducts a search of the house, only to find Elizabeth's body in the cupboard that Anne locked her in, her nails torn and her fingertips worn and bloody, deep pits in the back of the door where she'd tried to claw her way out.'

'No way. That is some dark shit,' says Lucas as he follows Zach along a corridor.

'In his grief, Elizabeth's father shut himself up in the old house, refusing to take visitors,' Zach continues. 'A family friend, worried about him, eventually forced his way into the house, only to find Edward standing in front of the ornate gilt-framed mirror in his bedchamber, a knife held at his throat. "I can no longer live without them," he's supposed to have said into the mirror, before drawing the blade across his flesh.'

'No. Way.'

'Finding his daughter's lifeless body had been too much for him, and it's said that those days alone inside the huge, empty house had driven him mad.'

'Man, no word of a lie, I got the biggest chill then, like the temperature's dipped.' Lucas stops. 'Dude, come and stand here. Is it me or is it colder here? Like there's something standing right here.'

Zach walks back to where Lucas stands.

'I don't know, man,' says Zach. Then he reconsiders and says, 'Yeah, actually, you're right. It is a bit colder. We should go get the EMF reader, take some readings . . .'

'Well, I can't feel a thing,' says Byron, standing in the exact same spot as the boys had months ago, while Zach continues to speak: a small, tinny voice from the camera.

Byron steps aside so that Molly and I can take his place.

'Me neither,' I say with a shrug and a shake of my head to camera, before turning it around to get Molly in frame.

She has her eyes closed and her head slightly lowered in concentration. Her mouth is set in a line. After a moment, she gives a little sigh and opens her eyes. She scrunches up her face and to camera, she says, 'Nothing. But that doesn't mean there wasn't something here when they shot that footage. It just isn't here now.'

'Yeah. Sure,' I say. 'Maybe.'

Earlier, sat on a couple of sleeping bags bundled in the alcove of the bay window in our base camp, we scanned through mostly useless footage of Zach and Lucas leaving the London flat they share; some driving shots; Zach eating chips outside a parade of shops that looks a lot like Hillthorn's high street, though I can't be sure; and a video of them messing around in the front gardens outside Thornhanger House; until we found this video, where their investigation begins. We've decided to use the footage as a virtual map, to retrace their steps through the house. That way, we hope not to miss any clues as to what happened to them here.

On-screen, the boys head back to the entrance hall, to get the EMF reader from their gear, and we follow. EMF readers – electromagnetic field readers – detect any electromagnetic energy in the area, which is *supposed* to indicate the presence of spirits. But they can be triggered by any electrical devices, such as mobile phones, or power lines and outlets, and camera equipment. When an electromagnetic field is present, the energy is registered by a series of lights, from blue, through green, yellow and orange, to red: the stronger the energy, the higher the colour will spike, with red being the highest. During paranormal investigations, EMF readers can be used alongside monitoring things like temperature and humidity, to keep track of any unexpected and unexplained changes and add to the overall picture of an investigation, rather than any spike necessarily *proving* that there's a ghost in the vicinity. I guess Zach and Lucas liked the drama of a device spiking. It makes for a good bit of footage and, who knows . . . But when they return to the cold spot, no lights flash at all. Nothing happens when they call out to any spirits present, and they end up heading straight back to the central staircase, where the video ends. So, we stay put and, perched on a step a little way up, we watch the next piece of footage.

To see where it will lead us.

9

'CHECK IT OUT,' says Lucas, shining his torch at the same mirror where I scared myself earlier. 'I wonder if that's the mirror Elizabeth's dad killed himself in front of,' he says.

'I don't know, dude. But a lot of the original items from the house are still here,' says Zach, who now has the camera and is filming Lucas standing in front of the mirror.

Lucas shoves the EMF reader into the front pocket of his hoodie. Staring at his reflection, he mimics slicing his throat, pulling a tongue-out death face, while making a gargling noise, as though choking on blood. He bursts out laughing.

'Lucas, man, you really are doing everything you can to piss these spirits off,' Zach says from behind the camera.

The EMF reader emits a faint crackle, which sounds a

little like crickets chirruping at night. Lucas pulls it out of his pocket and holds it up to the mirror. Both boys release excited *Whoa*s and *Oh my god*s, and Zach zooms in on it with the camera as the lights go from green to yellow and orange.

'Maybe it's picking up Elizabeth's dad?' says Zach. 'Strange how it's going nuts in front of this mirror. I mean, there's no power in this house. It shouldn't be going off at all. Dude, look at it.'

The EMF reader spikes at red, then settles back to green.

Lucas, ever the joker, laughs and says, 'D'you think if I say his name three times while staring into the mirror he'll come and haunt me? Like Bloody Mary.'

'I think Bloody Mary is thirteen times, dude.'

'I'm pretty sure it's three times. Or is it five?'

'Five is Candyman, who isn't even real. But whatever. Try it. See what happens.'

'What was his name again . . . Edmond . . . ?'

'Edward. Edward Turner.'

'Edward Turner, Edward Turner, Ed—'

'*Buuut*,' says Zach, cutting Lucas off before he can complete the incantation, 'you should know that in the 1980s this place was being renovated to be turned into a hotel. But it was never finished. The foreman slit his own throat with a box-cutter, while staring into the large ornate mirror that had once hung in Edward Turner's bedchamber,' he says, recounting a detail that I didn't know. I knew someone died during that time, from my own research, but I didn't know who or how. I throw a glance up the stairs behind me, catching a glimpse of the mirror, inky black in the dark. I don't want to turn my back on it, unease making my spine prickle, but I do. My eyes find the flip screen in Byron's hand, as he sits between me and Molly.

'No way,' says Lucas, his grin dropping. 'Just like Elizabeth's dad?'

'*Exactly* like Elizabeth's dad.'

Lucas smooths his straight, black fringe out of his face with his fingers. His hand comes to rest for a moment in the short hair at the back of his head, as he puffs out his cheeks. 'Man. I should really do my research before I come to these places.'

'Yeah, instead you always leave it to me,' says Zach.

'But you're so good at it, dude,' says Lucas, looking into the camera. 'I can't believe I almost cursed myself in some haunted mirror.'

'Well, we don't know if it's this actual mirror. But it's meant to still be here somewhere.'

'So, they just stopped doing up the place?'

'Yeah, after the foreman died, the labourers refused to go back on-site. Thornhanger House has been empty ever since.'

'I am *so* not looking in any more mirrors in this place,' says Lucas, as he climbs the rest of the stairs, heading to the left.

Lucas lights the way as he and Zach edge down a corridor. Zach can't be seen, as he is filming, and he hangs back a bit so that Lucas is in frame, shot from behind and slightly to the right.

'Where are we heading?' asks Lucas, without looking back.

'To the roof. For the next part of the Thornhanger House legend. The story of Grace.' This piques my interest, as I have no idea who Grace is. 'And I'd like to get up there while it's still light out. I want to get a good shot of the woods from up there, and see if we can see the stream and the property line.'

'Oh yeah, the woods where Anne died, right?' says Lucas. 'If we get fifty thousand likes for this video,' he says as he continues to walk, throwing glances back to the camera, 'we'll come back to Thornhanger House and camp in the woods for the night.'

'Oh man, I think we'd need nearer a hundred thousand likes for me to do something like that,' says Zach, laughing. He turns the camera on himself and pulls an I'm-worried face.

'OK, dude. A hundred thousand likes and we'll stay the night in the haunted woods. You hear that, people, hit that "like" button, and we'll be back.'

They turn right at the end of a corridor. It's darker here, with no natural light, and it's hard to see the edges and corners of walls with just one torch. The boys pass through a series of rooms, some with dusty, forgotten belongings, others bare, and out into corridors, as they wind deeper into the house. Suddenly, Zach stops in a corridor.

'Dude. Lucas. Wait up. Did you hear that?'

Lucas halts and turns to camera. 'What?'

'Shhh. That . . . did you hear it? Footsteps. Listen . . .'

Zach holds a shot of Lucas, as they both remain silent and still, Lucas with his head to one side, listening.

'Again – you hear that? You must have heard that.'

Lucas slaps a hand across his mouth. His eyes bug out.

'Footsteps, right?' says Zach.

'Right above us,' whispers Lucas, lowering his hand.

The boys remain still for a few beats.

'It's stopped. I think it—'

'Oh my god – again!' Zach points the camera upwards, as if he expects a ghostly foot to come right through the ceiling.

'I heard it.'

'You think the camera is picking this up?' says Zach in a hushed but excited voice.

It's not. I press myself into Byron's side, straining my ears as I watch the footage, but I can't hear a thing from the recording. Molly gives me a little shake of her head to indicate that she can't hear it either. I turn my attention back to the screen.

'Let's go check it out,' says Lucas.

We watch Zach and Lucas tear along corridors until they find a set of stairs which take them up to the next floor, making enough noise to announce their arrival, for good or for bad. In a large room above where they heard the footsteps all appears still. But as they edge around the room, which is partially converted into a boxy hotel room, the EMF reader starts going off, from green to yellow, all the way through to red, where it stays for three beats of my heart.

10

'SO, IT'S JUST gone nine thirty p.m.,' I say into camera, pointing it at myself as I walk along a corridor on the first floor, 'and we're retracing Zach and Lucas's steps to where they heard sounds in a room above them.'

'We're going to stand where they stood,' begins Byron, Zach's Canon in his hand. I swing my camera round so that it's on him and Molly as they walk just ahead of me. 'To see if we can hear anything and hopefully start discounting any likely causes.'

'Professor Byron Miller there everyone,' I say, playfully, turning the camera back on to myself, 'ensuring that we stick to strict ghostbusting protocol.' We catch each other's eye and swap a small smile. I think I see his cheeks flush a little, but it's hard to tell in the torchlight.

It's near dark through the corridors, and so we use torches to light our way. Mine keeps flickering and cutting out, and then being fine again, giving more of a disco vibe than a scary-house vibe. Molly says that it's a spirit trying to grab our attention. I don't disagree but I'm guessing it's probably damaged from when I dropped it, when I scared myself on the stairs earlier. As we walk, I open doors, searching for cupboards, as I'm determined to find the one Anne used to lock Elizabeth in. I know from watching their footage that Zach and Lucas have checked the doors along here. But I want to see if they missed anything. Somewhere in this house, if the legend is to be believed, is a door with deep grooves on the inside of it from Elizabeth's nails, and I want to find it.

'So, does anyone have any theories as to what happened to Zach and Lucas?' I say.

'Well, we didn't see their car out front,' says Byron, flicking a glance back to the camera. 'So, it's possible they left in a hurry and crashed.' He stops a moment to replay a little more of the footage of Zach and Lucas making this same journey, his eyes flicking up to a doorway on the left and back to the screen. Sure it's the one he's looking for, he heads towards the door, adding, 'That might explain why their stuff is here and why they never made it home.'

Molly and I follow Byron into a large room filled with old junk – bits of furniture, some stacked crates and odds and ends: lamps, piles of books, a glass vase so dusty that it has turned opaque, candlesticks . . . I wonder how this stuff hasn't been looted over the years.

'But that doesn't make sense,' says Molly, as she pauses to peruse some of the knick-knacks dotted about. 'Surely someone would have found the car by now?'

I spot a stack of old paintings leaning against a wall. On my haunches, I shine my torch on a dusty portrait of a pretty young woman, looking off to the side, her golden hair up and adorned with flowers. She wears a white dress, edged with pale blue to match the flowers in her hair. I wonder if it's Charlotte Turner. I place my torch on the floor and riffle through the other paintings: the same woman, dressed this time in green, holding the reins of a silky black horse, outside Thornhanger House; a small girl in a navy dress, reading a book.

'And even if no one's been out here,' continues Molly. 'Zach and Lucas would most likely have been driving back the way they came – we would have passed the car, wouldn't we? If it crashed, we probably would have seen it.'

I start at the next painting: a portrait of a striking but sour-faced woman, with a mouth that turns down at the edges and pale skin stretched over high cheekbones. Her hair is scraped back, with a centre parting. But it's the eyes that get me – so dark and piercing, I feel her judging me from out of that canvas. And I don't think I'm going to like any judgements she makes. *Anne?* With an internal shudder, I let the other paintings fall back against it. Grabbing my torch, I stand and say, 'Yeah, you're right, Moll. It doesn't add up.'

'None of this adds up,' says Byron, idly flicking through the pages of a musty old book. 'And I don't like it.'

'Because you can't explain it.'

I join Byron, just as he says, 'I can't explain it *yet*,' and he pokes me in the side when he says *yet*, for emphasis. I go to poke him back, but I remember Molly, though she's just discovered the paintings and is cross-legged in front of them. I stop myself anyway. *Progress*. 'But there's a rational explanation,' he continues. 'There has to be.'

'Yeah, the explanation is that they either never left the house and disappeared into thin air, or they left the house and disappeared into thin air,' I say from behind the camera. I film one last sweep of the room, before we head back into the corridor.

'That's not an explanation,' says Byron from ahead of me. 'That's a recap of the scenario.' He flashes me a wry smile. 'And no one vanishes into thin air. Maybe the car went off the road and crashed in the undergrowth so we didn't see it?'

'Something happened to them here. I'm sure of it,' says Molly, as we turn the next corner. 'You can just feel it, right? Something's here, right?' She shoots a glance at me behind the camera, rather than Byron. 'There's a weird energy,' she continues. 'Like sensing someone's already in a room when you walk into it, only there's no one there.'

Molly was raised by her grandmother. Her dad drowned in a fishing accident when she was five. At the funeral, her mum told her dead husband that she'd see him soon. Two weeks later, she died in her sleep. Her heart just stopped. Sudden Arrhythmic Death Syndrome. Or as Molly's grandmother tells it: a broken heart. Like it's some big tragic romance, rather than just a fucking tragedy that a five-year-old lost both of her parents in the space of a few weeks. That's where Molly's fascination with the supernatural comes from, because if ghosts and the afterlife are real, it means that her parents aren't gone completely. That they are somewhere waiting for her, and they are looking out for her until she gets there.

It's how she copes.

That's why, like me, she needs this.

'Like when I felt someone watching us in the ballroom,' I say to Molly, and I place a hand to the back of my neck for emphasis as she glances round at me.

'It's probably just your expectations, influenced by the location and your preconceived—'

'A simple *no* would work, By,' Molly snaps.

Feeling a seismic shift in Molly, I switch to an uncharacteristic diplomatic mode. 'Well, everyone take note of how you feel as you move around the house. Any cold spots, feelings of a presence, or of being watched, touched, and— Jesus . . . crap!'

'Fuck me!'

'What?' Molly bumps into the back of Byron as he stops suddenly, and she makes an *Oof* sound.

'Did you guys see that?' I say.

'I saw it,' says Byron. 'But it couldn't . . .'

'*What?*'

'Jesus. That door,' I say to Molly, pointing with my torch to a door on the left, a little way down the corridor. The torch flickers and cuts out. I bang it against my thigh and it comes back on. 'It opened by itself. I swear it did.

You saw it, right, Byron?'

'Yeah. But—'

'Ugh, I can't believe I missed it,' says Molly. 'Did you get it on camera?'

'I don't know. I don't think so. It just sort of happened really quick. I wasn't ready.'

'Damn . . . I wish I'd seen it.'

'It's just an old wonky hinge,' says Byron, and Molly shoots him an extremely chilly glare.

'Wonky hinge?' I say, as we reach the door. 'Do you have the pocketbook version of *101 Ways to Explain the Unexplained to Annoy Your Friends While Ghost Hunting* on your person or something? It was a door that opened by itself, Byron.'

He snorts good-naturedly at my comment. 'Doors don't just open by themselves,' he says, running his torch beam up the hinge-side of the jamb, inspecting it.

'Exactly. And this one did. And you saw it,' I say.

I nudge the door open further with my foot, not wanting to touch it, as if I think I'll catch ghost lurgies.

'It's dark. I don't know what I saw.'

'You saw a door open by its freaking self!' Frustrated, I swing round to face him, my back against the door frame.

Byron looks at me, eyes wide, and I think he's going to say something, but, instead, he grins and snorts. And he bursts out laughing. And I'm like, 'What's so funny?' and Byron mimics, '*You saw a door open by its freaking self!*' and I glare at him a moment, before saying, 'And what's so funny about . . .' and I don't get any further because I snort and then I'm laughing too, as adrenaline wears off enough for me to see that, actually, this is sort of funny. I mean, doors opening by themselves – as if! And Byron and I are lost in giggles as Molly stares at us, looking for a way in. But all I can do is laugh and laugh, and maybe it's just the reaction of the adrenaline leaving me after the scare but I double up, reaching out to grasp Byron's arm to steady myself, when Molly says, 'I think something wants us to go inside,' and barges between us, disappearing into the room.

Our torch beams skim over chairs and small wooden desks, the type with a top that lifts to reveal a compartment to keep books in, all stacked at the far end. A blackboard hangs on the wall behind them. An old classroom.

To my right, a wooden cabinet runs the length of the room. Doors hang off hinges. Some of the shelves above it have collapsed. I use my torch to pick out some of the old junk that still occupies the cabinet's surface while I film: stacks of old decaying hardback books and piles of papers. An abacus. A globe, with a dark-wood base and a brass meridian.

A framed photograph leaning against the wall catches my eye. Shifting closer, I shine my torch at the faded photo beneath the cracked glass. Serious-faced children lined up in rows outside Thornhanger House. Those in the front are cross-legged on the ground, with the next row sat on stiff-backed wooden chairs. Behind them stand a line of older children, followed by the final row, who must be standing on a bench or something, as they are a good head and shoulders above the children in front. At the left and right ends stand two women with tight smiles, both with neat hair, wide-collared shirts beneath smart button-up cardigans, one pink and one pale yellow, and knee-length skirts. They are quite clearly teachers. The children wear dark grey blazers with a red trim over light grey shirts and trousers, or a below-the-knee-length pleated skirt for the girls, with the younger children in grey shorts or pinafores, socks pulled up to their knees. The older kids look to be about ten or eleven, and some in the front row look as young as four or five. As I study each innocent little face, I remember Vera, the old lady from town, saying that there had been some deaths and disappearances, before the school shut down.

Which of you never made it—

I jump at a sharp bang from behind me. Turning, I see Byron standing beside a desk, looking sheepish. 'Sorry,' he says, lifting the desk's top a little way up and down again. 'It slipped out of my fingers.'

'Jesus, Byron,' I say, 'you almost gave me a heart attack.'

'Sorry,' he says again.

'I think I peed myself a little bit,' says Molly, so sweetly that even if she had, it would be the most adorable thing in the world. Cuter than an internet kitten.

'Guys, look at this old photo,' I say, getting it in frame with the camera. They both crunch over to where I stand. 'Some of these kids must have died in this house.'

'Oh, look at them.' Molly leans in for a closer look. 'Why don't we try to call out to them,' she says excitedly, as she straightens up and puts a hand on my arm. 'Make contact.'

'How about we challenge ourselves to see how long we can stay in here in total darkness, just listening, after someone calls out,' suggests Byron, as he sidles up to Molly to study the photograph. 'There are no windows in here,' he adds, turning and shining his torch around the walls, 'so it'll be pitch-black.'

I grimace. I do NOT like the idea of *total darkness*.

'Come on,' he says, beckoning us with a flick of his head as he strides to the middle of the room. He turns and says, 'I'll prove to you both that there's nothing to be scared of. In the dark or with the lights on, it's just an empty old house.'

He switches off his torch and raises an eyebrow in a I-know-you-want-to-hmm-hmm kind of way. Molly shrugs and, with an eager grin, she follows Byron.

'Okaaay,' I say hesitantly, leaning in for another look at the photograph. I'm not thrilled by the idea of not knowing if something is creeping up on me in the dark. But then, on second thoughts, if it brings us closer to finding out the truth about this house – to stopping Byron from leaving the channel – I'm all for it, so I turn back to the others and say, 'Yeah. OK. Let's do this.'

I set the Canon up on the cabinet, checking that Molly and Byron are in frame, before ducking into shot to say,

'So, you won't see anything for a while, as it'll be too dark for the camera to pick anything up, but I'm going to keep filming anyway – just in case . . .'

Switching off my torch, I leave it with the camera and join the others. With only Molly's light, the room grows smaller, as the darkness draws in around us. I give her a nod, and she switches her torch off. We're plunged into blackness. The type that makes you wonder if you have fallen off the face of the earth.

'This is creepy,' I say.

'Only in your head,' says Byron.

'You saying I have a creepy head?'

I hear Byron chuckle, and Molly says a polite, 'Shush.'

'Yeah, let's get on with this,' I say.

And after a beat, Molly says, 'If there is anyone here, one of the missing children who used to go to school here, please give us a sign.'

Silence.

We stand in the Total. Pitch. Dark. My ears strain. I hear my thumping heart. My ragged breathing. A scrape, followed by a hushed voice from beside me that says, 'Sorry, that was me', while another voice says, 'Shush!'

I peer into the darkness, not knowing where I end and it begins. Eyes wide, I start to imagine that I see shadows shifting. Something even darker than the dark itself. I glance left and right, but it's as if the movement is always in my peripheral vision.

Just your imagination.

Shapes swirl in front of me. Faces form: pale and small.

Coming closer. Closer. I shut my eyes. I can still see the pale faces. And I know that they are just the faces of the children from the photograph imprinted on my mind's eye.

I gasp when I hear a creak.

'Sorry. That was me again,' comes a hushed voice.

'Shussshh!'

I open my eyes. But it makes no difference, so total is the dark. Is there something creeping up behind me? Is there something just about to touch my neck with a cold finger?

What if something snatches one of us away in the dark?

Fear constricts my heart and my lungs at that thought. I know the fear is irrational. That I'm just spooking myself. But I can't breathe. My head snaps in all directions, sure something is in here with us. I'm about to call time, when I realize that I'm afraid not only of what is in the dark but of what I might see when the lights go on. What if someone is stood right in front of me? Their dead face centimetres from my own. What if—

'Wait,' I say. 'Can anyone hear that?'

'Sorry,' says Byron. 'That was me again. I moved my feet. Creaky floorboards.'

'No. Not that,' I say, my voice hushed. 'There's a faint whirring sound.'

'I don't hear anything.'

'Shush. Let me listen,' says Molly.

Silence.

'There it is again. How is no one else hearing that?

Someone switch a torch on. Quick!' I say with urgency. 'I'll get my cam—'

'No! Wait. I want to hear it.'

'Moll, if there's something happening, I have to get it on film before it stops.' I take a step to the left, feeling blindly for the cabinet, hoping I don't touch something cold and dead in the dark. 'I can't find . . . Christ! Someone put their torch on!'

'Wait. You'll scare . . .' But Molly's words trail off as my knee connects with an open door and its hinge squeaks. My hands fumble along the surface of the cabinet, until I feel my torch. Snatching it up, I switch it on. It flickers. Once. Twice. I groan and shake it and it's fine again. I pan the torch's beam along the surface of the cabinet, where we saw the class photograph. 'There!' I say, as the light finds the globe. It is gently turning, making only the faintest mechanical whir as it slows. 'See. I told you I could hear something.'

Molly gasps – a long, inward sound. 'Holy cow – it's moving!' She switches on her torch and shines it on the globe but stays back.

I grab the Canon, pointing it at the rotating globe as it slows. I film Byron as he comes over to inspect it.

'Did either of you—'

'No!' Molly and I say together.

'I haven't moved from this spot,' says Molly.

'And I just picked up the torch and my camera.'

'Then one of us must have knocked it with an arm or something, when we were looking at the photograph,' says Byron. He stops it with a finger. And to demonstrate, he leans forward as if to look at the class photo and when he moves back, he brushes the globe with his arm, sending it spinning again. 'See, easily done. And these things go for age—'

'No,' says Molly, firmly.

Byron and I turn to face her, staring back at us from the middle of the room. Her eyes sparkling in the torchlight.

'I asked for a sign. And they gave us one.'

11

SO, WE'RE BACK on track and heading down the corridor where Zach and Lucas heard footsteps above them, and Molly is all: 'Something – not us – spun that globe,' and Byron is all: 'Moll, either one of us brushed it with an arm, or one of us sneaked over there and spun it intentionally.' And I'm like: 'In the pitch-dark, in an unfamiliar room, with junk all over the floor without making a sound?'

At Byron's request, we reviewed the footage from when I was setting up the camera, but the globe was not in shot. No way of proving when it began to spin.

'But they're the only two plaus—' Byron begins, but Molly flings out an arm and says: 'Wait! Stop moving.'

Byron and I halt, both of us staring at her. I frame her in the camera screen.

There's a deep pause, before she says, 'Did you guys hear that?'

'What?'

'Shhh.' She puts a finger to her lips and whispers, 'Listen. There,' she points her finger above us.

I hear it. Footsteps. Slow and steady. They grow in volume to creaking thuds. Right above us. Right where Zach and Lucas heard them too.

'You all hear that, right?'

'Yep. Byron?'

He nods to the camera.

'Well, Professor Miller, any theories . . . anything you want to discount or hypothesize?' I say.

He gives a slight shake of his head. 'Not yet.'

We come across a narrow staircase, different from the one I took up to the second floor earlier, which I'm glad of, as I'm in no hurry to pass those weird turret windows again. The windows that don't let in light. At the top of the staircase, I pause. There's a door across the landing that is smaller than the others. There is a keyhole but no key. I don't remember Zach or Lucas checking this one, as they were in too much of a hurry to track the footsteps.

'I won't be a second,' I say, as I let Molly and Byron go on up the corridor ahead.

And to camera, I say, 'So, I'm just going to check the back of this door quickly, to see if it's Elizabeth's cupboard.'

You've gotta be here somewhere, you damn death-cupboard you.

How I'm going to keep track of which doors I've

checked and which I haven't when there are so many, I don't know.

Shoving my torch under my arm, and with the camera in one hand, I grip the doorknob. I pull, but it's stuck. I worry, for a moment, that it is locked. I give it a good tug, and it gives, making me stumble back a little way. Shining the torch inside, I see a small, windowless space and I shiver. 'Imagine being trapped inside there,' I say from behind the camera. 'In the pitch-black. In the suffocating, dusty airless space. It's just too horrible to . . .'

My words trail off and I lower the camera as a sudden nausea sweeps over me, and I have to lean against the door frame. I breathe deeply until it passes. 'Ooh, I felt a bit weird there for a . . . moment . . . and I . . . Oh . . .' My voice is strained as another wave of sickness hits. Light-headed, I grip the door frame as I take deep breaths in and out. The nausea eases, and, to camera, I say, 'I'm OK. Just feeling a bit . . . a bit woozy.' Breathe in. Breathe out. 'Probably just a waft of stagnant air from inside this old cupboard,' I hypothesize, pasting a smile on to my face to camera. But it looks more like a grimace in the flip screen. 'I'm fine.' And with my back against the door frame to steady my shaky legs, I shine the torch at the back of the door. It flickers briefly, and then it's fine. 'No scratch marks,' I say, disappointed. Nothing. Just the back of a door, its solid wood marred only by time and damp. I had been certain that this was the one. I straighten up as the nausea continues to recede, but I'm still feeling a little off. There's a sickly knot in the pit of my stomach, and an unsteadiness to my legs, a bit like seasickness.

I take a beat to compose myself, and draw in a few deep breaths, then I close the door and head for the corridor to catch up with the others. I could have only been a minute, but already I can't see Molly and Byron at all.

'Guys?' I listen for them.

Silence.

'I've lost them,' I say to camera. 'Great. Alone in the bloody dark.'

Byron has Zach's camera, but I'm certain I can remember the way to the room where he and Lucas thought the footsteps had emanated from, so I carry on. I'm feeling better now, but not a hundred per cent. There's a lingering tightness in my stomach. My torch lights the way, flickering only now and then. Each moment of darkness makes my heart skip.

'Guys?'

Nothing.

I quicken my pace, sure that I'll catch up with them soon. But with each lonely step, my skin bristles with unease, while I try to soothe the burn of irritation that they didn't wait for me.

I edge along corridors and through a series of rooms, all of which have been gutted back to the brick and timbers, ready for the hotel renovation that was never completed. The bare, echoey rooms make me feel as though I'm walking through the carcasses of great beasts, bones stripped clean by scavengers: there is the sad sense of something mighty having fallen. Eventually, I reach what I'm sure is the room above where we heard the footsteps. But it is empty.

'Okaaay,' I say to the camera, as I take a few tentative steps into the room. 'This is where we and Zach and Lucas heard footsteps coming from. But there's no sign of the others. Hello?' My ears strain, while I shine the torch and swing the camera around left and right. It doesn't make sense – where did they go?

Am I in the right place?

I think back to Zach and Lucas's video. I thought I had retraced their steps through the building. And I recognize where sheets of plasterboard cover the original brickwork on three walls, and the boxy, built-in wardrobe, bed and dresser – the room is just a garish bedspread away from being a 1980s hotel bedroom. But I wonder if I may have confused myself. This house is so large – so much larger even than it looks from the outside – with corridors that twist and turn.

Maybe I'm disorientated . . . Maybe I've come out in the wrong spot?

'Guys?'

Silence.

Where are *they*?

Back out in the corridor, I head back the way I came, to see if I can work out where I went wrong. 'Byron?' My torch flickers and for a moment I'm in pitch-darkness. 'By?' I halt, and I'm overwhelmed by the urge to cry.

Deep breath.

I whack the torch against my thigh and it comes back on.

'Molls?'

Nothing.

'Guys?' And to the camera, I say, 'I've lost them. How did I completely lose them? I was only just behind them.'

I carry on, swinging both the torch and the camera left and right. I'm back in an old section of the house, which looks as if it hasn't been touched since Elizabeth's time, with its wood panelling and elaborate but decaying cornicing. I search every corner, adrenaline pumping, imagining that at any moment something horrible will crawl from the shadows – shadows so ingrained into the edges and corners that my torch beam struggles to penetrate them.

'Byron?'

'Molly?'

I speed up, keen to be somewhere, anywhere else than alone up here in this silent, dark and narrow corridor. It seems to be getting narrower and narrower by the second, but I know that it's only my imagination playing tricks on me. I hate being confined. I always need a way out. Never ever in a million years would I go potholing. I like a nice, clear and accessible escape route. But these corridors. So narrow. So constricting. I can't breathe. My torch starts flickering rapidly. On. Off. On. Off. Like a strobe. On. Off. On. Off. On. Off. Then I'm plunged into a darkness that seems to last an age.

'Shit!'

I give the torch a shake, cursing it some more. It flicks

back to life, and I let out a steadying breath. The door to my left is wide open. I shine the beam of my torch through the doorway. The light picks out the frame of a four-poster bed straight ahead of me, one corner completely collapsed, so that only three posts are standing. I don't remember this room from Zach and Lucas's footage. I'm about to carry on when I hear something from inside: a footstep, followed by what could be a door closing.

'Guys?' I call as I step over the threshold.

Silence.

I swing the torch around to the right and almost have a heart attack at the row of pale faces staring back at me – dolls. Horrible, creepy, ugly old dolls. Sat on top of a dresser, their faces chipped, hair matted, cheeks grubby, dead eyes that follow me around the room. 'Just look at these dolls,' I say for the camera's benefit, as I frame them in the flip screen. 'So sinister.' I edge towards them for a closer look. But I only get so far, before I'm like: 'Oh, hell no. Just *no no no* to you, you freaky, evil dolls. I've seen the movies. I know that you're all possessed with the spirits of demons or dead psychopaths.' I back up, just as my torch flickers.

Off. On. Off.

'Come on, you stupid thing,' I say, rattling the torch and hitting it against my thigh again, imagining those dolls coming after me in the dark.

On.

Off.

On. Illuminating a tall figure at the window beside the dresser.

Their pale face is reflected in the glass, their dark eyes in the reflection lock on to mine, just for a beat, before the light goes out completely. Male, I think. But it happened so fast. I'm not sure. And I'm in the dark. I can't see anything. I gasp. Too numb with shock and terror to manage anything other than that feeble gasp of air. *That face. That pale face . . .* And in this moment of blackness, I'm paralysed, my breath caught. My eyes wide, as if I think that will help me see. I peer into the darkness.

Waiting.

'B-Byron?' My voice is a strangled whisper.

No reply.

'By?'

The light flashes on. I'm prepared to scream. To turn and run from that tall figure and its pale, pale face. But there is no one there. Hardly able to believe it, I draw in a ragged breath. My back hits one of the bedposts. My legs turn to jelly.

Where could they have gone? Had they fled past me in the dark? Through the door? But I would have heard them. Felt them. I shiver at the thought of them passing me. So close. And there wouldn't have been time for them to get across the room in that brief moment of darkness. A moment that had felt like an age in the dark, but that had been just a moment, nevertheless. Did I imagine it? I must have. I probably just caught my own reflection in the glass and my imagination filled in the rest.

I'm just freaking myself out in the dark.

I back up, my eyes fixed on the spot in the glass where I thought I saw that pale – oh so pale – face. One step. Two steps. Heart throbbing. Torch flickering. Expecting, in each flash of the light, for the figure to reappear. Closer. Closer with each flicker. Until . . . Suddenly fearful of what might be behind me, I swing around. The strobing torch intermittently lights the corridor beyond the doorway. It's empty. I swing back. No one there. I turn and tear through the door and down the corridor, glancing over my shoulder as I run.

But there is nothing there.

Around the corner, I slow my pace a little. Sweat trickles between my shoulder blades, down to the small of my back. My heart races. I can't breathe in the confines of the narrow corridor. It's stifling, like being sealed in a coffin. *Keep it together. Keep it together*, I tell myself. That figure – it had to have been my imagination, stoked by the creepy surroundings.

But I can't get that pale face out of my head.

Just. My. Imagination.

My torch is working OK now. Which is a small mercy, at least. And I remember I'm still filming. 'Jesus,' I say to the camera, holding it up. I think I've been recording the floor this whole time, since I saw . . . whatever the heck I saw. 'This is creepy as hell. I saw something back there. Someone. At a window.' I turn into another corridor. I'm not sure if I recognize anything from Zach and Lucas's footage. I take a deep breath. And another, trying to ground myself while I figure the way out. 'Ugh! I don't know where I am. How is this house so big? It's like the Tardis. Unless I'm going round in circles. But I'm OK. I'm OK,' I say, my voice breathy. 'Well, I will be when I find the others.'

Corridors twist and turn. I'm disorientated. Trapped. My breaths come short and fast. I'm overwhelmed with an urgency to get out. Out. OUT. Panic rising. I have the strangest feeling that I'm not alone.

Did they follow me . . . that figure? That pale, pale face.

But there was no one there.

It was just my imagination.

I glance over my shoulder as I scurry down the corridor, sure I feel a presence at my back.

No one there.

'I just need to keep going. Molly and Byron have to be around here somewhere. I just . . .'

I realize, with relief, where I am. I've crossed the entire second floor and I'm in the landing off the staircase I came up earlier. It's still creepy as hell, but at least this is familiar creepy, rather than unknown creepy. I stop, panting hard. I feel my heartbeat in the way that you would feel the vibrations of an aftershock. The torch is still working fine and I run its beam over the walls, along the floor; but as it shines across the turret at the end of the landing, it's as if the darkness eats up the light and I can't see all the way to the windows. It's a strange effect, and I'm reminded of how the twilight didn't seem to come through the windows at all earlier.

I shift closer.

'I don't know if the camera is picking this up,' I say, as I run the torch beam across the opening of the turret once more, 'but I swear it's too dark in that spot. You see how the light from my torch is being swallowed up by the darkness, and there's no moonlight coming in? It's like someone is standing there, blocking the light.'

I can't shake the feeling that I'm being watched. I'm flooded by the need to run away from this spot. Right now. Just run. Run and don't stop. But I can't make my trembling legs move. I balance the torch in the hand with the mini tripod and, to prove to myself that there is no one there, I reach out my free hand. The torch beam flickers.

'Not again,' I groan, halting. 'Please, you stupid, sodding torch.'

It stops flickering and I plunge my hand into the darkness. It's cold and damp, like mist and . . .

Off.

On.

At the flickering of the torch beam, I come to my senses. I back up, turn and tear down the staircase, so fast that I become disoriented and I can't see one step for the other and I'm scared that I'm going to tumble and break my neck. And I'll be forced to haunt this horrible house for all eternity. Or worse – whatever is up there will catch up with me and . . .

. . . I'm down, on the first floor, a smudge of moonlight

coming in through the three large windows, creating shadows on the walkway. I feel lighter here, less like I'm being watched, but I don't slow my pace. I make for the central staircase. For a heart-stopping moment, in my haste I lose my footing at the top and I grab for the balustrade to stop myself tumbling all the way down. *Steady.* I scramble down the steps two at a time, and I don't stop until I reach the very bottom. Where I run right into Byron.

12

'IRIS!'

I fling my arms around Byron, taking him by surprise. It takes half a beat for him to wrap his arms around me. And when he does, he does so tightly. He's wearing one of his oversized woolly jumpers. It is soft and comforting, and I bury my face in it and it smells like him: laundry powder and lavender soap, and a hint of something musky. We stay like that a moment, but then I pull back, feeling suddenly awkward. And worried that Molly will catch us like that, even though it's just a hug.

'Are you OK?' he asks.

'Yeah. No. I don't know.'

'Which is it?'

'I'm not OK,' I say. That pale face. The turret windows that eat light and spit out darkness. Someone watching me. Lost and alone. 'I . . .'

He goes to tuck a stray curl behind my ear, but he stops himself. His hand lingers in the air, so close to my face. I can't read the words behind his eyes. At the sound of footsteps, he drops his hand and looks away, sheepishly.

'Iris, what happened to you?' says Molly as she appears from around the left of the staircase. 'Where did you go? We were so worried.'

I don't have a chance to decipher what just happened between me and Byron. '*Me*? Where did you guys go? I looked for you. Right above where we heard the footsteps. In the room Zach and Lucas went to. But you guys weren't there.'

'We were.'

'You weren't.'

'We were, Iris. It's *you* who wasn't there.'

'But I just hung back for a minute. Just one minute,' I say, confused, glancing from Byron to Molly and back again, while they gaze at me with wide eyes. Like they think I've lost it. 'And you were gone. I couldn't find you.'

'This place is a maze,' says Byron. He looks as if he's not sure whether to hug me again at the sight of my continued distress. He's not really one for physical contact – we're both socially awkward types. It's Molly who is a hugger. But she's staring at me with her big eyes as if my befuddlement may be catching. 'You probably just took a wrong turn and missed us,' he continues.

'I . . .' I stop and shake my head. 'You guys didn't look for me?' I breathe in as my cheeks flush and my eyes sting with tears at the way they abandoned me. Am I a third wheel now? Is that it? Do they want to get rid of me? I mentally shake myself at how crazy that sounds, confused as to where the thought even came from. Byron would never do that to me. *Would he?* I hold the breath a moment, before letting it out slowly.

'We *did* look for you,' says Molly, as she takes a step closer to me. She reaches out a hand and rubs my upper arm. 'We were looking for you this whole time. Then we figured you'd head back here.'

'Guys, I saw something upstairs,' I say, raising the camera to film the exchange.

'What?' says Molly. Her hand stops, and her fingers squeeze into my flesh, just a little. 'What did you see?' she urges.

I shake my head. 'I saw . . . I still can't believe it . . . I mean, you both know I'm not sure I even believe in this ghost stuff, right? But . . . what I saw. It's undeniable.'

'*What?*' Molly's fingers dig in a little deeper.

'I stopped to check out a cupboard, but I felt really sick all of a sudden and—'

'You did? Really?' says Molly, cutting in. 'And did it pretty much go as quick as it came?'

'Yeah. I mean I still felt a little off, but . . .'

'Sudden fleeting nausea is a sign that a spirit is present,' says Molly, her eyes wide with wonder.

But Byron says, 'Come on, Moll, it was probably the stuffiness of this place, or a wave of claustrophobia. Iris hates confined spaces.' I glance at him and give him a wan smile. I like that he knows me so well as to know details like that.

'The dislike of confined spaces is because you're a Sagittarian,' she says to me. 'But sudden nausea is a well-known indicator of an otherworldly presence. Same with sudden headaches and nosebleeds.' And before Byron can protest further, she says, 'Is this when you saw something?'

I shake my head. 'No. No, this was before that. I was trying to find you guys and I was in this bedroom and my torch was flickering . . .' I raise it to show the others, but it's working completely fine. Of course it is now. Typical. 'And in a flash of light, I saw someone standing in front of a window. Right in front of me. Clear as day. I swear.'

'You saw someone?' says Byron, incredulous, his brow creased. 'A living person. Here . . . in the house?'

'Not someone *living*. I saw a full-body apparition!'

'You saw a ghost?' says Molly.

'Just for a moment, because this thing cut out,' I say, waving the torch, before shoving it in my hoodie pocket. 'But yeah. Yeah, I did.'

'You actually saw a ghost? Do you remember what they looked like?' Her eyes are wide with wonder.

'Tall. Male. Old-fashioned clothing. Maybe early thirties,' I say.

'Edward – it has to have been Edward,' says Molly. 'Or possibly Lord Thornhanger.'

'And then in another spot, I . . .'

'Oh my god, Iris. *What?*' urges Molly, as she grips my arm tighter. Uncomfortably tight.

'I *sensed* someone . . . more than sensed,' I add. 'I saw the shadowy figure of someone standing right in front of me. It was blocking the light from these windows in a turret, if that makes any sense.'

'That's amazing,' says Molly, unable to contain her excitement. 'You saw a ghost – maybe two ghosts. Or a ghost and a shadow person. Have you any idea how lucky you are? An actual full-body apparition! Did you get them on camera?'

I shake my head. 'Not the apparition. It took me by surprise. And my camera didn't pick up the shadow. I couldn't see it on-screen, anyway. Just with my eyes. But hopefully it picked up something in that area. Like how the light wasn't coming through the window.'

'We should all go up there and check out both locations.' Molly releases me and starts to pace as she rattles off plans, a little manic in her enthusiasm. 'We could call out or do a seance or—'

'Molly, slow down,' says Byron. 'Don't get carried away.'

'Do you remember exactly where you were standing when you saw the apparition?' she continues, ignoring Byron. 'We have to test angles, see if it could have been your reflection, or—'

'Of course it was her reflection!' snaps Byron. 'What else could it have been, other than Iris's reflection and imagination? Jesus Christ, Molly. You're obsessed.'

Molly stares at him, wide-eyed for a moment, before her face crumples into hurt. She recovers herself with a wan smile, and says soberly, 'I'm going to replace the batteries in my torch. It's starting to get a bit dim,' and she spins and scurries off towards the base camp.

Byron watches after her for a moment, a confused look on his face, mouth hanging open, as if he can't believe he snapped at her like that. I can't believe it either – it's so un-Byron-like. Bit of a grumpy sod, yes. But mean . . . never. I expect him to go after her but, appearing to mentally shake himself, he turns to me. He slips his right hand into my left one and positions himself so that we're standing face to face. I feel the cool metal of the rings on his fingers – the fidget ring that he always wears on his thumb; the wide silver band on his forefinger that I gave to him last Christmas; the Celtic design he wears on his middle finger – and, looking deep into my eyes, he says, 'I'm gonna have to keep a closer eye on you so you don't go getting yourself lost again.' The words are reassuring, after my scare, and he gives me a wry smile, before tucking a curl behind my ear with his free hand.

We stay like that for a moment, an awkward silence between us. It's then we hear Molly shout, 'You guys. Come here. Come here now!'

13

'MOLLY?'

'Molly!'

We sprint through the entrance hall and into the next room. Our base camp. By the light of Byron's torch, I spot Molly. She is standing next to where we set out our stuff to sleep later, just looking down at the floor. Byron reaches her just ahead of me and shines his torch along the ground, while I film. Molly's backpack is lying on its side next to her sleeping bag, and its contents are sprawled across the dusty floorboards, all the way to the recess of the bay window. This isn't just the usual Molly-mess; her belongings have been ransacked.

'What the . . . ?'

'I did not leave it like this,' says Molly, as she crouches down beside her spilt clothes. She looks as if she doesn't want to touch anything, as if it's a crime scene, and we're all waiting for the guys in hazmat suits to turn up and start bagging stuff for evidence.

'Are you sure you didn't just knock it over before we went upstairs?' says Byron. 'Or maybe you left it at an awkward angle and it fell over on its own?'

'No. I know how I left it. I left it lying flat with the zip fastened. It didn't fall and spill. Look at it! *Something* did this.'

'Molly . . .'

'This is physical proof that something is in here with us,' she says, her voice a mixture of fear and wonder and excitement as she motions with her hand to her belongings. 'And the footsteps. And feeling watched. And what Iris saw up—'

'None of that is proof,' says Byron, cutting Molly off. 'Not unless any of it was caught on camera. We've got nothing.'

'But . . .'

'How do we know it wasn't you?' says Byron, turning to me.

'Wait. What? Why are you blaming me?'

'Someone did this,' he says, nodding down to Molly's things. 'Molly and I can account for each other. But where were you *really* when we lost you, Iris? Did you come down here and mess with Molly's stuff to make it look "ghostly"?' He uses air quotes around the word *ghostly*.

'What . . . ? Why would I do that?' I say, incredulous.

'For the video. What would you do to get a good video, eh, Iris?'

'It wasn't me. I swear I did not mess up Molly's things. How would I even have had time? I only just got down here when I ran into you guys in the hall.'

'But you could have come straight down when we lost you, trashed Molly's stuff and ran up again. And invented a story about being lost and seeing ghosts.'

'Oh, come on, By. You know how seriously I take this stuff. It means so much to me. Especially this search. And especially now that we've actually found Zach and Lucas's stuff. Why would I risk the credibility of what we've been building up together?'

'Maybe you did it for attention?' says Molly, a hard edge to her tone that is so unlike her and that leaves me speechless for a moment and makes my cheeks redden.

'What do you mean by that?' I manage to say.

'Maybe you just wanted By—'

We all fall silent as a dull thud from somewhere nearby cuts across Molly's out-of-character bitter words.

'You all heard that, right?' I whisper, after a collective pause.

Byron shines his torch in the direction of the noise, towards the entrance hall.

'What *was* that?' whispers Molly.

We stand, ears straining. I can feel the darkness closing in around us. I pull my torch from my pocket. It's still working fine. But I don't have a chance to feel grateful for that before we hear something heavy being dragged along the floor, this time unmistakably from out in the entrance hall.

'I think we can all agree that isn't me,' I say in a whisper.

Fear rising, I point my torch in the direction of the doorway.

'Turn it off.' Byron's words are hushed and fast. He has already switched his torch off, leaving us in near darkness.

'What? Why—?'

'Just do it,' he hisses.

I do as he says, freaked out by the urgency in his voice, just as much as the strange sound itself. We're plunged into total darkness. The dragging stops. Silence. Adrenaline courses through me as I stand, listening. But all I can hear is the rushing of blood in my ears.

It's Byron who speaks first, barely a whisper, drawing closer to me in the darkness. 'If it wasn't Iris who moved Molly's stuff then we have to consider that maybe she *did* see someone upstairs.'

'What?'

'Maybe there is someone else – someone very much alive – in this house with us.'

14

WE'RE CROUCHED SIDE by side, silent in the darkness, our backs pressed against the wall where the room splits round into the L-shape. Our ears straining. Our breath held.

Now that my eyes have acclimatized to the dark, I can just make out the lines of our belongings, spread out across the floor, as well as the outlines of the windows across the room, where a little moonlight filters in. Rattled by the sound, we make ourselves small and invisible in the shadows. Eyelids heavy with weariness, but held up by adrenaline. Byron has Zach's camera clutched so tightly, I worry he's going to crush it, while Molly is sitting with her chin cupped in her hands, listening intently; her lips pressed together as if supressing excitement or fear. I can't tell which. Probably both in equal measure. We haven't heard anything from out in the entrance hall for a few minutes. But we have no way of knowing if whatever

– whoever – is out there has actually gone. And if so, where. Or if they are just waiting.

Like a spider awaits a fly.

I glance at my watch: 12.08 a.m. The night is stretching out, long and endless.

'OK. Listen. I think we should make a run for it to the car,' whispers Byron. 'If we go through—'

'No,' I say with a shake of my head. 'We can't leave.' My words are a hushed hiss. 'Not before we've finished retracing Zach and Lucas's steps.'

'Iris . . .'

'That's the only way we can figure out what happened to them. We don't even know who Grace is yet.'

'Iris, stop it,' says Byron.

'We *need* to understand what happened.'

'Don't be stupid,' he rasps, so close to my ear that I can feel his breath on my skin. 'Not with someone else here. They could be *responsible* for whatever happened to Zach and Lucas.'

'Come on. It's probably just kids messing about,' I offer, trying to placate Byron. 'Maybe it's that kid, Justin, from town. Maybe he's come out here with some friends to freak us out? They'll go away.'

'You want to take that kind of risk?' hisses Byron. 'It could be anyone. If someone is here, we have to go.'

'It's one of the spirits that haunts this house,' says Molly, her voice a breathy whisper. 'I vote we try to communicate with it. Now, while it's active.'

'Moll—'

'But we'll miss it.'

'Seriously, now is not the time to start calling out. Not with someone—'

'Guys, we're probably freaking out over a fox or something,' I say, cutting Byron off. 'Look, this is getting silly,' I add, tired of hiding in the shadows. Of talk of leaving when we've barely started watching the footage. 'It was a fox. Let's just go and see, instead of hiding here like three dumbasses in the dark.'

I stand and move to step around Byron, but he shoots out a hand and grasps my wrist, halting me.

'Iris, what are you doing?' he hisses, staring up at me.

I pull my wrist from his grip and say, 'I'm not wasting our limited time in this house by being scared of kids or a wild animal. Or even a ghost, for that matter.' And I edge along the wall.

'*Iris!*'

I glance back to see him on his feet, his eyes glinting in the moonlight as he glares at me.

I ignore him and carry on until I reach the end of the wall, where it turns into the wider section of the huge room. I peer around the corner towards the door. It stands partially open, blocking my view out into the entrance hall. Nothing stirs. I switch on my torch.

'Turn it off.'

'No,' I say, glancing back at Byron, my voice no longer hushed. 'I'm going to prove that you are just as guilty as me and Molly for letting your imagination run away with you. And then I'm going to do what we came here to do –

I'm going to investigate what happened to Zach and Lucas.' Hitting record on the Canon, I turn from him and I stride towards the entrance hall, my desire for answers and a good video making me reckless. But my heart thumps and my hands sweat and my guts twist and turn – because I could be wrong.

Oh god, what if I'm wrong?

What if there is someone out there?

With a big butcher's knife and a mask made of human skin and—

'Iris, stop!'

'No. Whatever is out there,' I say, my camera held in front of me, 'I want it on film and—'

Scrape.

I stop halfway to the entrance hall at the sound, as if caught in a searchlight. Louder. Closer than before.

Scrape.

I switch off my torch but keep the camera rolling, despite the darkness, and I stand, wide-eyed, staring towards the door.

Scrape.

'Iris!' I hear Byron hiss from behind me, his voice urgent. 'Iris, hide.'

But there's nowhere for me to go. There's no time.

Scrape.

I'm caught. I stare at the back of the door, with my heart beating against my ribcage so hard that I'm sure if I looked down, right now, I would see it. Straining. Like in that scene from *Alien*, where the alien bursts through the man's chest in a fountain of blood. I imagine my heart slithering away to hide in the shadows, leaving me to face whatever is coming this way on my own.

'*Iris!*'

Scrape.

My eyes flick to the shadows that now shift across the threshold.

Scrape.

I open my mouth to scream.

Scrape.

I ready myself to turn and run.

Scrape.

And in the moment that it should come through the door, there is . . .

Nothing.

Silence.

Stillness.

I'm paralysed. Incredulous. Breath drawn. Waiting. Ears straining. Eyes fixed on the strip of floor where moonlight and shadows spill into the room from the entrance hall. My thumping heart didn't escape my chest after all and has, instead, taken refuge in my mouth. The shadows remain still.

Are they waiting for me to make a move?

When nothing stirs after a few heartbeats, I turn my head to glance back at Byron. He's at the corner of the wall, frozen in a state of motion. Molly beside him. In the gloom, I can't make out his features clearly, but I can see the sparkle of fear and gravity reflected in his wide eyes: as if he wants to pluck me out of the path of whatever is waiting, ready to burst through that door at any moment. I take a deep breath, but I don't retreat. And as if he knows what I'm about to do, Byron shakes his head at me – slowly at first, and then more urgently.

As I turn back to the door, I hear him hiss, 'Iris, no!' I hear his feet against the rough floorboards as he comes after me. But I've come too far to turn back now. I need to know what is waiting behind that door. *Think of the views. The likes. The subs.* Switching on my torch, I tear towards the entrance hall, not giving myself a chance to back out.

'*Iris!*'

I don't stop. I keep putting one foot in front of the other. My cheeks burn with all the blood pumping around my body. With the adrenaline coursing through my veins. My heart pounds. I don't stop until I reach the door. I hold my breath. I fling it open all the way, so that there is no barrier between me and the hallway beyond.

And
there
is
nothing
there.

I scan the entrance hall with my torch beam.

Nothing.

I jump as something touches my arm from behind.

Gasping, I glance back to see Byron, his fingers curling around my upper arm.

'There's no one there,' I say, breathy, shaking my head. 'No one there.' I give a small, slightly hysterical laugh. And it's then that I realize my whole body is trembling, and my legs are jelly as fight or flight deserts me, and my head is swimming, and I think I'm going to fall.

Byron guides me back, so that I rest against the door frame, and with his hands on my shoulders, he says, 'You OK?' as my breath judders from the shock.

And then Molly is there, a hand on my upper arm, taking over from Byron. 'Just take a steady breath in and out,' she says competently, me trying to bat her away, saying, 'I'm fine. I'm fine, for Christ's sake,' while Byron shines his torch around the entrance hall, swinging the beam left and right.

He glances back to me and growls, 'That was so stupid, Iris.'

I gaze at him. I see the intensity in his eyes as he frowns at me.

'Really stupid.'

'I had to know.'

'You shouldn't have gone off like that. You could have put us all in danger.'

'But she didn't. So just drop it,' says Molly.

I glance at her, eyes wide with surprise that she should snap at Byron like that. Especially in defence of me. There's a darkness in her eyes that I've never seen before.

It's unnerving. She needs this every bit as much as I do. Proof of the supernatural. Proof that she'll get to see her parents again one day.

My gaze finds Zach's Canon, where it dangles from Byron's wrist by its strap. Lifting the camera, I pull it from his wrist. 'Let's get back out there,' I say, as I glance between Byron and Molly. 'Right now.' Holding the camera before me, and with my eyes locked on to Byron's, I add, 'Because we're not leaving. Not until we've tracked every last step of Zach and Lucas's journey through this house.'

15

WE'RE SITTING IN a circle, cross-legged on the dusty floorboards in a large room on the first floor. The next piece of footage on Zach's camera led us here. The video includes a grainy, static shot of the room, where neither boy is in frame. Rain can be heard lashing against the window, and what miserable, grey daylight manages to penetrate the glass offers the only light in the room. Off-screen, Zach shushes Lucas when the camera's audio captures someone whispering: it's a mixture of hissed and jumbled words and it's hard to make out what is being said or how many voices there are, especially over the beating rain, and, as Byron says, as Zach and Lucas are not in the shot, we don't know if it's them faking or messing about.

The footage continues with Zach getting stroppy when Lucas keeps making stupid noises while he is trying to call out to Anne during a seance. The video cuts short after Zach can be heard saying, 'For Christ's sake, Lucas, man, I fu—' and it throws me a little, hearing Zach lose his temper. Like I just imagined, from watching their channel, that Zach and Lucas had this magical friendship, where they never fight. But I guess that's the sort of thing that gets edited out. Their seance had been uneventful, but the weird audio intrigued us enough to carry out our own seance in here.

I have already set the camera up on its tripod, so that I can record all three of us. Three fat white candles in the centre of our circle provide the only light. Furniture and old paintings, age-tarnished and dusty, are stacked against the right side of the room. Some of the bigger pieces are covered with large sheets. I can smell the mustiness of them from where I sit. To my left, along the wall beneath the window, are the moonlit outlines of children's toys, which, when we ran our torches over them earlier, look as if they date back to Elizabeth's time. Some look undisturbed, as if she had only just finished playing with them, this half of the playroom unaware that the other half got turned into a storeroom for some of her family's belongings, probably when the place became a school. I guess there was no family left to come and claim them.

Closest to me is a child-size wooden table, laid with a miniature porcelain teapot and two chipped cups, each with a little saucer. Sat on one of the small chairs pulled up to the table is a moth-eaten teddy bear, wearing a long white dress, the yellowed lace hem of which grazes the floor. The other has been vacated, I imagine, by whoever set up the tea party. Behind that is a blackboard, which hangs from a broken easel. If there is anything written on it, I couldn't make it out through the thick layer of dust. Further along is a doll's pram, empty; a small, cubed tin, which I assume is a jack-in-the-box, and which I hope doesn't suddenly pop out with a sinister cackle at the wrong moment; a spinning top; an age-stained rag doll; and a rocking horse in the far corner. Along the far wall is a dresser with a large jar of dusty marbles, full to the brim. Right now, in the candlelight, I can't see into the edges or corners of the room, and that makes me uncomfortable.

Molly likes us to start a seance with a moment of quiet contemplation, eyes lowered, alone with our own thoughts. And while Byron doesn't believe in this stuff, he is respectful of the rules. I tend to think that, deep down, he does believe, but he just enjoys the challenge of the debunk. Tonight, though, I fidget a little, feeling wired from the can of energy drink that I downed before heading up here. All it's done is give my tiredness a sharp edge. My head buzzes. Adrenaline is lending the caffeine a hand, keeping my scratchy eyelids artificially wide. I jump at every sound. My eyes flick to the rocking horse – *Did I see it rock? Don't be silly.* It remains perfectly still.

I glance at my watch: 2.15 a.m. God, this is a long night. So much has happened already, in just one evening. I never expected us to get this much activity – whether ghostly in origin or not – in the entire weekend.

'Is everyone ready?' says Molly, after a moment. She

runs a hand through her hair. It falls back into place perfectly. Unlike mine, which – even if I could run my fingers through my curls without snagging – would stay sticking up at all angles and puff out with frizz as punishment for my mistake. I've put mine up in a messy bun, to keep it out of my face.

'Yeah, I'm ready,' I say.

'Ready.'

'Who wants to call out?'

'You do the honours, Molly,' I say, knowing that she lives for this stuff.

She flashes me a small smile. 'Right. OK,' she says, steeling herself, as we each join hands. She makes a little delicate noise as if clearing her throat, and after a breath, she begins. 'We come here tonight with respect in our hearts. We welcome any spirits present and invite you to speak with us. If there is anyone here who would like to communicate with us, could you give us a sign?'

Silence, other than for the drum-rhythm of my heart.

'If there are any spirits present, please, could you make a sound, or blow out one of the candles, or move something. Use one of the toys. Anything, so that we know you are here.'

Ears strain against the silence.

Eyes squint into dark corners.

'If there is someone in this room with us, please, come forward and make yourself known.'

I listen and watch. Mouth dry. Hoping. Doubting. Fearing. Hoping. Hoping. Hoping.

Nothing.

Molly continues to call out, '*We mean you no harm*' and '*We just want to talk*', but nothing answers, while the darkness of an entire house presses in around us. Next to me, Byron's shoulders begin to sag. I fidget, wiggling my toes to stave off pins and needles from sitting still on this cold, hard floor. '*Is there anyone here with us tonight?*' I focus on the candle in front of me, the gently flickering flame causing the white wax to glow a warm, translucent orange. '*Please talk to us.*' My head grows heavier on my shoulders. Heavier. Heavier. '*Give us a sign.*' And my eyelids become ten-tonne weights which I struggle to keep aloft. '*Can . . . you . . . please . . . show . . . us . . . a—*'

Thud.

I'm jolted awake by the distant sound. 'Ohhhh. Did you guys hear that?' I say, sitting bolt upright.

'I didn't hear anything,' says Byron, sluggishly.

'I heard it,' says Molly, her eyes wide as she stares at me across the candles; her body tensed. There is the hint of a smile of wonderment at the corners of her mouth. 'A thud from somewhere overhead, when I was asking for a sign.'

'I thought it was from somewhere out in the corridor,' I say, with a chill and a whole lot of hope that I wasn't wrong to talk Byron out of his *There's someone else in the house* theory.

'Try again,' says Byron, sitting up straighter.

'Thank you for communicating with us,' says Molly, excitedly, and I admire her unwavering ability to believe that whatever it is, it is, without question, supernatural. 'Can you do something louder? Maybe something in the room with us?'

We listen.

Silence.

'Is there anyone in this room with us?' says Byron. 'Make a noise or—'

Thud.

'Whoa . . .'

'Holy crap!' Even Byron can't help reacting to that one.

'That was louder this time.'

'It sounded like it came from that corner of the room,' I say, nodding towards the far corner behind Byron, to the right of the dresser. I wish that I could see into the corners and I'm glad that I can't, both at the same time.

'Anne, is that you?' I ask.

Silence.

'Whoever is in the room with us, do you wish to speak with us?' I say, taking charge of the seance.

Every last trace of weariness has gone from the room. The air is charged, and we're all buzzing with anticipation and excitement.

Tap.

'They want to speak to us,' says Molly, clearly thrilled.

'It's just the woodwork cooling down, Moll.'

'Byron, stop.'

'I was just—'

'Not now.'

'Do you have a message for us?' I continue.

I hear what sounds like the *clink* of a teacup.

'Holy crap . . .'

'Elizabeth, is that you?' I ask, my eyes fixed on the tea things on the small table to my left. Watching and waiting for the slightest tremor of movement.

Stillness.

'Do you have a message for one of us in particular?'

Silence.

'For all of us?'

There's a scratching sound that comes from somewhere behind me. I gasp and shiver and resist the urge to turn around. I don't want to see.

'It's for all of us,' says Molly, interpreting the scratching as a ghostly *Yes*. 'Do you want to hurt us?' she asks.

And I wonder why she had to ask that question of all questions. I hold my breath while we wait for the answer, and breathe out when, after a few pounds of my heart, we hear nothing.

'Does someone other than you want to hurt us?'

Nothing, then . . .

Thud!

The sound was sharp; as sharp as my intake of breath. It sounded like one of the dresser doors slamming.

Byron's hand grips mine even tighter, and this small action – from our resident non-believer – is what makes my heart flip out, like a fish on land.

'Are we talking to Edward Turner?'

Silence.

'Did you used to live in this house?'

Silence.

'Is this . . . is this *Zach*?' I ask tentatively, feeling my cheeks flush a little at how ridiculous that must have sounded.

Silence.

'Are we talking to Lucas—'

Thud!

I scream. The sound had come from right behind me. I feel something cold on the back of my neck – lips or a fingertip brushing – and the candle in front of me blows out.

16

I WAKE WITH a start. Something woke me. A sound. A short burst of crackling – faint and chirrupy, like the EMF reader. It didn't appear to be working when we tested it, after I found it during the search of the house. No lights would come on at all, even when we waved it in front of our phones and the cameras. As I lift myself on to my elbows and strain my ears, I can't hear anything. I glance at the EMF reader, over by our gear, but it is silent. No lights flash. I must have dreamt it.

We called it a night at 3 a.m. Now, it's still dark. Just. I check the time: 4.06 a.m. I've barely slept. But I didn't think I'd sleep at all, after that seance. Did we speak to Lucas? Some of those noises had come from inside that room with us. *Floorboards creaking as they cool down in the cold of the night; mice; a bird flapping its wings; bats in the rafters; a bug infestation in the woodwork; old, crumbling plaster falling from the walls . . .* Byron reeled off explanations like a mantra. That one candle blowing out: *You screamed, Iris. It was the air from your lungs that blew it out.* Lips or fingertips on the back of my neck: *You were spooked by your surroundings. That's all there was to it.*

Groggy, I rub my eyes with the heels of my hands. I pull the band from my hair and gently ruffle my fingers through my curls. Rolling my shoulders to release the tension from sleeping on a hard floor, my hand goes to my left shoulder to massage a tight spot. The scratches don't hurt any more, and the initial angry marks have faded to faint lines of red, the skin barely having been broken.

Molly and Byron are motionless lumps beneath their sleeping bags to the left of me. I can't get used to seeing them like that: Molly curled up in the crook of his arm, sticking out of his sleeping bag. And I feel the familiar sharp pang of regret that I let him go. That I got carried away with the fantasy that Zach would take one look at me at the meet-and-greet and fall head over heels in love with me. That I let my obsession with Zach get in the way of me and Byron. And that I realized just that bit too late how stupid I was to not take a chance on us.

I bury the feeling with a deep sigh and, biting a thumbnail, I look away. My eyes stray over the floor around us. Having tidied up after the 'ghostly' ransacking, Molly's belongings are starting to spread out, in a way only she can manage, like she's moving in. Unlike me and By, Molly is *not* a tidy person. I call it Molly-mess. Her bedroom is *Organized chaos*, as she calls it. And she manages to leave stuff round mine and Byron's all the time – though we don't hang out at Byron's often, because his parents aren't chilled like mine. It drives me crazy when I find she's left another hoodie or a pair of socks, a hairbrush or some make-up in my room. It's like she bleeds into the lives of others.

My eyes stray back. I watch the steady rise and fall of Byron's chest in sleep. I envy him and Molly right now. Wherever they are in their dreams, at least they are not here. In this creepy old house.

Molly has the hood of her top up over her head and is facing away from me, into Byron's chest, so I can't see any of her at all. Byron is turned towards me. A mop of green, tousled waves in his face. He sometimes uses straightening irons on his fringe to tame it. But I know from our various overnight stays in abandoned buildings that even if he does, the waves tend to spring back overnight, defiant. My heart aches at how cute he looks when he's sleeping. He's cute when he's awake, too, in an awkward, gangly, geeky sort of way. Sort of like a teenage Benedict Cumberbatch, but with green hair and eyeliner.

I lay on my side and watch him, my head propped up on an elbow. I follow the line of his long, straight nose down to his lips, parted slightly. In sleep, he looks like that little boy I used to make mud pies with in my garden; the one my dad caught in the shed eating a piece of coal because it smelt like winter, his favourite season. The one who used to tickle me until I couldn't breathe, and he'd stop, and I'd squeal at him to do it again. The one who used to tell people that we'd get married one day, and to which I would say, *Ew, I think I'll decide who I'll marry. Thank you very much!*

I bite my lip as I study him, as a wave of something between panic and excitement and longing and loss runs through me like a lit fuse.

The little boy grew up.

He had wanted *me* once. Where did those feelings go? And I wonder if I just . . . He makes a snorting sound in his sleep and turns his head to the other side, making me lose my train of thought. Probably just as well. I must *not* continue that thought.

If I just tell him how I feel.

I roll on to my back and stare at the cracked ceiling. Even if Molly was out of the picture, it would never work between me and Byron. We've been friends for far too long. I fix my eyes on the decaying plaster above me. I think, *What if it all comes crashing down on me?* I tell myself that this place has stood for a couple of hundred years, and I'm sure it will still be here in another hundred. But, still, I sit up, not wanting to look at that ominous crack any longer.

Cross-legged on my sleeping bag in the dark, with two sleeping bodies, I can't help feeling so alone. I pick up my phone and fiddle with it to distract myself. I wish I could get online to check how many views the teaser trailer has. No internet is killing me. I settle for flicking through some photos of my dog, Casper, and some from my eldest sister

Poppy's last gig, while I twirl a dry, frizzy curl around a finger.

Poppy, Amba and my seven-year-old sister, May, all have perfect warm-brown springy spirals, though Amba currently has the ends of hers dip-dyed purple. They always look flawless. While my dull curls are prone to copious amounts of frizz. I'm constantly torn between wanting to chop the lot off and knowing that I'll regret it if I do. Besides, I know I'll eventually find THE leave-in conditioner that will transform this unruly mess into a mass of silky curls that even Amba will envy.

As I sit, I'm suddenly overwhelmed by the feeling that someone is standing over me. I can't move for a moment, thumb poised over my touchscreen, so sure there is someone there. Right behind me. So close, I can feel them. My heart pounding, I see nothing in the reflection of my phone. I lower it and keep my eyes fixed on the floorboards in front of me, expecting to see a shift in the shadows. The back of my neck prickles. Hairs stand on end. The feeling intensifies. I almost imagine that I will feel breath on the top of my head. I'm paralysed by the thought that if I look behind me right now, I'll see someone darker than night looming over me. But that's crazy! *Is it?*

There's no one there.

No one there.

No one.

To prove how crazy it is, I make myself twist around and see . . .

No one there.

Of course there isn't!

You're letting your imagination get the better of you.

But I just can't shake the feeling that there is someone else in the room with me. Someone I can't see. Just like Molly said she experienced, right from when we first got here. Just like I experienced in the turret. And during the seance.

I shiver.

My eyes dart nervously around me, my vision bouncing off walls, digging into the dark corners and tripping over the shadows. My gaze pauses at the open doorways, too scared to linger long, in case something should lurch through as I sit here waiting for the others to wake up; as I sit here waiting for something to crawl out of those creepy-arsed shadows; as I sit here waiting for something to jump on me from behind.

I consider waking Byron up to have someone to talk to. To take my mind off the dark and the creepiness. But we might disturb Molly, so I decide not to risk it. She may be the nicest person you ever could meet, BUT that is on condition you don't wake her up before she's ready. I know from past experience that she can be a real grouch if she's not quite ready to face the day.

But I do have a good reason.

Do I?

You're just creeping yourself out.

There is no one there.

No one.

No. One.

I'll think it until I believe it.

No one no one no one no one no one no one.

My eyes fall on Lucas's camera, over by my backpack. We left the majority of Zach and Lucas's belongings where we found them during our initial search of the house, not wanting to disturb any evidence. Between us, we located two backpacks, one belonging to Zach and one Lucas's. Zach's we found downstairs when we first arrived, its contents strewn across the floor, along with his camera, spare batteries for his Canon, his notes, water bottles and two sleeping bags. Lucas's turned up in one of the small attic rooms – again, his clothes, spare batteries and a memory card for his camera and his wash stuff were all over the floor. Byron spotted Lucas's camera, a Sony Alpha A5100, in a stairwell, and then there's the dead mobile he found on the first floor and Zach's smashed laptop I found on the second floor. Everything was so scattered around the house. We have no idea why, or if there is any pattern in it.

What the hell happened here?

I could almost burst with the frustration of not knowing.

What. The. Hell. Happened?

We haven't found another mobile. No idea if Lucas brought his laptop.

The only items we took with us were Zach and Lucas's cameras, the spare batteries and the EMF reader, before we realized it wasn't working.

I stand, bundle up my sleeping bag, and tiptoe around the others, careful not to activate any creaky floorboards. I stop when Molly stirs and rolls over. Breath held, I wait a beat before bending down to grab the Sony. I'm keen to start watching and retracing some of what Lucas recorded, as we've only looked at Zach's camera so far. Then I settle myself down in a nest in the alcove of the bay window, so as not to disturb the others. With a wall behind me so nothing can creep up on me in the dark, and wrapped in my sleeping bag to ward off the chill, I go to the first video and press play.

17

'GUYS! YOU NEED to watch this,' I say, clambering to my feet and letting my sleeping bag slide from my shoulders. The sun is up; it rose, unnoticed by me, as I watched Lucas's footage from his and Zach's first day. The sun's rays are weakened by the grime on the windows, but I'm sure if I were to go outside and stand in an unshaded spot, it would already feel hot on my skin. Inside, though, I still need my hooded top on to ward off the chill. 'Guys, wake up.'

I'm no longer afraid to wake them. I need to show them what I've found on Lucas's camera.

'Wake up!'

Byron groans and lifts his head a few centimetres off the ground.

'Guys.'

His eyes open to slits. Brow furrowed, he glances about

himself as though trying to work out where the hell he is and what his life is about right now. Then, as if it all sinks in at once, he sits bolt upright, sloughing off Molly, who, amazingly, just rolls over and continues to sleep. He stares at me wide-eyed. 'Iris, what's going on?' His voice is a little groggy with sleep and confusion but edged with dread. 'Are you OK?'

I ignore him for a moment, and I kneel beside Molly, giving her a shake. 'Molly? Moll. Wake—'

'What the actual . . . ? Iris,' she growls as she peels her eyelids up a slither. 'Go away, I'm sleeping!' She strikes out at me, but it's half-hearted and misses me completely, and she curls herself up into a tight ball.

'Molly, you have to watch this,' I say, my excitement making me immune to the dose of morning evil. 'Both of you. I need you to confirm that I'm not going completely mad.'

'Huh?' Molly has her eyes open and she's looking up at me from beneath her hood. She's definitely still evil-Molly, but I can see curiosity is thawing her out. Before she can protest her wake-up call any further, I wedge myself in the space that's opened up between her and Byron, and I press play.

The camera pans around a small, empty room. There is no natural light, and a torch beam flits through the frame.

'If there is anyone here with us, make yourself known,' says Lucas from behind the camera.

There's a shot of a grey, peeling wall, its surface pitted

where old, dead plaster has come off.

'Nothing,' says Zach from somewhere off-screen. A beat later, booted feet crunching on dust and debris can be heard, marking the boys' retreat from the room. On-screen, the walls rush jerkily by, as the camera is swung round, until Zach is caught in shot, just the back of him, as he heads through the doorway ahead of Lucas. He runs a hand through his gorgeous-without-even-trying tousled hair. 'So just down here are a set of stairs to the second floor,' he says as he walks, turning to the left and flicking a look to the camera.

'Hey, have you noticed how there's no graffiti in this whole place?' says Lucas from behind the camera, as he follows Zach. The autumn sunlight is bright as it falls through the three large windows at the end of the walk-way. Light spills over the balustrade and down to the entrance hall below.

'Oh, yeah,' says Zach, glancing at the walls. 'Yeah, you're right.'

'I mean, when have we ever come to an abandoned place and there's been no graffiti?'

'Never, bro.'

'Isn't it a bit weird?'

'Yeah, I guess. But I also guess no one really comes all the way out here. I mean, it's miles away from anything.'

'Or they're just too scared,' says Lucas.

'Most likely. I know how they feel.'

'Dude, d'you think we should split up later?' says Lucas.

Zach glances over his shoulder to the camera. 'Could do. You sure you want to? I mean this place is creepy as anything.'

'It'll be a laugh.'

Zach shrugs. 'You've got a messed-up view of what makes something funny, bro,' he says to Lucas. Then to camera, he says, 'Anyway, we're just about to head up to where Anne, the evil aunt, used to stand at a window for hours on end, keeping watch over the woods and the meadow to make sure that the ghost of Elizabeth's mother wasn't coming to get her.'

'She was well sketchy, that Anne,' says Lucas.

Zach puts his hands up, claw-like, and says 'Rah!' into the camera with a grin, before turning to go up the stairs. When the camera catches up with him, the staircase is gloomy with shadows.

'D'you feel that?' asks Zach, as he pauses halfway up the stairs. He flips the hood of his hoodie up and pulls on the cords to tighten it a little around his face.

'What?'

'A temperature drop.'

The camera draws closer to Zach, who stares out from the screen, with wide, ocean-blue eyes, as Lucas climbs more steps to stand in line with him.

'Yeah. It's colder here, right? Like a sudden drop.'

The camera draws back from Zach, as Lucas goes down a few steps. He turns the camera so that his face is in shot. 'Not cold,' he says. He walks up a few steps. 'Cold.'

He goes back down a step, but stops when Zach says, 'Whoa', as the EMF reader begins to crackle. Zach holds it up to the camera as the lights go from green to yellow: a small spike. 'Man, I'm getting chills right now.'

'Me too. Look, I've got goosebumps. There's something here, dude.'

'Let's carry on up, see if it gets stronger.'

The camera follows Zach as he climbs the rest of the stairs.

'It's dark up here,' he says.

'Dude,' says Lucas, swinging the camera around to the turret at the end of the landing. The same turret where I have sensed something twice now. 'Is this where Anne's window is?'

'Yeah, this is it,' confirms Zach. 'This is where she used to stand.' He points to the window that looks out in the direction of where the woods lead down to the stream and the meadow beyond. I imagine Anne standing there, keeping vigil. In my head, she's dressed all in dusty black: a dress with full, ruffled skirts, and a long veil of black lace over her face. The turret is small enough that, if she stood there, she would block the light from all three windows. I imagine her there in that moment, head turning – slowly, slowly – until her dead eyes are fixed on Zach and Lucas. Watching them silently. Those high cheekbones. That downturned mouth. Face as pale as ash. Eyes as dark as coal. I shiver at the thought, just as, on the flip screen, Zach moves towards Anne's window. Lucas's hand can be seen shooting out and grabbing Zach's arm to stop him.

'D'you notice how the sunlight isn't coming through the glass?' says Lucas.

Zach studies each window in the turret and then the floor and back to the windows. 'Man, you're right.'

'The turret's on the same side as the windows at the bottom of the staircase, right? Or have we come out on a different side of the house?'

Zach goes back to the top of the stairs and looks as if he is tracing the way back down in his head. 'No, it should be on the same side,' he says, glancing at the camera. He slides his hood down and runs his fingers through his hair, his brow creased.

'So, why's no light coming through?' Lucas's hand emerges from behind the camera and he waves it through the space between him and the windows. Outside, the sun shines strong and defiant from between the dark grey clouds that are trying to engulf it. 'You know what I mean, right? It's like you can see the daylight on the other side of the windows . . .' Lucas shoots directly into the turret. He pans it slowly to show each window as a square of daylight, each like a lightbox that a doctor would place an X-ray over in an old TV show . . . 'but it's not shining through to the inside. There's no shadow or patches of light on the floor. It's darker here than it should be, right? For this time of day. It's too dark.'

'Yeah. It's like something's blocking it. Like, you know when someone blocks your light when you're trying to read something?'

'Yeah. And it's cold. You feel that, right? I mean, even

colder than on the stairs.'

'You're right,' says Zach. 'But then some of the glass is missing, so maybe a draught is getting in.' He takes a couple of steps towards the windows. 'Whoa!' He holds the EMF reader up as it spikes yellow – orange – red. 'You see that? This thing is going crazy!'

'This is freaky. D'you feel like . . .'

'Like what?'

'I dunno, like someone's up here? Someone's with us right now, watching us?'

Zach takes another step towards Anne's window. He stops. I see a shiver run down his spine. If he reaches out a hand, he'll be able to touch the remaining glass. 'Is there anyone here with us?' he says, holding the EMF reader in front of him. It spikes red and stays there a few beats.

'Whoa! Oh man.'

'Jesus! I've never seen it that crazy before.'

Zach takes a step back. 'I don't like it here, man,' he says, glancing back at the camera, an uncertain grin on his face. 'This is freaking me right out.'

'Yeah, maybe we should just—'

I pause the video, freezing Zach and Lucas right where they are, and I lead the others up to the turret.

'This is big, right?' I say, pulling my hooded top around me against the sharp chill on the landing. There's a nervous grin on my face, as I film Molly and Byron studying the three windows: I may be able to see a perfect blue sky through the glass, and I may have the others with me this time, but I don't feel any less uneasy about being here. As if something in that unnatural gloom is waiting for one of us to get *just close enough* . . . Molly and Byron must sense it too, even though Byron would never admit it, because they both hang back on the landing.

'Twice yesterday I passed this turret,' I continue, 'and twice I noticed how light didn't seem to come in through the windows. You see it, right, it's like there's someone standing there, blocking the light. But there is no one there. Well, no one that you can *see*. But it's like you can *sense* someone there, right? Remember I mentioned it? When I bumped into you guys downstairs, before we realized Molly's stuff had been messed with.'

Byron shoots me a glance over his shoulder. 'I thought you said you saw a shadowy figure. But that's not what you're saying now and not what Zach and Lucas saw.'

'No. I meant that it's *like* a shadowy figure is there,' I say. 'But one you can't actually see. You can just sense it. And the video of Zach and Lucas here is proof, right? That something is going on in this house. Something . . . something supernatural.'

Byron gives me the side-eye.

'Yes. Oh yes! There's something there,' says Molly excitedly, as she takes in each pane of glass in turn, and down to where the strong sun should be illuminating the floorboards but isn't.

'*Moll* . . .'

She ignores Byron, switches on her torch and shines it into the shadows. The beam is swallowed up. 'Someone's blocking the light,' she says, glancing at me and then back to the windows. All wide-eyed and flush-cheeked. She takes a tentative step forward. Just one. 'Anne . . . Anne Turner, are you here with us?'

Silence.

'Hey, we should do a seance here when it gets dark,' I suggest, wondering, as I say the words, if it is the best idea. If my nerves can take it. But then I think of the footage we could get and decide that it *is* a good idea. 'See if we can make contact.'

'You two need to stop getting carried away,' says Byron.

'No,' I say, turning to him. 'You know what, By, the old me would convince myself that what I've seen and heard is down to mice or my own reflection or an overactive imagination. But the new me knows that there's something very weird and very creepy going on here. And this proves we're on the right track.' I pull Lucas's camera from my hoodie pocket and thrust the screen towards Byron. His eyes flick to where Zach is frozen in a place he wants to run away from and back to me.

'This is nothing more than evidence that Zach and Lucas freaked themselves out because they knew that there's a legend attached to a window in this house that suggests it's haunted. But it isn't. It's the power of suggestion, which is also influencing you and Molly, watching them being spooked.'

'OK, Byron,' I say, 'if you're so clever, explain how come I had the *exact* same experience as they did at this *exact* same window before I even saw this footage and when I didn't know that part of the tale, huh?'

'Easy, you must have read about Anne standing at a window in a turret when you were doing your research but you didn't retain that piece of information, not in your conscious mind, but it was still there in your subconscious, and your subconscious used it to play a trick on you.'

'I didn't do much research. Not like I usually do, and not at that level of detail. I didn't have time. I had an essay to write, and I didn't want to put off coming here until next weekend, because I knew. I just *knew* this was the place. But I didn't know about that window. I swear. Besides, you see it too, right? It's not just me and Molly. Byron, you can't deny something is wrong here.'

He regards me through narrowed eyes a moment. 'OK, well, there must be something in the atmosphere,' he says, brow furrowed as he turns back to the windows. 'A natural gas or a high damp level confined to this area, which causes mild hallucinations. Or maybe the floor level is off.' Byron looks down, his head turning left to right as he scans the length of the landing, all the way to the turret. 'Just enough to disrupt the sense of balance and fool the brain into seeing and sensing things that are not there.' He presses down heavily on the floorboards with a foot to check for movement.

'Oh, please. Grasping at straws much,' says Molly, but she manages to sound cute, rather than nailing the sarcasm she was going for.

Byron is quiet a moment. 'OK. Then there has to be something outside,' he says. 'Something blocking the sun.'

He strides towards the windows but halts, about a metre away. I see a shiver run through him, and he backs up, muttering, 'Nope, nothing out there. So, it's just some sort of optical illusion,' while refusing to catch my eye.

And when I suggest we don't linger too long, neither Molly nor Byron argue with me.

18

WE'RE SITTING ON our sleeping bags in our base camp, scan-watching some footage of Zach and Lucas hanging out in this very room and in the entrance hall, just chatting and messing about and sliding down banisters, and a video of Zach searching for Lucas during a game of hide and seek somewhere upstairs. We alternate between the cameras, while we munch a breakfast of rice cakes with peanut butter and some croissants, which we fill with chocolate spread. We only have one knife – a small paring knife that I nabbed from home, because it's sharp and useful for all sorts of cooking needs, but small and compact enough to pack safely – so there's chocolate spread in the peanut butter jar and peanut butter in the chocolate spread jar. But, hey, it still works.

As we eat, I'm aware of Byron casting lingering looks at me when he thinks I don't notice. I do. Just in my periphery. But when I try to catch him, he looks away too quick for me to see if it's concern in his eye – *does he think I'm losing it after the trip to the turret . . . imagining things that aren't there?* – or if it is something more. I focus on the footage, so that I don't have to think about what it means, even though I hope he doesn't stop. There's not much more to note on Zach's camera, until they decide to head up to the roof. This grabs my attention, as I remember Zach saying that's where he'll tell the next part of the Thornhanger House legend. And I want to know what else they know that we don't.

To get to the roof, the boys take the same narrow, winding staircase we took yesterday evening up to the attic, and along a corridor with doors on one side and sloped ceilings on the other. As I watch the flip screen, I find myself turning or tilting my head, as if I'll be able to see around corners that Zach and Lucas have yet to turn into, in my eagerness to know if anything is there. They come to a small set of steps, which lead up to a door to the outside. On the other side of the door is a section of flat roof, which stretches above one side of the house, edged by a waist-height ornate stone wall. As the camera pans around, I can see that the other side of the house rises in a pitched roof, beneath which must be the attic rooms.

Molly, Byron and I watch as Zach comes to a stop by the wall, standing in a corner so that he can film the back and side of the house's grounds – all of which are bigger than I realized. Though what would once have been immaculate lawns and rose gardens, pathways and hedges and neat flower beds, are now reduced to tangles of weeds, brambles, scraggly bushes and trees, and gnarled brown creepers that threaten to strangle the lot, and that smother the tumbled remains of garden walls. A ruin of what it once was. He moves the camera wider, to take in the view, revealing just how in the middle of no-freaking-where this place is. The sky has a cool violet hue, dappled with ash-grey clouds, with just a hint of frosty orange on the horizon as the day shifts towards dusk. I see rolling hills, trees and open, rocky moorland, where everything is awash with yellow and orange and red, as autumn is in full flow. Zach sweeps the camera round too fast and it's dizzying, until he stops on a shot of where the sprawling woods become denser to the right. Those leaves that haven't already shed from the twisted trees are mostly a sickly yellow, with splashes of blood red. I can just make out the stream that runs at the edge of the property line at the side of the house, and the wild meadow beyond.

'So, that's the section of woods where Anne's body was found,' he says.

'Oh, where they lead down to the stream. That's where Elizabeth's mum's ghost can't cross over the property line because she died outside of it, right?' says Lucas, who is standing to Zach's right. His profile is just in view at the edge of the screen. A soft breeze ripples the back of his hair.

'Yep. That's the one,' says Zach, turning himself and the camera around so that he is standing with his back against the wall. He and Lucas are in shot, with the distant woods and even more distant rolling hills framed in the background. Lucas continues to look out across the landscape, so we can only see his back and a little of his profile. 'And there's more to the story of the woods,' continues Zach, pulling his notes from his pocket with his free hand. He swings round again, turning the camera to the right, in the direction of the woods. He zooms in for a closer shot. 'But this part happens decades— Wait . . . what *is* that?'

'What?'

'There.'

'What, dude? I can't see anything.'

'There. There's . . . Shit, I . . .' He zooms in some more, but the camera doesn't pick anything up, other than flashes of tree trunks and undergrowth. Then the camera zooms out and there's a blur and a shot of the stone floor, as Zach lowers it to his side. 'Never mind. I just thought . . . it's nothing,' he says off camera.

'What . . . did you see someone down there or something?'

'No. I . . . just spooked myself. That's all.'

'You sure, man? I mean, it's probably just a hiker or—'

'I *said* it was nothing, OK?' The words are spoken between gritted teeth.

'OK. OK, man. But if—'

'It's cool. I'm cool. Look, it's getting a bit late to get a good shot up here.' The camera tracks along the ground as Zach appears to be backing up, away from the edge. 'We should come back tomorrow morning or something.'

'You OK, mate?' Lucas's voice sounds concerned, less of the perpetual joker.

'Yeah. Yeah. I just want to get off this fucking roof,' says Zach, a little too short. A little too snappy.

'Yeah. Sure. No worries, Zee.'

'I just . . . You know, it's getting late.' Zach's voice has none of its usual energy. 'Getting dark, and I—'

The recording ends.

'What did we just watch?' I say, as the three of us stare at the screen, half-eaten rice cakes held, forgotten, in our hands.

'A guy freaking himself out,' says Byron. 'Or he might actually have seen someone out there,' he adds. 'Someone messing with them.'

'Don't start that again,' I say. 'I really don't think there's anyone else here, By. We've found no evidence.' Byron's jaw tightens.

'It could have been Anne's ghost,' says Molly. 'In the haunted woods.' She breaks off a piece of rice cake and pops it in her mouth.

Byron groans. 'Look, I'm just saying that we should consider—'

'All right then,' I say, cutting Byron off, 'perhaps he saw a deer.' I'm trying to talk his language – the language of the non-believer – before he can suggest leaving, if he thinks someone is here. 'There are bound to be deer out there. And maybe he got embarrassed about freaking himself out over a deer and didn't want to admit it to Lucas.'

Before Byron can respond, I stand and head towards the door, purpose in my stride.

'Where are you going?' Byron calls after me, but I ignore him. I cross the entrance hall and head into the library. By the time I get to the ballroom, I can hear two sets of footsteps following me.

On my knees, I rummage around in Zach's things.

'What're you looking for?' Byron asks.

'This,' I say, as I pull Zach's notes from his backpack and wave them in the air.

We retrace Zach and Lucas's journey up to the roof, using the footage on Zach's camera so that we don't get lost. As soon as we step outside, I have to squint and my skin prickles from the full force of the sun's rays, with nothing to shade us up here. Byron films me and Molly as we stop where Zach and Lucas had stood months ago. We scan the vast landscape: silent, eyes wide, as we take it all in. Then, with a quick glance to camera, I open out Zach's notes. I want to read them up here, where Zach had intended to. More dramatic that way, for the video.

'With its tragic history, Thornhanger House remained empty until the 1930s,' I begin, 'when it belonged to Harold Brooks, his wife Margaret and their two grown-up daughters. Not much is known about their brief time at the house, other than they and their entire staff vanished overnight, leaving all their possessions. Perhaps the result of Harold Brooks's involvement in some shady business dealings, forcing them to take off in the night, after paying off and dismissing all the staff. Or perhaps murdered by Brooks's enemies, they never left and still roam the walls of Thornhanger House unseen . . .' I flick a glance to camera and widen my eyes – partly for dramatic effect and party because this information is completely new to me. 'Then, in 1976,' I continue, 'it was opened as a boarding school. It was closed within a month, however, after a pupil, who had been seen fleeing in a panic from the second floor of the house, fell to their death from the central staircase . . .' I pause, breath caught, at the memory that I almost tripped in the exact same spot when I ran from Anne's window, freaked out at feeling watched.

'You OK?' asks Byron.

My eyes flick towards him. 'Yeah. Yeah, it's nothing,' I say, trying to shake it off, though something snags in the back of my mind, playing like a scratched record: *what were* they *running from?* I clear my throat and, locating my place in the notes, I continue. 'While two more pupils went missing from the premises. They were never found. A teacher's body was discovered in the meadow with a broken neck, just prior to the closure. Her death remains a mystery and foul play was not ruled out.

'The housemistress, a Miss Grace Foster – Ah, Grace. This is who Zach mentioned before,' I say, glancing at the others. 'A Miss Grace Foster,' I continue, 'claimed to have seen a distraught woman in the meadow the day before the teacher's unexplained death, frantically searching for a way to cross the stream, despite it being no deeper than an ankle. According to local legend, the woman Grace saw that day was Charlotte Turner's ghost, desperately trying to reach her beloved daughter, Elizabeth, locked and slowly dying in a cupboard, but forever shut out as she had died outside the property line. So great was Charlotte's despair that Grace was forever changed from that day, as though she had discovered a dark secret not meant for her, and that she now had to bear always.

'Some months after the school was closed, Grace, now a shadow of her former self, moved back to Thornhanger House. She lived there alone. And when children began to go missing from local villages, rumour had it that Grace, haunted and driven mad by Charlotte Turner's anguish, stole the children for her, hoping that they would in some way appease her.

'Apparently, Grace's body was found on the steps outside the back of the manor house by police officers, when they went to question her.' I pause to glance over the stone wall around the roof, to catch a glimpse of the steps. But the drop makes me dizzy, so I lean back again, before continuing. 'Some say that the rumours drove Grace to take her own life as a protest of her innocence, while far more believe that either the burden of guilt at stealing the children was too great, or that she jumped from the roof terrace because she could no longer stand the torment of Elizabeth's mother's sorrow; a sorrow never ended, no matter how many stolen children Grace led into the woods.

'Dun dun duuuun,' I add to the end, for effect.

'I've got to admit, that's a cracking story. But it *is* just a story,' says Byron from behind the camera.

'But isn't that all any of us are,' says Molly, her eyes fixed on the woods. 'Just stories that haven't yet had their endings.'

19

BEAMS OF LATE-MORNING sunshine break through the tall trees as we walk, giving the ruined grounds a hazy, otherworldly beauty.

After the roof, we switched to Lucas's camera and followed some of his footage through a series of corridors and rooms on the second floor, until it led us to a narrow and windowless set of stairs we'd not seen before. We retraced Zach and Lucas's steps down the dusty staircase, using Molly's torch to light the way, and through a door on to the balcony that overlooks the ballroom. Stopping with my hands resting on the balustrade, I surveyed the desolate room and said, 'Remember when I felt someone watching us from up here when we first arrived?' Glancing round at the others, I added, 'I thought I was imagining things then. But now I'm convinced a spirit had been up here. The Thornhangers must haunt this room.'

To which Molly nodded in furious agreement, while Byron said, 'I think I preferred you as a sceptic,' and gave me a lopsided smile. On camera, Zach and Lucas pause briefly on the balcony to get a shot of the vast room below, before continuing down the stairs and out into the ballroom itself. Nothing to note on the footage and nothing that we hadn't seen ourselves when we found Zach's gear in there. Through into the library, the boys decide to head out the broken window to explore the grounds.

We follow the same route as Zach and Lucas from the left of the house. On-screen, it grows darker as black clouds move in like sharks; soon it's raining so hard that the boys decide to head back inside, and the video ends. Molly, Byron and I decide to carry on, as we have no idea what is over this way. Unlike the right, which leads to the dense woods and the stream, and which we plan to explore later, before it gets dark (*loooong* before it gets dark).

Our feet crunch on fallen twigs and mulch, while rich green ferns and long grasses soak our jeans with morning dew. In a small clearing, six ivy-covered stone steps lead us up to a raised garden, where the statue of a woman stands. Naked, with her arms positioned modestly, she has a long braid down her back, stone flowers woven into it. Her eyes are closed, head lowered and slightly to one side. The picture of sorrow. Lichen of green and yellow and patchy black mould give the impression that she is transforming into something else – a forest sprite, perhaps. We wander on through the sparse trees, and through a crumbling stone arch which looks as if it was once part of a tall wall, now mostly in ruins and reclaimed by the wild woodland. It's cool in the shade of the trees. I smell earth and freshness. Other than the soft crunch of our feet, I hear birdsong and the creak of the old trees that hem us in.

I'm filming intermittently. We hardly speak. We're in awe of our enchanted surroundings. It's so perfectly peaceful out here – a welcome distraction from the strange events inside the house. We all needed to get out of there for a bit. Get some fresh air and clarity.

Eventually, we stumble upon an old chapel, disguised, until we are almost on top of it, by ivy and shadows. It's not very big, maybe the size of a small cottage, with a vestibule that juts out from the front aspect. As we emerge through a break in the trees, I raise the camera to get a shot of the stone cross on the top of the steeply pointed roof. 'A chapel in the woods,' I say to the camera. 'That's not creepy. At. All.'

The three arched windows at the front of the building are boarded up, so it's not much to look at, really, just greying, creeper-covered, crumbling stone, with slates missing from the mossy roof here and there. I jump at the sound of harsh cawing, and glance up to see a largish black bird in the branch of the tree closest to us.

'A crow,' says Molly. 'Look, there are more.' She points to the trees around us. 'One, two, three, four, five . . .' she counts . . . 'six. Huh.'

'What?' I ask, curious at the *Huh*.

'Crows can be a sign of good luck, according to superstition.'

'Can be?'

'*Yeaaaah*,' she begins, drawing the word out. 'But six crows are meant to signify that death is nearby.'

'Oh, great,' I say. 'Just what we need to hear right now.'

Byron shakes his head, a wry smile on his lips, as we carry on towards the vestibule, obviously not willing to give any more of a response. As we draw closer, I'm not holding out much hope that the tall arched door will be unlocked, but when Molly twists the iron handle and gives it a shove, it opens right up, with a creak and a scrape of the weather-worn wood along the concrete floor slabs. It's cool inside the roomy vestibule as we step inside, the air musty and damp, and I get a shiver down my spine. Ahead, the heavy inner door is closed. I halt, heart thumping, when I spot two dark shadows beneath the door, as if someone is standing on the other side. They shift, slowly and purposefully. I fling an arm out to warn the others, and I indicate with a flick of my head to the crack of light that runs beneath the door, just as the shadows quicken, flitting to the right. And then they're gone.

Lips tight, eyes wide, I stare at the others, in a *What do we do now?* kind of way. Molly goes down on to her hands and knees, and with her head to the ground, she looks beneath the door. Following the line, left to right. She glances up at us and shrugs her shoulders, before standing and reaching out a hand towards the door handle. Byron grasps her wrist, halting her, and she shoots him a look. His face stern, he releases Molly and points with a finger to the outside, silently indicating that we should *Go. Get out. Now.* I shake my head, and his eyes widen so far that I think his eyeballs might actually fall right out of their sockets.

He mouths, 'Someone. Is. In. There.'

I stare into his eyes, biting my lip. We haven't found any evidence that anyone is staying inside Thornhanger House. We'd have seen some sort of trace: food wrappers, an old mattress with bedding, clothes. We've found evidence of squatters during other explorations. We've even come across used syringes before, so we have learnt to be careful. There's usually a smell, too, if people are using a place to sleep in: stale unwashed bodies and clothing. Urine. Faeces. Rancid food. Heavy and cloying. We have never actually seen anyone, but we've smelt them. Sensed them. But I suppose it is possible that someone could have an off-the-grid hidey-hole out here, and a little place in the woods like this could be ideal. A proper live-off-the-land type, who snares rabbits and knows what mushrooms won't kill you. *If someone wanted* not *to be found, what might they do to someone who stumbles upon them?*

But if there is someone in there, they could have vital information on what happened to Zach and Lucas. Blinded by how much of a scoop that would be, getting someone on camera who knows the truth of this place, I mouth, 'Just. A. Fox.'

I raise the camera before me by the tripod like it is Gandalf's staff, prepared to use it as a weapon if I have to, as it's all I have. Mouth dry, body trembling with fear, I lunge for the cast-iron door handle before Byron can stop me. He hisses 'Iris!' but beside me Molly clenches her fists, ready to dive in and throw some punches if she has to.

My heart is pounding so hard, I'm afraid it's going to break loose and I'll choke on it. I just have time to think that if there is someone inside, with the windows all boarded up, they are probably trapped – *a cornered animal is a dangerous animal* – before I fling the door open.

'Holy shit!' I cry, and I hear Molly and Byron shriek as a blurry shape sweeps towards us from the dusty shadows.

Thinking we're under attack, I duck, while Molly covers her head with her arms, and Byron says, 'It's a bird! Just a bird.' Straightening up, I dart to the outer door, holding on to the wooden frame as I follow the line of his pointed finger, just in time to see a wood pigeon flying off into the treeline.

I stand a moment, back against the door frame, to catch my breath. I glance from Molly to Byron, their faces pale with shock.

'Well, I guess if there's anyone in there, they now know we're coming,' I say, my words hushed nonetheless.

We pause at the inner doorway. I angle the camera around the edge, my eyes on the flip screen. Narrow beams of sunlight break through the many gaps in the boarded windows. Like tiny searchlights, they fall on the few rows of pews, wood dull with age and dust. At the very front of the chapel, which is no bigger than a good-sized lounge-diner, there is an elaborately carved altar. I see no one. As I edge further in, filming left and right and up and down and around as I go, I think how cold it is. Icy, in fact, and breath forms in small clouds in front of me. The rubber soles of my Converse make slight slapping sounds on the paving slabs, but other than our footsteps, the air is heavy with silence and stillness. No sign that anyone is living here. There are no other doors. Just this one small room, which rises to the rafters. Satisfied we've seen all there is to see, and that there is nowhere for anyone to hide, but with the question of what we saw moving in the strip of light beneath the door remaining unanswered, we head back out into the welcoming warm summer air.

Behind the chapel, we find a dank graveyard. Row upon row of ivy-smothered headstones stretch off into the thick undergrowth. I imagine it would have been well-tended once, maybe by a gardener, with freshly picked flowers laid on the graves by mourning loved ones. But now all those who cared about the dead buried here are themselves long gone, and the wonky, lichen-covered headstones are cracked and crumbling. Many are plain slabs, with simple inscriptions, but some are elaborately carved into grand statues, weeping angels and tall crosses.

As we wander, we find one small headstone that is separate from the others, over to the far left. I bend down to read the inscription, but there isn't one.

'An unmarked grave,' says Molly, going down on to her haunches beside me. 'And you see how there's no grass growing over it . . .' she adds, nodding to the rectangle patch of dirt over where I assume the body lies. I stand and study the other graves for comparison. They are covered in grass and weeds and thick moss. 'Well, according to superstition,' she continues, rising to her feet, 'if nothing grows over a grave, it's a sign that whoever is buried there lived a wicked life.'

'Oooh, maybe this is Anne's grave,' I suggest, liking the drama of the story. 'Or Violet. She murdered two people. I'd say that was pretty wicked.'

'After everything Lord Thornhanger promised her . . .' Molly pauses, shaking her head. 'Violet was betrayed by someone she loved. There's nothing worse than that.'

'Honestly, you two,' says Byron. 'Someone's character has no effect on what grows over their grave.'

Molly shrugs. 'I'm not saying that I believe it,' she says, a tightness to her tone and a stiffness to her smile. 'I just find it interesting.' And, mellowing, she adds, 'People used to believe some wild stuff, like you should hold your breath when passing a graveyard, so that you don't breathe in the spirit of someone recently buried. And if you leave a tooth from a living person on a grave—'

'Yeah, OK, Moll,' I say, half joking, my palm out towards her. 'A creepy graveyard in the middle of nowhere is not the place to be telling creepy superstitions about graveyards.'

She gives a little snort and says, 'Fair point.' And with an excited shoulder shrug, she adds, 'Let's see who can be the first to find Elizabeth's grave,' and she practically skips off among the headstones, like a kid in a toyshop.

Byron snorts, shrugs and says, 'She won't stop until one of us finds Elizabeth's grave. I'll make a start on the other side.' He nods his head over to the right.

'OK, I'll take the middle.' It will be a scoop for the video to find Elizabeth's grave. Or any of the Turners from the legend of Thornhanger House. Or even Lord Thornhanger himself.

Byron disappears between the trees, and I raise the camera. 'So many graves,' I say in my camera voice as I start walking, weaving between the stone slabs and statues. 'I guess this chapel must be older than the house itself.' I go down on to my haunches and point the camera at the inscription on the headstone in front of me. It's worn, but I can mostly make it out:

IN L   VI   G MEM   Y
OF
TH   MA   AU   TIN
B   RN SEPT   BE   176
DIED JULY 1796

I move on to the next stone; again, it is pretty weather-worn.

'In life we . . . something, something . . . on a wind we

– what's that . . .' I read aloud for the camera. 'Something, something . . . until we meet again. William something . . .' With a shake of my head, I give up and move on.

I'm lost in trying to decipher inscriptions and filming *spooky* graveyard shots to maybe use as a montage in the video. I assume the others are similarly engrossed nearby, though I can't see either of them. Swinging round to film the far end of the graveyard, I halt a beat, before crying out, 'Molly? Molly! Oh my god, Molly.' Manoeuvring around a headstone, I take a tentative step forward. 'What have you done? Moll—'

'What?'

I jump at the voice, which had come from a little way behind me. I spin round to see Molly weaving between the graves towards me.

'Moll? But . . .' I turn to where I had been looking just now and then back to Molly as she approaches, her eyebrows raised questioningly. I glance from her face down to her hands. 'I . . .'

'Iris, what's wrong?' she says, placing a hand on my arm as she draws up in front of me. 'What were you looking at?'

I shake my head. 'I . . . Where were you just now?'

Her brow furrows, confused, no doubt, by my strange tone. 'I was just over there –' she points between the trees behind her, in almost the opposite direction to where I was filming – 'looking for Elizabeth's grave. I couldn't find it. Have you had any—'

'I saw you.'

'*Okaaay?*' she says, questioningly.

'I saw you over there. Just a second ago,' I say, swinging round and pointing to the other side of the graveyard.

Molly squints against the sun as she follows the line of my finger. 'I haven't been over that way.'

'But I saw you. How did you get from there to here? And your face . . .'

'What about my face,' she says. Unnerved, she raises her hands and touches her fingertips to her cheeks. She stares at me, confusion and a spark of fear in her eyes, while I stand, mouth open, not sure what to say to her.

Over Molly's shoulder, I spot Byron heading towards us through the trees. 'Hey. What's going on?' he calls, frowning as he draws closer. He must sense that something is wrong.

'I'm not sure,' says Molly. 'Iris?'

They both stare at me, wating for an explanation for my odd behaviour.

'I . . . I saw someone standing between the graves over there. Just a shadow against the sun through the trees at first, but . . . Molly, it was you. I recognized the outlines of your jeans and hoodie.'

'I wasn't over that way,' says Molly.

I shake my head. 'That isn't even the strangest part,' I continue. 'I didn't think much of it at first, and then in a blink-of-an-eye moment, the sun was blocked by a branch and –' I take a steadying breath – 'I could see your face, Moll. It was blank. Eyes glazed. And the blood . . .'

'Blood? Iris, what are you going on about?' asks Byron.

'And then the sunlight broke through the branches again,' I continue, ignoring him. 'Blinding me. But – oh god, Molls . . .'

'*What?*' she urges.

'Blood was running down your cheeks. Clumping in your hair. Staining the front of your T-shirt and hoodie. Your hands were all bloody and held out in front of you.'

Molly's face drains of colour, and she fixes me with wide, glassy eyes, mouth open but nothing coming out.

'Whoa, Iris, slow down,' says Byron, palms out towards me. 'You're not making *any* sense.'

'You saw me . . . covered in . . . in blood?' Molly says, finally.

'Yeah.'

'And you're sure it wasn't Elizabeth's ghost? Or . . . or Anne, maybe?'

'No. It was you, Molly.'

With a hand over his eyes, Byron scans the area. Turning back to me, he says, 'If you saw something over there, it was probably just shadows and glare creating some sort of illusion. You said yourself you had the sun in your eyes.' His brow is creased with what could be concern or confusion as he speaks. 'Or maybe you mistook one of those stone angels – probably spooked from Molly's superstitions.'

'No,' says Molly, firmly. 'Iris saw my doppelganger.'

'Your doppelganger?' says Byron, incredulous.

'Yeah. In supernatural terms: a ghostly or demonic double of a living person. They're considered a bad omen.

Oh god. Oh holy . . .' Molly hugs herself, as if trying to contain her rising panic. 'It's a warning,' she says, glancing from Byron to me. 'I think something bad is going to happen.'

20

HAVING ALREADY GOT some great footage this morning from the turret and the grounds, we leave Lucas's camera in the base camp and methodically follow some more of Zach's footage from their first night and into their second day at the house. All the while searching for Elizabeth's cupboard: the door with the scratches on the inside of it still eludes us.

We didn't find her grave. Or those of Edward, Charlotte or Anne. But that's not surprising, as many of the headstones were too weather-worn to read. Though Byron suggests that maybe there never was an Elizabeth, Edward, Charlotte or Anne, and that, yes, the Turner family did once own this house, but the stories are nothing more than that . . . stories. Based on some fact, maybe, but mostly invention. Developing over time to eclipse any truth of this house, which is probably much more mundane, and nothing more than people were born here, lived here and died here. And probably the Turner family had a financial misfortune, which lost them the house. Molly shakes her head and says, 'You can feel them here. You can.' She's been mostly quiet since the graveyard and what she believes was a sighting of her doppelganger, which makes me feel bad, but not as bad as it probably should. That is why we're here. For the video. And it was good for the video. She's chewed a hole right through the cuff of her hoodie sleeve so that her thumb pokes out. As we follow Zach and Lucas through the house, she chews on the skin around her thumbnail, making it bleed.

In a dark, windowless room with toilet stalls and brown-stained washbasins, Zach feels something touch his arm. We feel nothing. In a large dormitory, Lucas hears faint tapping on a wall, but by the time Zach gets there with the camera, the tapping has stopped. When we stand in the same spot, our ears against the crumbling plaster, we hear nothing. As we retrace their steps, we stop now and then to call out for any spirits that would like to speak with us. Nothing stirs. Nothing shifts. No bangs or thuds or footsteps. Not a thing. No clues. Just the best part of an afternoon gone and a lot of useless footage on my camera. Though I notice that Molly's eyes dart around the shadowy corners of the house ever more frantically, and she jumps at the slightest sound.

On the flip screen, Zach and Lucas head downstairs to get something to eat, and with our stomachs rumbling and not much else happening, we decide to do the same.

When we get back to the base camp, Lucas's camera is sat in the middle of the room, several metres away from where I put it down.

'Are you sure that's not where you left it?' says Byron.

I pick the Sony up off the floor and turn it around in my hands, my brow creased.

'I'm sure. I know I didn't. I left it on the sleeping bags after we got back from the chapel this morning.' I glance from Molly to Byron. 'Did either of you . . .'

'I didn't touch it,' says Molly. 'Something wants us to watch what is on that camera,' she adds, before resuming gnawing at her bloody thumbnail.

'Molly, *come on*,' says Byron.

'Whoever is haunting this house,' she persists, 'has a message for us.'

'There is no such thing as a haunted house, Molly,' says Byron, plonking himself down on his sleeping bag and fiddling with the zip of his backpack. 'There is *always* a rational explanation,' he says. 'Everything that anyone has heard, seen or felt can be explained. Rationally.'

It was just a bird.

A bird or a bat.

It was just a bird.

A mouse or a rat.

It's beginning to sound like some creepy old nursery rhyme.

I sit cross-legged beside Byron, and I stare at Lucas's camera in my hand.

'Really? You think Iris seeing my doppelganger can be explained?' Byron doesn't dare speak, and, turning to me, Molly adds, 'Play it, Iris.'

I glance at Molly, her eyes fixed on the Sony. I feel the weight of it. Wondering how the secrets inside it – waiting to be discovered – can weigh so little. Wondering where the footage will lead us next. Is Molly right, does some spirit in this house want us to watch what is on here? Or did one of us unknowingly knock the camera across the floor with a foot? I switch it on, because maybe, just maybe, Molly is right. Weary, I lean my head on Byron's shoulder, like I've done a thousand times. Molly lays down heavily and tugs her hood over her eyes as far as it will go. No one speaks, while I find the next video on Lucas's Sony, all lost in thought. Thoughts of birds and bats and mice and rats.

Ghouls and ghosts: what do you fear most?

I jump when Molly sits bolt upright. Frowning at me and Byron, she says, 'What?'

Neither Byron nor I move for a beat. We both stare at her, wide-eyed.

'*What*, what?' I say, confused.

'You said something,' says Molly.

I shake my head.

'You whispered something between you.'

'No. We didn't,' says Byron.

'You did. What were you saying? Was it something you didn't want me to hear? What's going on – what don't you want me to know?'

'*What?*' I say with a snort. 'Nothing's going on. What

do you even mean by that?'

I don't like the intensity she is staring at us with. So un-Molly-like.

'I heard you.'

'Why would we . . .'

'We didn't say anything, Moll,' says Byron, sliding over on to her sleeping bag and slipping an arm around her slender shoulders. 'You're tired. We can watch the footage later. Iris and I can go and explore the woods and the stream, while you stay here and rest.'

'I don't want to be alone,' she says, shaking her head.

'Look, we're all tired and frayed,' Byron glances at his watch. 'It's getting on for four already, and we've barely slept since we got here, and this house is getting in all our heads. Maybe we should think about going—'

'No way,' I say, cutting him off. 'There's still more footage to retrace.'

'Iris, come on. We've got a lot of stuff recorded. Enough for a video,' says Byron. 'We've discovered Zach and Lucas's last known whereabouts.'

'But not what happened to them,' I huff.

'I really think we should inform the police sooner rather than later. We can film the trip to the station, make it a big thing for the video. Us handing in the evidence. The police can take it from there.'

'But the video won't be a hit unless *we* discover what happened here,' I groan. 'Not the police. Us.' And, not willing to discuss it any further, I play the next video. As I watch, Molly draws up beside me. After a moment, even

Byron sidles up, resting his chin on my shoulder, his eyes glued to the screen.

'Yo. Hey, guys,' says Zach, as Lucas points the camera at him. Zach is standing at the top of the central staircase, where it branches to the right. He has one hand on the dark-wood balustrade, and in the other he holds his camera. A torch can be seen poking out of the pocket in his black hoodie – which carries the Zach and Lucas merch logo of a red Z & L in a gothic font and, below it, a crude red smiley face, dripping as if painted by a finger dipped in blood. Some light is coming in from the big windows, which are behind Lucas, at the end of the walkway. It's muted, as though it's starting to get dark outside.

'So, Lucas has talked me into us splitting up and carrying out a bit of lone exploration,' he says with a nervous laugh.

Lucas's laughter, which morphs into a mock-sinister *mwahahaha* can be heard off camera. 'You know you live for this stuff, dude,' says Lucas.

'Yeah, I love it,' says Zach, with a half-grin. 'Who wouldn't love being all alone in a big old creepy-as-fuck house?'

'Where no one can hear you scream, *mwahahaha*.'

'Yeah, thanks, Lucas. Why would you say that?' says Zach, with a mock-scowl. 'Let's get this over with, OK?' He starts to move off but stops. 'Um, how long are we doing it for?' he says, glancing at his watch.

'An hour?'

Zach screws up his face. 'An hour? Dude, that's a long time.'

'This is a big house. An hour's not that long.'

'Ah, you're killing me.'

'An hour will fly by. I think we'll need more—'

'An hour's good,' says Zach, cutting in. He gives a cute lopsided grin to camera.

'That's the spirit,' says Lucas, behind the camera.

'How are you so calm about this?' asks Zach.

'What's the worst that can happen?'

'Yeah, there's probably a big, long list to answer that question.'

Both boys laugh.

'So, we're going to do this. I'm going to take this floor,' Zach says into Lucas's camera. He lifts his camera and points it back at Lucas. 'Say hi to the boys and girls at home, Lucas,' he says playfully.

'Hiya.' Lucas puts on a silly, high-pitched voice, which can be heard from behind his camera.

'And Lucas is going up to the second floor, so that we don't end up running into each other.'

'And scaring the bejesus out of each other,' adds Lucas.

'Yep. Anyway, let's get this over with before it gets too dark. And before I lose my nerve.'

There's a bit where Zach and Lucas almost collide as they move off, and Lucas, from behind the camera, says, 'Dude, I'm going that way . . .' He swings the camera to the left. 'I am *not* going past those creepy turret windows again on my own.'

The camera traces along the balustrade around the staircase, then catches a glimpse of the ornate mirror above the landing of the main stairs as he descends the steps on this side and crosses over to the left. Zach can be heard calling out, 'Anne's going to get you,' in a spooky voice.

'She's going to get you, dude. I'm too fast for her. She'll never catch me!'

Lucas points the camera straight ahead, as he climbs the stairs that lead him to the left side of the house. He edges down a corridor. It's dark. There's a rustling sound, a *click*, and then a torch beam lights the way. There are doors on either side of him, along the long, narrow corridor, the first of which is ajar.

Lucas turns the camera so that he is in the frame.

'Right, plan is,' he begins as he walks and talks, 'I'm going to go up and wander around for a bit, see if I can find Elizabeth's cupboard, as we've not found it yet. And then maybe I'll find a spot to stop and call out for— Crap, what was that?' says Lucas, swinging the camera round to get a shot through a door to his left. He stops. 'I think I'm just freaking myself out,' he says, before carrying on.

The camera shows jolting glimpses of the wood panelling on the bottom half of the walls, the crumbling plaster above, and door after door, as Lucas edges down the corridor, not really paying that much attention to what he is pointing it at as he moves it left and right. He turns into another corridor. Another. Another.

'Hope I can remember where the bloody staircase is,' he says as he zooms the camera to the end of the next corridor, and back out again. 'This place is a maze. I don't— Oh crap, what was . . .' The camera swings round and back again. 'Stop freaking yourself out, man,' he says to himself. 'This place is creepy. I mean, we've been to some creepy places, but *this* place is some next level . . . Stairs. At last. We're on our way,' he says as he shines his torch up the staircase.

The camera traces the wall as Lucas climbs the stairs. At the top, he pauses, panning the camera left and right.

'Which way to go . . .' he ponders. 'Straight up, or right?' He yanks open a small door off the landing, which opens outwards, and shines the torch on the back of it. 'No scratch marks in here.' He swings the torch and shines it straight up the corridor. 'I'm going to go that way and see if it circles round.' He leaves the cupboard door open and walks along the corridor.

'So, I'm going to— What was that?' The camera swings to the left, to an open door. 'Christ.' Lucas turns the camera on to himself. 'I keep thinking I see something moving from the corner of my eye,' he says, his eyes darting left and right as he speaks into the camera. 'But when I turn around, there's nothing— What was . . .'

The camera swings around to the end of the corridor, back the way he just came. He doesn't seem to notice, as he doesn't comment on it, but the door to the cupboard that he left open is now closed. He turns the camera back around to the way he is going.

'Argh. This is scary, man. I swear I'm seeing things moving.'

He continues down the corridor a few steps.

'OK. OK,' he says, stopping outside a closed door. 'I'm going to check in a few rooms, see if I can find somewhere to stop and call out. See if I can contact anyone. Get some action.'

Lucas's hand can be seen on the doorknob. He turns it, pushes the door a little way, shining the torch through the gap. There's a pause, then the door opens wider. I immediately recognize the collapsed four-poster bed and I go cold inside. The camera pans around the room and – yes – there are the creepy AF dolls, with their grubby faces and eyes that follow you and the you-are-going-to-die-tonight sinister smirks. Lucas is in the room where I saw the pale face reflected in the window. I want to shout, '*Run! Get out!*' But just like when you hope a movie you have already watched will have a better outcome for a character the next time around, I know it will do no good. Whatever Lucas's fate is, it is sealed.

'Jesus!' says Lucas, as he catches sight of the dolls. 'Horrible, creepy, ugly-arsed things.'

It's probably just me being spooked, but I'm sure the dolls are in a different order to when I saw them. I make a mental note to check my footage.

Lucas moves the camera around the room, and as it skims the window, I hold my breath. But there is no one there. *Breathe.* A glimpse of outside shows that it is already darker than when he and Zach were stood at the top of the central staircase. And there are streaks of cool violet and angry-bruise purple across the sky.

The *crunch crunch* of Lucas's boots can be heard as he walks across the room. Past the collapsed bed. The camera shows a narrow door set into the grey, pock-marked wall. Lucas's hand comes into view as he grips the doorknob. With a tug, he pulls to reveal a small, windowless room or a large cupboard space. One that I missed because I'd been so desperate to get out after seeing the figure. Lucas shines the torch on the back of the door.

'I don't think this one's Elizabeth's—' He stops and swings the torch beam towards the door to the corridor. 'I heard something. I'm not sure if the camera picked it up, but it sounded like a footstep out— Again,' he says in a rushed whisper. 'Something's outside this room.'

His breathing can be heard, fast and heavy. Nothing moves for a moment. Then he says, 'Christ. I really think there's something out there. Oh man.' A pause. 'Crap. I don't know what to do.'

The sound of his breathing is punctuated by the sound of him swallowing.

'Zach, is that you, man?' There's a tremble in his voice. 'You'd better not be messing with me.'

Silence.

'What was that? There's someone out there. Fuck, there is someone . . .'

Another pause, and then the camera tracks Lucas's jerky movement as he creeps across the room, stopping to the side of the door frame. Again, his breath can be heard. He swallows, and whispers, 'Come on, dude. You can do this. You can do this. Get it together.' And, as though he has just counted inside his head – *One, two, three* – he launches himself around the door frame, the torch and the camera swinging to the right.

Nothing.

A scuffling, like a foot dragging on wood, can be heard, though it's not clear where the sound comes from. The camera spins to the left, and Lucas can be heard crying out, 'Holy crap! What was that? That was someone . . . someone's leg. I swear I saw someone's leg disappear around that corner.' Though nothing can be seen on the screen. The footage shakes as Lucas tears down the corridor after the figure. His breathing is ragged when he stops at the end, pointing the camera in the direction that the 'person' disappeared. 'I don't . . . know . . . if the camera picked . . . that up,' says Lucas, incredulous, 'but I swear I just saw someone walk around this corner and go up there. But there's no one there. I mean, they would've been just ahead of me.' He turns the camera around to himself. His eyes are wide, skin pale. 'I don't know if—'

Click.

Lucas directs the camera back down the corridor. 'That sounded like a door closing,' he says. 'There really is someone . . .' He stops for a beat. 'That sounded like footsteps.' He begins to edge down the corridor. 'I mean, it's possible that it's Zach. But why would he come up? Hello?' Lucas stops, camera pointing towards the end of the corridor, where it branches left and right. 'Hello? Is there anyone—'

Bang!

'Shit!' The footage shakes again as it traces Lucas running towards the end of the corridor. His feet can be heard pounding on the floorboards. The camera swings round to the right. It captures what can clearly be made out as the reflection of a figure – just a glimpse of someone's reflection in the window as they turn around the corner of the corridor. Male. Tall.

'Zach? Zach, is that you, man?' Lucas's ragged breath can be heard from behind the camera. 'It didn't look like Zach. But . . .' He pauses. 'Crap. There's someone here. There's someone here.'

The end of the corridor recedes as Lucas backs up. He turns back the way he came. The camera shakes, and all that can be seen is a blur of floorboards and walls and doors and twists and turns and stairs and walls and doors and more stairs, until it stops. And Lucas turns the camera on to himself. He's sat on the central staircase, just a little way down, bunched against the banister. 'There's . . . someone . . . someone in here . . . with us,' he says through gasps for breath.

His eyes dart left and right as he presses himself up against the wooden rungs of the banister.

'Holy crap. I have never been so freaking scared.' He glances at his watch. 'Zach's due back in a few minutes. Oh god oh god oh god.' He looks into the camera. 'There is someone in this house with us.'

The recording ends.

21

'RIGHT. THAT'S IT,' says Byron. He's on his feet, shoving possessions into his backpack. He chucks in a sweatshirt of mine and Molly's washbag in his haste.

'No!' I say, leaping up. I put a hand on his arm, halting him. 'Please, By, we're so close. We can't leave now. We have to retrace Luc—'

'You saw that video, Iris,' he growls, cutting into my words. 'There. Was. Someone. There. In the house with them. They could still be here somewhere. With us. Or they could come back. It's probably them that's been messing with us. Stalking us. We need to report this to the police. Now. This could be a murder investigation. For all we know there could be bodies buried in the grounds somewhere. Zach and Lucas – and maybe others. We don't know.'

'I saw someone in the house, too, remember?' I say,

recalling when I saw someone – something – at a window in the room with the dolls. 'But they weren't really there. They couldn't have been. They were there and then they were gone – *poof* – just like that. My torch only cut out for a few seconds. They couldn't have got passed me.'

'Perhaps there's a secret door,' says Byron.

'What?'

'A secret door. These big old places all have them in the movies. There's probably a network of secret passages.'

'Oh, come on. *Really?*'

'Maybe that's why we haven't seen their stuff.'

'Oh what, because they live in the walls?'

'Maybe.'

'Jesus, Byron. Psychos and secret doors – this is starting to sound like something from *American Horror Story*!'

'So, what . . . you're saying that what we saw on Lucas's camera was a *ghost*? That what you saw was a *ghost*?'

'Yes. That's exactly what I'm saying!'

'Don't be ridiculous, Iris!'

'She's not being ridiculous, Byron,' says Molly. She stands, fists clenched, glaring at him. 'There is something in this house. Something not living. How can you deny feeling it?'

'There's nothing to feel.' Byron puts the heels of his hands to his temples. 'Because ghosts aren't real . . . Agh!'

'OK,' I begin. 'You're the one who's usually finding the logical explanation. Well, the logical explanation here is that it was Zach. Maybe he was messing with Lucas?

Maybe they were both in on it and it's all a big fake. Maybe this is one big internet prank and Zach and Lucas are just hiding out in some supercool hotel somewhere in LA, and they're going to upload a *gotcha* video any day now. We don't know.'

'That's stupid,' says Byron, brushing his unruly fringe from his eyes. 'And you know it is. But you're right about something: *we don't know*.' He pauses a moment before adding, 'We don't know who might have been in the house with them. With us. Right now.'

I draw in a breath, mouth open, ready to rebuff Byron, even though in the privacy of my head I have to admit there is a possibility that he could be right, although I am so, so, *so* sure he's wrong, when Molly says, 'Guys. Look, I agree with Iris. Whatever is going on here is supernatural.'

'See!'

Byron narrows his eyes at me.

'*But . . .*' Molly continues, 'I think that whatever entity or entities are in this house, they are powerful. I mean, to be able to move stuff and to appear in a physical form. That takes a *lot* of energy. And we don't know their intent. They could just be trying to get our attention, to make themselves known. To be listened to.'

'Or?' I prompt when she pauses.

'Or they could be dangerous.'

'Ghosts can't hurt the living, Molly,' I say with conviction.

She lets out a sigh. 'I think we have to consider the possibility that they can, Iris. The doppelganger. They're bad luck. More than bad luck. Doppelgangers are portents of sickness, evil, death . . .'

I shake my head in disbelief, before adding, 'So what are you saying?'

'I'm saying that Byron's right. We should leave.'

'But . . . Molls, you're really into this. We're on the verge of getting proof of paranormal activity on camera. Of finding out what happened here. Just one more night. *One more night*,' I say, trying to win her back.

'Oh my god, Iris,' snaps Molly, her eyes wild. 'Don't you get it – if we stay something bad *will* happen!'

'You guys, come on. This is silly. You're both over-reacting. Let's just—'

'If it were safe,' says Byron, cutting me off, 'Zach and Lucas would've come home.'

I open my mouth to speak, but my words shrivel up and die on my tongue.

If it were safe, Zach and Lucas would've come home.

'He's right, Iris. It's dangerous here. The doppelganger, it's a sign. A warning. I should have insisted we leave right away, when you first saw it. But I—'

'I lied!' I say, spitting out the words before I can change my mind.

'What?' Molly stops and stares at me, open-mouthed.

'What do you mean you *lied*?' asks Byron, his tone warning.

I ignore him for now and say, 'Oh Molly, I didn't think you'd freak out like this. I didn't see anything in the grave-yard. I made it up for good content.'

'You terrified me for views on social media?'

'I know. I'm so, so sorry. I don't know what to say . . . I just wanted a good video so that Byron wouldn't leave the channel. Because I . . .' My words fail as I glance at him: his eyes grow wide as they look into mine and they swirl with a mixture of emotions, and I can't tell which is more dominant – anger or surprise. Confusion or relief. Disgust. Hope. 'I didn't mean to freak you out,' I say, turning back to Molly, 'and make you want to leave. I—'

'So, are you sorry for scaring me or that the scare has made me want to leave?'

'Yes. No. Both. Oh my god,' I say, throwing my arms up. 'For scaring you, obviously.'

Molly shakes her head, letting out a little snorting sound.

'So, it was all you?' says Byron. 'You've been faking everything? Molly's stuff being ransacked – I knew that had to be you. I knew it. You lied to my face, Iris! And seeing the apparition . . .'

'No. Look. Ugh . . . OK, I confess, I made a few things up.'

'I knew it!'

'No, listen,' I say, putting a hand out, as if trying to defuse the situation. 'OK. Cards on the table. I faked feeling like we were being watched in the ballroom. I made that up to stop you guys from leaving when we first got here. I made the scratches on my back.'

'Iris . . .'

'And I spun the globe. I gave it a good spin when I set

the camera up and just hoped you guys wouldn't notice before the torches went off, or that it wouldn't stop before I was ready for the big reveal. But that's it. I promise. I'm sorry. I didn't mean any harm. I just . . .'

I glance from Molly, her eyes glistening with tears and her mouth hanging open, to Byron, who is slowly shaking his head, expression halfway between accusatory and smug.

'You've been playing us for fools this whole time,' he says.

'No, I promise.'

'I trusted you,' says Molly.

'Moll, I . . .'

'The *full-body apparition*.' Byron mimics me when he says it. 'You fake that too?'

'No. No, I swear I saw that. That was real. But . . .' I let out a sigh. 'I may have exaggerated . . . just a bit.'

'Iris!'

'I saw it. I swear. Just a flash. Just enough time to see a pale face in the window. I think it was a man but I'm not sure. It happened so fast. And – for the sake of transparency – I exaggerated the tears on my hand and the shadow figure in the turret. Those things happened,' I say quickly when I see Byron about to go off at me again. 'Just not as dramatically. Everything else – Molly's stuff being messed up, the door opening on its own, the footsteps, the activity during the seance, Lucas's camera moving, the shadows in the chapel – it all really happened. And I believe now. Don't you see? I may have faked a few minor

minor things –' I raise my hand and pinch my forefinger and thumb together with a slight gap between them for emphasis – 'all for a good cause. But the stuff that really happened, it's been enough to make me a believer. In the paranormal. In this house.'

'Why should we believe you?'

'By, please don't. You and Molly saw and heard some of that stuff yourselves.' I pause for a beat. 'Look, the point is, there was no doppelganger. No *bad omen*.'

'The fact that you think that's the point is the reason I'm done with this,' says Molly, her words heavy. 'You deceived me, Iris. And doppelganger or no doppelganger, this is still a bad place with some seriously negative energy. We. Are. In. Danger. I want to go home.'

I want to cry with frustration as I feel the investigation slipping away from me.

'Guys. Come on. *Please*. That was the last video on Lucas's camera. We're so close. We just need to watch what's left on Zach's. Finish retracing their—'

'No.' With his backpack in one hand and a jar of peanut butter in the other, Byron looks me deep in the eye. 'I'm done too.'

'By . . .'

'Get your stuff. We're going to the police,' he says measuredly as he goes back to throwing things into bags.

Not wanting the others to see my tears, I turn and tear across the room, out into the entrance hall, while Byron calls after me, 'Iris, come back. Iris, stop . . .'

I pause for a minute, my cheeks burning with shame

and frustration – where do you storm off to when you're in a creepy-arse house in the middle of no-freaking-where?

'Iris, don't be a . . .'

I don't hear the rest, because I run to get away from Byron's words.

Into the library, I spot the broken window. Air – I need air. I climb through the window, my feet crunching on the weed-infested paving on the other side. The air is heavy with early-summer warmth, even more noticeable after the best part of two days breathing the chill, damp, dusty air of the house. The sun on my skin is like slipping into a warm bubble bath. I breathe in deeply before heading round to my left. I follow the side of the house, all the way round to the back. And, out of sight, I go down on my haunches, my back against the cold, grey stone.

I'm so close. If only Byron would just believe . . .

The rewards for seeing this through, finishing this video and seeing it go viral will be worth the risks. And the others will thank me then, when we are famous YouTubers. When we have our own merch. When we have fans, who love us and *like* all our videos. And subscribe. Subscribe. SUBSCRIBE. They'll love us, whatever we do. Because we'll be famous. And that's how it works.

You can't do great things without taking risks. Mountains couldn't have been conquered, seas couldn't have been charted, the skies couldn't have been mastered without taking risks. Why can't they see that?

I breathe in, savouring the fresh air and the earthy scents of the overgrown grounds.

If we go, I'll be letting Zach and Lucas down. But Molly and Byron . . .

What if Byron's right and there really is someone else in the house? What if Molly's right and the entities inside the house are just too strong and dangerous?

I sit for a moment, just breathing the summer air – in and out. In and out. In and out. Tension eases. My head clears. The boiling in my veins cools to a simmer. I mean, who am I kidding? I'm not climbing mountains or sailing uncharted seas or exploring the limits of the skies. I'm making a YouTube video.

Why am I insisting on putting my friends in danger for the sake of a video?

Byron's earlier words replay in my mind: *If it were safe, Zach and Lucas would've come home.*

I take a long, deep breath in and let it out slowly.

If it were safe, Zach and Lucas would've come home.

With my face in my hands, I let out a groan.

If it were safe . . .

I sigh heavily. Even if we hand over Zach and Lucas's cameras to the police, we still have enough footage of our own to prove that they were here and that weird shit has happened in this house, especially if we keep quiet about my little *exaggerations*. Even if we don't get to track the whole of their journey through the house. Even if we don't solve the mystery.

I suppose we have enough.

With another deep, steadying breath, I wipe the tears from my cheeks with the back of my hand, and I stand, ready to head back inside. But something makes me pause for a moment – something more than delaying my tail-between-my-legs return – and I find myself with an urge to see the grounds. Just a little. This is the first time I have been out the back. I've only seen it from the roof and more closely on Zach's camera. It all looked so different then, with its yellows and oranges and reds and browns. I mostly see green, everywhere. In the thick, dark ivy that clings to crumbling walls, and in the moss in shades of emerald and yellow-green. The lush green grass, and the brownish green of the tall meadow grasses. Dandelions, bindweed, cow parsley and creeping buttercups add a variety of colour. There are tangles of weeds and brambles and scraggly trees, with grassy paths weaving between them. Some are worn, as if they are tracks taken by wild animals. It's so overgrown out here that I can't see as far down as the woods.

I know I have to get back to the others. I know we need to leave. Right now. And I will go back. In a minute. But I just want to walk a little way. Just a little way. Not far. Just so that I can see the edge of the woods. The woods where Anne died. Where stolen children were taken to appease a dead mother. I just want to see the woods with my own eyes. I mean, we've come all this way. It doesn't seem right to come all this way and not see them.

I take a step. A few more. Down a set of stone steps. On to the overgrown lawn. Past a sundial, discoloured with mildew and lichen. I walk, veering to my right, to where I know that the woods are the thickest. To where they lead to the stream. Even though I know I shouldn't be going this way. I should be going back inside to Molly and Byron. To get our things and go. Go. GO. But my feet keep moving forwards and, as they do, a tight ball in my stomach that I hadn't even known was there starts to unwind and unravel and I'm lighter. I walk further, surrounded by birdsong. Down a grassy path, my jeans snagging on the probing tentacles of prickly brambles. A bee buzzes busily past my ear. The heat is stifling. So hot and sticky. The air thick. Like a rainforest. I hear the whoosh of the long, straw-like grass against my legs; and it's almost as if it is the whispers of the garden welcoming me.

I should go back, but I don't want to. I want to go deeper and deeper. Through the dense undergrowth, where some weeds are as tall as me. Taller. I want to go all the way to the woods. Into the woods. I long to feel the darkness of those woods. The cool shade. I want to feel the shadows on my hot skin. I want to hear the muffled sounds of my feet on a bed of mulch and dead things. I want to sink into that soft, damp, musty mulch. Cool and dark and earthy. I swipe branches and tall grasses out of my way. Sweat trickles down my back, and I pull off my hoodie and tie it around my waist. I still can't see the woods, so I have to go deeper. I have a vague memory that I'm supposed to be doing something. Going somewhere. But I can't quite hold it in my thoughts. I almost have it. Just there, teetering at the edges of my mind. Something about . . . about finding . . . the woods. Yep, that's it. The woods. I want to see the woods before we— We? Who's we? There's only me. I mean, I, before I . . . I can't remember. Why can't I remember? I hate that I can't remember. It's frustrating. I hate . . . I hate . . . Everything. I fizz with a rage that bubbles up from my toes to the pit of my stomach, and my pace increases. I'm so angry. But I can't remember what I'm angry about. It's just there, inside me. Rage. Furious anger. Why? At what? Who. It's a who. I'm so angry at . . . at who?

Who am I—

'Ow!' I say as something tears my flesh. I stop and look down to see two long, deep scratches on my upper arm, blood oozing freely. The branch of a thorn bush, of what might once have been a rose bush but has long since gone to seed, is still attached to the sleeve of my T-shirt. I gently unhook it, careful not to lacerate my skin any further. And I release myself.

I do a double take then, glancing around, and wonder what I'm doing in the middle of the grounds.

Where was I going?

I really have no idea. Then I recall a vague notion of wanting to see the woods. *Needing* to see the woods. And feeling so angry. Anger like I have never experienced. Rage. A rage that started somewhere in my toes and that erupted like lava. A horrible disconnected rage. But it's gone. I feel a breeze on my skin, so gentle that it doesn't sway any branches, but that causes the petals of white blossoms to fall on me like snow. And it reminds me of him. Byron. Of that morning last January when I woke to a blanket of white; thick snowflakes still falling. Of that stupidly lovable look of excitement on his face when I answered the door to him: all red-cheeked and grinning. Eyes glittering. The snowball fight in the park that had us soaked right through; balls of ice clumping in my hair. How we ran and dodged and laughed so hard we didn't notice the cold. We made snow angels. Laying in the snow, our woolly-gloved fingertips touching, we caught each other's eye and swapped a look that could probably have told each of us everything if only we'd just listened. It's just, I thought we had an endless number of days like that one ahead of us.

Molly.

I remember Molly and Byron, back at the house. They will be waiting for me. We're going. Leaving. *Why was I going to the woods?* I shake my head as I remember a pull, like a magnet . . . a compulsion to see the woods with my own eyes. To be inside them. But all of a sudden, the idea seems absurd. I don't want to go anywhere near those creepy woods. Not on my own. No. Bloody. Way. *What was I thinking?* Especially without my camera. I shiver at the thought. What had Anne seen in there to make her die of fright? How terrified must those children have been, abandoned in those vast woods? Alone.

With another shiver, I take a step backwards. I stumble on a bramble and I turn. I trek back the way I came, not wanting to risk getting lost while trying to find a direct route to the broken window – my pace quickening as the sky shifts into the softer hues of evening. I'm sure I'm imagining it, but it's as though grasses and brambles reach for me as I pass, trying to slow me down. To stop me. And I think I sense something following me. A presence. The thought makes me break into a trot, though I'm careful not to trip on the undergrowth. I have a burning desire to be anywhere but out here in this weird, enchanted garden that tried to lure me in. I'm not confident that it is going to let me get away so easily. There's a tight ball of anxiety in the pit of my stomach, and I'm waiting for creepers to wind around my ankles and drag me into the woods. But as I draw nearer to the house, my breath ragged from the exertion, as if I have just trekked through a jungle, I tell myself to stop being so overly dramatic. It's just a garden. It's just a wood. I'm so exhausted – so sleep-deprived – that I probably just zoned out and was sleepwalking or something.

And then I'm back, at the house. Up the steps. I pause for a moment, with my hand touching the cold, solid stone of the old building, letting it ground me. And it occurs to me how crazy things have become if I am looking to this house for comfort. But . . .

Something had been luring me to the woods.

That sounds so completely crazy, even inside my own head. I try to laugh the idea off. But the memory is still a little dreamlike, heavy on me, and I can't. Not fully. With a quick, wary glance back at the gardens, I scurry back around the side of the house, not stopping until I reach the broken window.

Inside, it feels colder and danker than ever, the warmth of the outside evaporating from my skin. With a shiver, I pull my hoodie back on, the fabric sticking to the blood on my arm. I barely have a chance to step away from the window when Molly and then Byron come through the door, loaded up. Byron has my backpack. My sleeping bag is over his arm, the end dragging on the dusty floor. They both stop when they see me.

'Where have you been?' says Byron as he crosses the room towards me. 'We were worried.'

I think about telling them how I had been compelled to go to the woods; how for a moment I had forgotten about the both of them. About myself. How all-consumingly angry I had felt. An anger that wasn't mine. But I decide not to. It doesn't matter. We're going. And Byron won't believe me. And Molly will say it's more proof that the spirits are strong and dangerous. And they are right. And I am wrong. So, sheepishly, I just say, 'I needed some air.'

'We were about to go and look for you,' says Molly.

'When you weren't back by the time we'd finished packing up the stuff . . . We thought something had happened to you,' says Byron, his words catching. 'Christ, we were really worried, Iris, and you were just getting some air. Did you not think—'

'Look, I'm sorry, OK! I'm sorry. You have to believe me,' I implore. 'It was stupid and thoughtless of me to go off like that. It was stupid of me to lie. I've really messed up. And I'm really sorry. But . . . I'm stupid, OK?'

'Yeah. Yeah, you are,' says Byron. 'And Iris is sorry –

that doesn't happen every day.' He gives the slightest smile that says he's joking a little. And that maybe he'll forgive me – eventually.

I take that, and say, 'I don't want to go, but . . .' I slide my backpack off Byron's shoulder and put it over my arm, 'you're right, our safety has to come first.' I glance between him and Molly as I choke back my disappointment.

Byron nods, and Molly gives my forearm arm the slightest *I'm on my way to forgiving you* squeeze, and I turn back to the window.

Outside, we trudge away from the house, each of us throwing intermittent glances over our shoulders, as if we think something is following us. Ready to drag us back. Our pace is as fast as our exhausted bodies and minds and the tricky undergrowth will allow. I fall back a little, as I swallow down the sense of longing that tugs at me – a feeling of loss and regret that grows and grows with each step. Just as something had tugged me towards the woods.

I want to go back. I hate the thought that I've let Zach and Lucas down. I've let the house down. I always let everyone down. I let myself down by not being good enough. I can't do anything.

As if he can sense my reluctance, Byron slips his hand into mine. I squeeze his so tightly. He shoots me a side-glance, and I let him pull me along, grateful for his touch and feeling the house's hold on me loosen. And before I know it, we're at the tumbledown wall. Over the wall and . . .

'What the . . . ?'

Each of us stands staring at the car, the hood up and the battery gone. As in, vanished. Not there. Seats are shredded. Belongings are scattered. Windows smashed.

'My mum's car!' Byron drops his stuff to the ground and goes down on to his haunches. 'What's happened to my mum's car?' He stands and puts the heels of his hands to his forehead. 'Who . . . How . . . What the actual . . . ?' He stops, lowers his hands and turns to me, his gaze so fiery, I can almost imagine the whites of his eyes turning red.

'Iris. What did you do?'

22

AT FIRST, I'M numb. Cold. Then my cheeks flush. Red-hot. I drop my backpack and square up to Byron, head back to look into his eyes.

'Wha . . . ?' is all that makes it out of my mouth, I'm so mad and bewildered. Stunned.

'You did this,' he spits.

'I never!'

'You didn't want us to leave so you made it so we couldn't, didn't you? Admit it. Just like you faked that other stuff. Where's the battery, Iris?'

'Byron, I wouldn't. Come on. You guys don't believe I could do something like this, do you? The car's wrecked!'

My eyes flick towards Molly, appealing to her. But she is standing with a hand over her mouth, her wide eyes fixed on the car. She's no help.

'You always have to get your own way, don't you?' he

says, staring down at me with an uncontrolled wildness to his eyes, which I have never seen in him before and that makes the silver of his irises swirl with something as dark as lead. He looks like he hates me.

'Byron . . .' I go to put my hand on his arm, but he flinches away from me. 'By, you have to believe me. I didn't do this. How can you think I did?'

'Because you're obsessed. So obsessed with likes and views and subs that you don't see the rest of us.'

'By . . .'

'It's like we don't exist.'

'That's not true!'

'We only exist when you want us to.'

'What? Byron I—'

'Where'd you go, Iris?'

'What? When?'

'When you stormed off, where did you go? You were gone for a while.'

'I just . . . I needed time out. To collect my thoughts. I . . .' I hesitate, wondering if I should mention how I was drawn towards the woods. How I didn't feel like myself. The rage inside of me. How I had forgotten myself. Just for a moment. Until the scratch. But I don't think it would be any defence, right now. It would just make me sound crazy and give him one more reason to doubt me. Because it *is* crazy, right? It was just the heat and lack of sleep. I just zoned out. *Right?*

'Did you come down here and trash my mum's car, and—'

'No! No, I never. Besides, this could have happened any time since we got our gear from the car. It could have been any one of . . .' I stop as a thought hits me. 'Byron, you're the one who's convinced there's someone else in that house. Maybe there is. Maybe it was them. Trying to stop us from leaving,' I say, my head spinning. Or is it my surroundings that are spinning? I just know that something is off balance, and I need something to hold on to. I had been so sure that Byron was wrong about there being someone else. But I'm at a loss for how this damage could have happened. Maybe it's me who's been wrong all this time? I don't know what to think any more. What to believe. Everything I have seen . . . everything I have felt and heard . . . could it all be a mixture of my imagination and someone messing with us? With something cold settling into the pit of my stomach, I say, 'Doesn't that make more sense than me doing it? Come on, Byron. This is a bit more than faking some paranormal activity for social media. You have to see that?'

I gaze up at him with wide, imploring eyes: eyes that are tearing up with frustration and shock and disbelief. Byron has never raised his voice to me. Never. Not before coming to this house. He has never looked so far away from me. It's like a gully has opened up between us.

I don't know how to bridge the gap.

Byron doesn't say anything for a moment, his brow furrowed, mulling it over. He glances about himself, as if searching for a stranger between the trees. His eyes flick back to me, and he says, 'Yeah, well, whoever did this –'

he gesticulates towards the car – 'it's still *you* that's got us into this mess. It's your fault we're stuck here.'

'How is it my fault?' I ask incredulously, while Molly's gaze flits between me and Byron as we argue. Her eyes are wide, and they crackle as if full of everything she wants to say, but she doesn't know how to cut through this thing between me and Byron.

'It was your idea to come here in the first place. Then you wouldn't go to the police, like Molly and I wanted to when we found their stuff. You wouldn't leave when I first suggested someone else is here. You didn't believe me then. And now it's too late. We're stuck.'

My mouth drops open, but I can't speak. I feel like I've taken a bowling ball to the chest.

'Byron, that's enough.' I feel Molly's hand on my shoulder as she speaks, but I don't take my eyes off Byron.

'By . . . I'm sorry . . . I didn't . . . I thought . . .'

He shakes his head. 'I'm going to take a look for Zach and Lucas's car,' he says, calmer, but I can still see the fire in his eyes. 'The key should be somewhere in the house with their stuff. If their car is still here somewhere, we might still have a way out.'

'I'll help.'

'No!'

I recoil from the sharpness in his tone.

'Stay here and wait with Molly. Somewhere out of sight. If it was someone else, they could still be out here.'

'*If?* By—'

'Stay away, Iris. I don't want—'

'What? You don't want me trashing their car too, eh?' I say vehemently.

But he won't look at me. He shakes his head, eyes to the ground, as he turns and strides away from me, down the narrow track.

'I'll stay here where I can't break anything,' I shout after him. Childish, I know, but I can't help myself. 'Or where I can't be blamed for something I didn't do!'

He doesn't turn back, ignoring me, and I stand for a moment, spent, as I watch him go. And I hate myself. I want to run after him and tell him I'm sorry. That he's right, it is all my fault we're here. I'm sorry I've lost his trust. I'm sorry I didn't believe him before. But I don't. I let him go.

Because I am going to have to let him go. He has always been there. Our whole lives. We grew up together. I don't know a time in my life when he hasn't been in it. But I'm going to have to get used to it. Because if it isn't Molly, it'll be someone else, or it will be uni or a job in another town. And he'll go. Leave me. Forever. I can't imagine a life without Byron in it. I don't want to imagine a life without Byron in it. But I'm going to have to.

I had my chance, and I blew it by being scared and believing in fantasies.

And now I've lost him.

If he wants to leave the channel, I'm going to have to accept it.

And let him go.

Molly's hand rubs my back. I breathe in deep. And let it out. Breathe in. Breathe out.

'We should find somewhere safe,' I say to Molly, as anger and frustration ebb back into numbness. 'Like Byron said. In case . . .' I glance around myself, wondering where could possibly be *safe* right now.

Her hand stills against my back, and she looks at me. After a brief pause, she says, 'Iris, I believe there's some-one in that house. But I don't believe they're a living, breathing person.'

'So, you think I did it.' I back away from her. Stung. 'Molly, I know I lied about—'

She thrusts a hand out and grabs my elbow, halting me. 'What I'm trying to say is I don't think this could have been done by another—'

'Yeah, thanks. I get it,' I say, trying to yank my arm free, but Molly's grip is tight.

'No, let me finish. I don't think it could have been done by another *living* person. But something bad is happening in that house. Something supernatural. I still believe that. And whatever is in there, if it can appear in human form like the face in the window or what we saw in Lucas's footage, and if it can move things, like my stuff and Lucas's camera, then . . .'

I draw in a breath. 'You think it could have done this.' I phrase it as a fact, not as a question. 'A spirit. You think a spirit did this? This much damage.'

Molly nods. 'Yes, I do. And look, if whatever is in there can trash a car and make a battery disappear,' she lets go of me and motions towards the wrecked car with her hand, 'then . . .'

'What else could it be capable of?' I finish for her.

'Exactly.'

'So . . . what . . . ? You think it could harm us physically? That it did something to Zach and Lucas?'

She nods.

We both fall silent. I shake my head, not fully believing that a spirit could ever be *that* powerful, but I'm running out of explanations for what happened to the engine. To what happened to Zach and Lucas. *Something drew me towards the woods*, I think with a shiver. *Something powerful.*

In a daze, and with my legs feeling as if they are about to buckle, I stumble to the wall – Molly's theory running through my head. *If whatever is in there can trash a car and make a battery disappear . . . What else could it be capable of?* I sit with my back to her, and watch the house, just visible through the wild gardens. The sky behind it is just starting to take on a tinge of silvery blue, stained with a sickly yellow on the horizon, as the day fades. It's just a house. Just walls and floors and ceilings. It will rot and crumble and waste away to nothing. What will happen to its ghostly occupants then? As I watch the house, the house watches me with its big, dead window-eyes, and it says, *Come back inside. I haven't told you all my secrets yet.*

Come home.

I feel it tugging at me. Tugging at my edges – just out of its reach.

It wants me back.

Molly perches beside me, but I don't take my eyes off the house. The early-evening air is cool and fresh in my lungs, though it is still pleasant on my skin. I hear birds singing all around me. They sound so loud in the absence of any other sounds. Damp from the mossy wall seeps in through my jeans. Without saying anything, Molly slides a hand over one of mine, and she squeezes.

We both jump at the sound of feet crunching on the dirt track behind us. I swing round to see Byron jogging towards us. He slows as he draws closer, coming to a stop by the car. He pants for breath as if he has run far.

'Well, did you find their car?' asks Molly, expectantly, as she scrambles down the wall and heads towards Byron.

He shakes his head. 'No sign. I had a look about for the battery too, but it could be anywhere out here or in there.' He motions in the general direction of the house with a nod of his head. 'I'm guessing whoever took it doesn't want it to be found.'

'What are we going to do? How are we going to get home?' says Molly, glancing from Byron to me and back to Byron.

'I don't know, Moll,' he replies, enveloping her in a hug. 'But we'll figure it out, OK? I promise.' I cast my eyes away. That's the last thing I need to see right now. I feel as if I'm in a dirty, manky, stinking gutter and people are kicking me. But I can't help my gaze flicking back. He has his chin resting on the top of her head, as they stand in each other's arms. No one speaks. After a moment,

Byron's head turns towards the car and he says, 'My mum's going to kill me.' And he turns back to Molly, holding her even tighter.

I want to scream.

But I don't. I stay where I am, sitting quietly on the tumbledown wall, and I bite a thumbnail while I watch them. While I pretend that I'm fine. That I don't want to rip my heart and my lungs out to be rid of the constant ache in both.

'We're going to have to leave on foot – before whoever did that to the car comes looking for us,' says Byron.

'Maybe we'll get a phone signal,' says Molly. She pulls out her phone and stares at its screen.

I slide my phone out of my pocket. The wallpaper on my lock screen is a selfie of me, Dad and Poppy. Poppy is pulling a face, but she still manages to look prettier and cooler than me. My curls frizz around my face and there's a spot breaking out on my chin. Dad's smile is broad, and it makes me think of his big, infectious laugh. So warm. So loud, it'll make you laugh, too, even if you have no idea what the joke is. One of his pots is in the background: every bit as vibrant as he is, with its tie-dye effect glaze, in green and yellow. I get an ache to hear his laugh right now, to break the tension that fizzes and crackles like static between me, Byron and Molly. No service. 'We might have to go miles . . .' I say, my voice cracked and raw.

Byron's brooding eyes fall on me, almost accusatorially. I look away.

'But it might be worth—'

'Listen,' I say, cutting Molly off and getting to my feet. 'We have to go back to the house.'

They both glare at me.

'No. I can't go back there,' says Molly, her voice is as fine and as fragile as spun sugar, while Byron growls, 'No way, Iris. That's exactly what they want us to do.'

'Look, I know neither of you want to,' I say, taking a step towards them. 'And I know you're mad at me right now, Byron. I get it. It's my fault we're here. I pushed and pushed this thing, but I . . .' I let out a sigh. 'Never mind. Look, it's going to be dark in a couple of hours. We're in the middle of nowhere. I don't think any of us want to be roaming around those little roads or cutting through moorland and over hills in the dark. I think we should head back to the house. Get something to eat. Find a secure spot to rest up for the night.' Byron opens his mouth to say something, but I put a hand up to stop him. 'Take turns on watch, just in case . . .' I don't finish that thought, leaving it to the others to insert whatever their *just in case* is. 'And first thing, we trek out of here. Hopefully find a phone signal or a main road or something.'

'Iris—'

I don't give Byron the chance to argue with me, and I cut him off. 'Would you rather stay out here – in the dark – with the mangled car? Are we any safer out here?'

Molly shrugs, her eyes wide. Byron bites a black-painted fingernail, glaring at me.

'Look, guys, if there is someone or something in that

house, they obviously don't want us to leave. If we set off now and we're out here in the dark, whoever it is – whatever it is – they know this land, for sure. We don't. We're in unfamiliar territory. They'll be on us in no time. And for all we know, us leaving could be the trigger that causes whoever or whatever it is to come after us.' Molly's eyes glisten with barely held back tears, and I think that I'm getting through. Byron, on the other hand, looks less convinced, his face stern. 'Maybe that's what happened to Zach and Lucas,' I continue. 'If something happened to our car, perhaps something happened to theirs, too. And maybe they panicked and left on foot in the dark and got lost. There's nothing for miles and miles. It would be easy to get lost out there. Have a nasty fall in the hills or get stuck on the moors somewhere. And maybe never be found. But if we wait and go first thing, we stand a much better chance.'

'There's something dark in there,' says Molly, imploringly. 'Something we shouldn't be messing with. You know there is, Iris.'

'OK. What if . . .' I begin, a plan formulating . . . 'we set up the cameras to catch *whoever*,' I say, looking at Byron, 'or *whatever*,' I say, my eyes shifting to Molly, 'is in there in the act?'

Molly opens her mouth but nothing comes out, so I continue. 'If we capture something on camera, something to prove who or what is moving stuff around and making noises. Then we'll know, right? We'll have a better idea of what happened here. To Zach and Lucas. And we'll know what we're dealing with. How to protect ourselves.' I pause for a beat. 'Just one more night.'

Byron lets out a breath. He runs his fingers through his hair. 'It's a big house, and we have, what, three cameras.'

'We've got our phones,' says Molly. 'So that's three more.'

'Good thinking, Molls,' I say. 'And the stuff that's moved since we've been here happened in the room we're camping in. We could set up the phones and cameras in there. But if we're going to do this, we're going to have to do it now – before it gets too dark to film in natural light. If we use torches, it'll give the cameras away.' I pause. 'Guys?' I urge when no one speaks.

Brow furrowed, Molly tucks her hair behind her ears and gives a slight nod. 'But we take turns on watch tonight, right?' I can hear the mixture of determination and trepidation in her voice. 'And we stay together. All of us.' She glances between me and Byron.

I nod. 'By?' I raise an eyebrow at him.

He glances from the car to the house, his jaw tight. 'I don't suppose we have much choice,' he says bitterly, his eyes settling on me. He sighs heavily. 'You're right about one thing, we're not going to get far on foot before dark. But first light . . .'

'We're out of here. I promise.'

23

WITH THE BASE-CAMP room's L-shape and with all the nooks and crannies, the windows and doors, it's hard to cover the whole area with our limited equipment. We change the batteries in all the cameras then set up my Canon in one corner, positioned to cover the door off the entrance hall and the big bay window to the left, and most of the left side of the room. Molly's phone is propped up against the skirting board, pointing down the length of the room, and it is covering the two windows at the back. Byron's phone is covering the door at the end of the long section, and Lucas's camera is positioned so that it has the last door in the room in shot, as well as a portion of the room to the right. While we can't survey the entire room, because it's so big, at least we've covered all the doors and windows, so we know that if anything moves inside the room, no one would have been able to get in or out without getting caught on film.

All the cameras and phones are positioned in corners or at the edges and are on ground level, and they are disguised as best as we can with debris. We have no idea if they will be spotted and moved or messed with in any way. But I guess that will be some sort of proof in itself, if only to ourselves. Worst-case scenario is that nothing happens. Nothing at all. And we will know no more than we do now.

While Molly and Byron set out our gear as if we're camping for the night, as we did last night, I take my phone out to the entrance hall. I'm going to position it across the door to the base-camp room and angle it to get as much of the entrance hall as possible and, if I can, the bottom of the central staircase too, as out here has also been a source of activity and strange noises.

I look at my phone's screen. No signal. No way to call for help. No way to speak to my family. I never usually give them much thought when we're on an exploration. It's like the rest of the world disappears, I'm so focused on exploring and filming. On the excitement of what could happen. What we could discover. What we could become. But, right now, I'd love to be at home, curled up on my bed with snacks, watching YouTube videos or Netflix with my sisters; or helping Poppy pick out an outfit for a gig with her band; or brushing May's hair into a bun, ready for a ballet recital. Or helping Dad tidy up in his potter's studio, because he never tidies up as he should as it's the *boring* part. Or listening to Mum recite her latest poem, with the passion and drama that she always puts into each performance, even when her audience consists only of her family. Or making her cups of tea, while she marks essays from her job teaching poetry and life-writing at the university near where we live. Christ, I'd even be happy to participate in one of Amba's annoying creative projects.

They all have their thing. Music, ballet, pottery, words, art. They're all so creative and talented. But me . . . I can't do anything. Other than make videos which no one wants to watch.

I have no talent.

I'm a dud.

I go down on to my haunches and open my photo gallery, and I flick through pictures from May's seventh birthday party last weekend. She's wearing a pink party dress that looks like a tutu. I smile at how adorable she looks. I stop on a video. Sitting cross-legged on the bare floorboards, I press play, and my heart swells as May wriggles and giggles on Mum's lap, as Mum tickles her. The sound of their laughter. Mum throws her head back, her straight, light brown hair cascading down her shoulders (us daughters all get our curls from our dad). Casper yaps, sitting beside Mum's legs, tail wagging. A reminder that he is waiting patiently for a cocktail sausage to fall his way. A chorus of 'Happy Birthday' breaks through the squeals and chatter. May slips off Mum's lap, and the camera follows her, as she pirouettes around the kitchen, her tutu billowing. She's beaming at being the centre of attention. Her friends crowd around her. So many friends. More than I've ever had, or ever wanted. I pause the video and touch the tip of my finger to one of her rosy cheeks.

I tell myself to get a grip, it's only been a couple of days. But with the car out of action, home feels much too far away.

But I want to be here.

To discover what happened in this house.

I exit the gallery and cling on to my phone for a moment longer; to the reminder of home. But then, as if I am a small child letting go of my mother's hand on my first day at school, I place it on the floor. I prop it up against some rubble, and I use pieces of age-worn wood to hide it, before going down on to my belly to check the angle. It covers the door and a section of the hallway, and I just have the base of the staircase in frame, too.

I stand, brushing dust from my front, and I pull Zach's camera from the pocket of my hoodie. I'm keeping hold of this one.

'All set,' says Byron, his voice not much more than a whisper. He avoids my eye as he and Molly join me in the entrance hall.

'I took some photos around the room, so we can tell if anything's moved.'

'Good thinking, Moll,' I say, trying to sound positive, and like I haven't just died a bit because Byron hates me and blames me for everything.

He's still mad at me for faking stuff. I can tell from the way he clenches his jaw. But whether he still thinks it was me who wrecked the car, I don't know.

I'm getting tired of how he's putting everything on me. I didn't put a gun to anyone's head.

I glance down to Zach's camera in my hand.

'We should go and watch the last of the footage on this, while we wait,' I say, holding it up. 'See this thing through to the end.'

24

WE SIT OPPOSITE the broken window, our backs against the wall. Being in a spot where we can see that window – the only way in and out – is where we feel safest, right now. The dying embers of the sunset break through the glassless window frame, and the cooling evening air filters in. It is fresh and alive and it speaks of outside. Of life far away from this gloomy, dead house. And it makes me feel just that bit more OK.

I skip through some random chatting on Zach's camera, and a bit of exploring where nothing out of the ordinary happens, and some messing about. There's a short clip, where Lucas has the camera but Zach is obviously not in the mood to be filmed. Lucas can be heard from behind the camera saying, 'Dude, what's got into you?' as Zach thrusts his hand palm out to the camera and growls, 'Turn. It. Off,' before the video abruptly ends.

Next, a happier Zach films himself on the roof, while he tells the story of Grace and the stolen children. This time, he gets through it without incident; though he shoots nervous glances towards the woods now and then. There is some footage where Zach raises his camera to film Lucas, while Lucas is filming him, just before they split up on their solo explorations. The one that ended badly for Lucas, when he caught the reflection of a figure on film. It is strange to see the same footage but from a different perspective, like shifting into someone else's body.

'Say hi to the boys and girls at home, Lucas,' Zach says playfully.

'Hiya.' Lucas grins as he puts on a silly high-pitched voice.

'And Lucas is going up to the second floor, so that we don't end up running into each other,' says Zach, from behind his camera, as Lucas continues to wave and pull faces, while filming Zach.

'And scaring the bejesus out of each other,' adds Lucas, pointing a finger-gun at Zach's camera, his silver skull ring catching the light.

'Yep. Anyway, let's get this over with before it gets too dark. And before I lose my nerve.'

Zach and Lucas almost collide as they both move off.

'Dude, I'm going that way . . . I am *not* going past those creepy turret windows again on my own,' says Lucas.

Zach swings the camera around to show Lucas

heading down the stairs to the small landing between the two sides of the house. He keeps the camera on Lucas while he calls out, 'Anne's going to get you,' in a spooky voice.

'She's going to get you, dude. I'm too fast for her. She'll never catch me!' says Lucas, as he climbs the set of stairs to the left side of the house, without glancing back.

Zach swings his camera round as he walks off to the right side of the first floor.

Unlike Lucas's lone exploration footage, Zach's time alone shows no activity, other than him complaining of cold spots, and hearing a scratching sound that wasn't picked up by the camera. He spends twenty minutes in a large room, which he deduces may have been the master bedroom, with dark-wood columns, wood panelling right up to the ceiling and a grand fireplace, where he proceeds to call out to Edward, with no success.

The thing that strikes us, as we sit huddled together on Byron's sleeping bag, with a blanket from his mum's car over our knees to keep out the chill, is that Zach's hour of lone footage shows he wasn't anywhere near Lucas on the second floor, when he saw a figure disappearing around a corner. Though as the footage is not one continuous take, and there are time gaps between some of the videos, we can't be one hundred per cent sure that he didn't slip up some stairs and follow Lucas.

As we watch, I'm aware of the sky outside darkening, and of the shadows in the room changing and growing longer as the sun sinks, nipping at our toes, until they fade and then disappear altogether as dusk falls; I'm aware of every creak, and of every scrape of branches against the windows; I'm aware of every hoot of an owl, and every swish of long grass from outside; I'm aware of my beating heart, and each breath as it begins to cloud in front of me, even though it shouldn't be that cold in June; I'm aware of how my ears listen closely to the camera's audio, wanting to pick up any footsteps or taps in the footage, but also how they strain for any footsteps or taps from around us; I'm aware of my dry mouth, my sweaty palms and my skin that prickles with goosebumps; and the blood in my veins that thrums with fear and excitement and anticipation.

As we view the video, I see Zach check his watch and notice that he is running a few minutes late to get back to the central staircase to meet up with Lucas.

I see Zach reach the staircase to find that Lucas isn't there, even though, from watching Lucas's footage, we know that he went to that exact spot to wait for Zach, getting there a few minutes early, having been freaked out by the figure whose reflection he captured on film.

But he's gone.

25

'SO, I, ER . . . I've been all over the house, and I can't find Lucas anywhere. He never showed up back here after the lone exploration. And I'm freaking out,' says Zach, the camera showing a close-up of his face, dark circles beneath his restless eyes. 'I don't know if he's gone out to the car. But he wouldn't do that without telling me.' His eyes flick around him as he speaks. 'And it's dark, so . . .' His head snaps to the left, as if looking for something. Back to camera. 'I don't know where—' He stops. Pauses a beat. 'What was that? Lucas?' The camera pans around to show that Zach is on the walkway on the first floor, the shot lit by his torch. 'Lucas! LUCAS! Shit. I keep thinking I see something out the corner of my eye. But . . .' He turns the camera back on to himself. 'I'm going to keep checking. He has to be . . .' His head flicks to the right. The camera swings round to his right, then to his left. He spins round to film behind him, the camera and torch moving erratically. 'He has to be here somewhere. Lucas? Where are you, dude? LUCAS!'

'OK, it's three a.m. and I've been searching for Lucas for the last few hours. I'm officially worried as fuck. All I can think is that he's fallen somewhere or is stuck or something. So, I'm going to have to check every single corner of this place. He may have gone outside. I'm not sure why he would. But I'm going to head out and do a circuit of the house. I can't really risk going too far into the grounds in the dark. I'll probably break my neck. But I'll give him a shout. I mean, he might have seen or heard something out there and gone to take a look . . . Maybe he fell. I don't know. I don't know why he'd go off without telling me. I'll be so mad at him if he's gone off somewhere without letting me know. I'm going to give it one last good look around, and then I'll drive back to Hillthorn for help. I don't have any other choice. I don't want to leave him here, but if I can't find him in the next couple of hours or so . . .'

Grainy, dark footage. Flashes of torchlight and someone's legs as they tear down a corridor while holding the camera. Turning around a corner, down another corridor. Doorways and wood panelling can be seen as they whizz past. The flash of someone at the end of a corridor. Just a shadow? Walls. Floorboards. Screaming can be heard. Shouting. But it's not clear if it's one person. Two. More than two? Or even if the screams are coming from the person holding the camera or from somewhere else in the house, because the sound is as distorted as the image is grainy. And it's confusing and disorientating. Down a set of stairs. Whoever it is stops. A flash of a mirror, a section of wall. The camera drops to the ground with a hard thud, followed by the torch. Someone's booted feet can be seen in frame, not moving.

The recording ends.

This scene, a scene we watched when we first arrived at the house and found Zach's camera, now makes sense in context of the other videos and of what we ourselves have experienced in this house. But it still makes no sense at all.

We don't speak. Don't move. Each of us staring at the flip screen as if we think it's going to offer up another video – one where Zach and Lucas come back on-screen and say, 'We hope you enjoyed our little movie, folks. See you next time . . .'

As we watched, Byron shifted closer to me, and his hand had crept into one of mine. But that's it. No more footage. But still so many unanswered questions. I burn with frustration.

'What the—'

I don't get any further. I feel the others flinch, their bodies pressing either side of mine at a distant, sharp *Thud!*

'Plaster. A chunk of plaster falling off the wall,' says Byron.

He must have been able to hear the metallic twang of that thud, the same as me; but I don't say anything. I'll let him believe in his plaster theory. Just for a little while longer.

'It came from somewhere out there,' says Molly, nodding towards the door and the entrance hall beyond.

We scramble to our feet. I want to run towards the source of the sound, and I want to climb through the window across the room from me and run and run . . . away from this place and never come back.

We're silent as we creep out to the gloomy entrance hall. A quick scan, aided by the light of Byron's torch, shows that nothing stirs. My mobile is still where I left it, propped up and disguised by debris. Stealthily, I make my way across the hall, the others close behind me, to the big L-shaped room. 'It has to have come from in here,' I say as I stop in the doorway. We survey the room, Byron sweeping the floor with his torch beam, even though there is still enough dying light breaking through the large windows to see. I don't spot anything out of the ordinary, until . . .

'There,' says Molly, pointing. My knife is laying on the floor near the back of the room, between the two windows. 'Was that there before?'

'No,' I say. 'It wasn't.'

26

THE KNIFE HAD been in the front pocket of my backpack. Most of my other belongings – a few items of clothing, my toothbrush, a hairband, food, bottles of water, my camera bag, deodorant, spare batteries and a memory card for the Canon – I had left out as bait for the 'mover', but the knife, well, health and safety . . .

And there it is, lying on the floorboards. It had gone from inside my bag to the floor, right there.

How?

'I promise you that was not there when I left this room.'

'Are you sure, Iris?' says Byron. 'You could've got it out and forgotten, and maybe one of us knocked it with a foot without realizing it? Or—'

'That thud,' I say. 'We all heard it. That only just happened.'

'It might not have been the knife, it might have—'

'Oh, Byron, just stop! Stop trying to explain everything,' I snap. 'Sometimes things just don't make sense.'

He looks at me, stupefied. But before he can say anything, Molly says, 'Look, I took photos of all our stuff and the floor around it before I came out, remember? We can check to see if the knife was there before.'

While Molly retrieves her phone, Byron and I gather the other phones and the cameras and place them in a pile on my sleeping bag. A tension has crept back in between us. Or maybe it never left from when he accused me of all sorts earlier. Molly is already there, sitting cross-legged on the floor, flicking through her phone's photo gallery. I kneel beside her, watching over her shoulder. She stops on a shot of the floor, right where we found the knife, but it isn't there. Molly glances from me to Byron, who is sat on the other side of her.

'This proves it,' she says. 'It wasn't one of us that either kicked or dropped it there by accident.'

'Or on purpose,' says Byron, suggesting I'm still a suspect in his mind, despite photographic evidence to the contrary.

'So, whatever happened, happened after we left the room,' I say, trying not to let Byron's words bother me.

To speed things up, we decide to each take a phone or camera and view the footage, and to shout if we see anything. There are two cameras that are most likely to have picked up the knife's movement: Molly's phone camera, which had been positioned to capture along the length of the room at the back, where the two windows are, and my camera, which was positioned at an angle to cover the main doorway, the bay window and some of the left side of the room. Though any of the cameras could show someone or some*thing* coming into or moving about the room. Byron starts with Lucas's camera, which had been set up to capture another of the doorways, as well as some of the right side of the room, not covered by Byron's phone camera.

No one speaks while we watch. We sit on my sleeping bag, with our backs together, forming a circle, facing outwards. No one suggested we sit like this. It just happened, as if having our backs together, facing out, makes us feel safer. More secure.

My stomach swirls with anticipation, dread and excitement.

Have we caught a ghost on camera?

Have we caught a psychopath playing with us?

Are we on the brink of discovering what happened to Zach and Lucas?

Adrenaline fizzes, and I have to take a steadying breath before I play the footage.

Immediately, I see that my backpack is at the edge of the frame to the right, the front pocket just out of shot. The rest of our belongings are right there. Right. There. But the backpack's pocket. Just. Out. Of. Shot.

'Crap.' I turn the camera so that the others can see why I'm disappointed. 'But it doesn't matter,' I say, remaining positive. 'We might catch something on the others.'

I continue watching anyway, hoping for a shadow, or a footstep. Or – the thing we all dread – a living, breathing person, coming into the room through one of the doors.

With each second of footage of the empty room, my stomach turns, and my eyes ache, and my heart pounds. All of my focus is on that screen. I don't move. I can't breathe. My eyes are wide. Expectant. Hopeful. And as each second crawls on, I become increasingly afraid of what I'm about to see at any moment, but even more afraid of what I won't see. On-screen, light changes and begins to fade, while off-screen, our torches lend some light as darkness falls around us. I watch and I wait for something to happen. Time creeps on. I'm reminded of watching the toaster: you know that toast is going to pop up, but you watch and you watch, and – *POP!* – it makes you jump anyway. I'm waiting for that toast-out-of-the-toaster *POP*. Only, this isn't going to be warm, golden brown toast, this is going to—

My eyes widen and I sit up straight when I see the backpack tremble, oh so slightly. I go back, just to make sure, and, yes, it definitely moves. A shudder. I bring the camera closer to my face as I watch and wait and— 'Holy crap!' I jump as a hissing flicker of blink-and-you'll-miss-it static rolls across the screen.

'What was that?' says Molly, shifting to glance at the flip screen.

'Nothing, sorry. Just a bit of static,' I say. 'Made me jump.' I go back and play it for the others.

'Pause it,' says Molly, coming closer. Byron, too, shifts so that he can see the screen.

I play it again and pause the blizzard of black and white. My eyes strain to make out shapes in the snow. But there is no ghostly face. No blur of a human form. I catch Molly's eye and shrug. 'It's nothing,' I say. 'Just static.'

'But it could be the camera picking up a spirit's energy,' offers Molly.

'It did happen right after my backpack shook,' I say.

'It did? Let me see.'

I go back once more, and play it for Molly and Byron, from where the backpack shudders, just before the static. I hear Molly gasp, and she draws closer to the screen. Byron watches with his mouth open. They both jump at the flash of static – the toast-out-of-the-toaster effect – and we continue to watch together, and, not long after the static, we hear the clanging thud of the knife as it hits the floorboards off-screen, at the back of the room. Then nothing. No one. No sounds, other than that clanging thud. Just a still, silent, empty room. Until the camera picks up our voices. Our voices grow louder, and Byron's torch beam sweeps past. Followed by the sound of our feet, crunching the floorboards. The recording ends soon after.

Molly stares at me with wide eyes for a moment, 'Holy moly,' she says. 'Do you think we caught anything else?' She retrieves her mobile and, cross-legged, she goes back to watching her footage, while I start viewing the recording on my phone.

After a few minutes, she says, 'Hey, watch this.' Byron and I look up to see her holding her mobile phone out towards us. We watch as a ripple of static precedes the moment that the knife lands, just in frame.

'Do you think we caught a spirit passing through the room?' she says, all big-eyed, like a little kid at a funfair who isn't sure if the rollercoaster will be too big and too fast for them, but they're going to go ahead and give it a go anyway. 'The static – it's a spirit, right? Moving the knife. We've caught paranormal activity on camera!'

Byron pulls a pained face. 'It's probably just static, Moll.' And I wonder if he means to shatter her hope, or if he is trying to protect her from disappointment.

'*Just static*,' she repeats. 'When have you ever got static on a video?'

Byron shrugs.

'Anyway, there's a whole load of nothing on Lucas's camera,' he says, still unimpressed by the static. 'Dullest hour of my life.' He places the camera down and rubs his eyes with the heels of his hands, smudging the remains of his eyeliner a little. I resist the urge to lean in and wipe it with a finger. Stifling a yawn, he picks up his phone. 'I'll go through this next.'

'It wasn't *just static*,' Molly says under her breath, and she sidles up to me, watching over my shoulder as I play the rest of the footage on my phone. It's not the best quality – my phone camera struggling with the descending gloom of the hallway – but I can see that there is no movement. And another hour or so later, we all have sore eyes, stiff, achy backs, and pins and needles in our feet from sitting still for so long. I'm exhausted and my eyelids are gritty and sore. But all the footage is watched. Not one of the cameras shows how the knife got from my bag to the floor. There was no more static on any of the other cameras. All we have is a bag that shakes briefly and a knife that lands on the floor and a bit of static on two cameras. But what each piece of footage collectively does prove is that no one could have got into the room to move the knife. No one could have got past all of the cameras without being seen. Not unless they could fly.

And what living, breathing human can do that?

27

'THERE IS SOMETHING in this house with us. Confirmed,' I say, doing a piece to camera, as we head down a corridor on the first floor.

'Not *confirmed*. It would only be confirmed if we caught some . . . *entity* –' Byron says it like a dirty word – 'on camera in the act of moving the knife.'

'*And*,' I say, ignoring him, 'if it's trying to communicate with us, we want to hear what it has to say. We're doing another seance.' I look intermittently at the flip screen and the way ahead, so that I don't bump into anything as I walk and talk. 'And, right now, we're heading to the room where we conducted the last one, when we contacted Lucas.' I get a chill down my spine as I remember the feeling of something unseen touching me last time. 'Or possibly someone trying to let us know what happened to him.'

'Or something trying to trick us into believing that they are Lucas,' says Molly.

'But why?' I ask, turning the camera on to her.

'Because they mean us harm.'

'A spirit can't really hurt the living, can they?'

Molly looks pained but she doesn't answer. I think back to Byron's mum's car. Something did that. But how can even restless or vengeful spirits such as Anne or Grace physically harm us when they have no physical presence?

But if that's so, what happened to Zach and Lucas?

Ugh. I feel I'm going round in circles, trying to mentally hash it out. I have to know. I *need* to know. I need to record some actual proof of paranormal activity. Something undisputable. Something not even Byron can deny. Something moving by itself that has no right, in the name of physics, to be moving by itself. The video series will go viral. It will make us. We'll be as big as Zach and Lucas. Bigger. We'll be set for life. Amba will never call the videos *lame* again.

And maybe Byron will stay.

But is it worth putting ourselves at risk for the sake of a video?

I remember that Lucas said something similar in a piece of footage: '*Is doing this shit really worth it for a video*?' Both he and Zach had laughed and agreed, '*Yes*.'

Because it is.

This is my life. It's everything. The likes, the subs, the views.

'For the record,' begins Byron, and I swing the camera

around to him, 'I don't believe that we made contact with anyone at that seance.'

'Byron, we've just proved that a knife moved in an empty room – how can you still deny we contacted someone?' I say incredulously, from behind the camera.

He shakes his head, looking down at his feet as he walks, his body tensed. 'I'm missing something with that knife,' he says, an edge of frustration in his voice. 'I know I am. But I just . . .' He lets the rest of his words come out in a deflating huffing sound.

We cut through a large, echoey room which I don't recognize. The walls are blistering and greying, and the room is empty but for a rocking chair in the middle, facing us. Beyond the chair, in the shadowy corner, is the dark outline of a low cupboard. It is in the eaves of a sloping section of ceiling, and its small door hangs open. I wonder if it's Elizabeth's cupboard. I angle my torch towards it, trying to see, but the beam can't reach that far. With each step I take into the room, I get a growing sense of dread, as if something isn't right. Something I can't place. Something that sits heavy and scratchy in my gut. Something that makes me not want to go over to that dingy corner and check the back of the door for scratch marks. Not right now. Later, perhaps. Or tomorrow morning, when it's light. I flick the torch's beam to the rocking chair.

What if there is someone sitting in it?

Watching.

Head slowly turning to follow us as we cross the room.

I shiver as my skin prickles all over. And, realizing that I've fallen behind the others, I quicken my pace to catch up.

'You really don't think anything supernatural is happening here, after everything we've seen?' Molly asks Byron, while I film them from behind.

'No. I don't. There's always—'

'A rational explanation!' I snap, getting tired of his *rational explanations*.

'Would you just stop.' Byron halts and swings round in front of me.

'Stop what?' I shrug. I go to move around him, keen to be out of the room and its creepy corner, but he grasps my elbow, pulling me back.

His eyes fix on to mine. 'I'm allowed not to believe.'

I lower the camera to my side as I square up to him. 'After everything we've captured . . . everything we've seen . . . the fact that two boys have disappeared off the face of the earth in this very house, you still think that there is some sort of rational explanation that doesn't involve ghosts?' My eyes flit towards the corner of the room and back. 'Ghosts *are* the rational explanation,' I continue. 'Why do you always have to doubt everything?'

'Iris, let's not forget you faked—'

'A few things, yes! But not everything. How many more times? Ugh! Byron, you know how important this video series is to me.'

'Of course I do, Iris. But that doesn't mean—'

'Then why can't you just for once open your mind to

the fact that we may have stumbled upon something big? Because of me. Because I didn't give up. Because I firmly believed—'

'It isn't always about you, Iris! You're not the only one who needs this.'

I'm so stunned by Molly's outburst that I stop, mid-sentence, and I turn to stare at her. I've never heard her raise her voice like that. Not ever.

'What?' I say after a moment, managing to unstick my words.

'Actually, no, it *is* always about you, isn't it?' she continues.

'What are you going on about?'

'I've been such an idiot for thinking he'll ever get over you,' she says, her eyes flicking to Byron and back to me.

I catch Byron's eye. His cheeks flush, and he looks quickly away. And to Molly, he says, 'Moll, I—'

But she cuts him off. 'I thought if I was the best girlfriend,' she says to me. 'If I showed him how much I loved him, he would forget about you. But, no, it's always *Iris Iris Iris*. Fucking Iris!'

'Moll . . . Christ . . . come on,' he says. 'This isn't—'

'You're in love with her. Just admit it, Byron. And then we can all get on with our lives,' she says, way too calmly. The sort of calm that means the only safe options available are to either run or to play dead.

I glance at Byron. He catches my eye but he looks away and down to the rubble-littered floorboards. What's going on in his head right now? What is he thinking?

Is it true?

'I put up with the fact that you're always there. Always,' she says, turning to me. 'Even when it's just the two of us,' she says to Byron. 'She's still always there, coming between us.'

I glance from Molly to Byron, my head spinning. I'm mortified that this is happening. But there's a thrilling, guilty relief growing inside me that maybe – just maybe – he still thinks of me that way. The lingering glances. The almost-moments. Molly has noticed them too. I feel excited and horrible and terrified. It's so wrong. He's with Molly. I lost my chance. But here he is, not admitting it. But not denying it either.

'He'll do anything for you if you just bat your pretty eyelashes and twirl your stupid, perfect hair,' she continues, using her index fingers to gesticulate spirals in the air as she speaks, as though to indicate my curls.

'My *what*?'

She shakes her head 'Why can't you just butt out of our relationship!'

'I'm not *in* your relationship!' I say, squeezing the torch and camera in my hands, as the dark, foreboding dread inside the room draws in around us.

Molly squares up to me. Formidable, despite being smaller than me. 'Aren't you?' Caught in my torch beam, she's all shadows and stark light. Her cheeks are washed out and her brow creased.

Am I?

'No. I'm not,' I say measuredly, denying it. Not

because I want to make her doubt herself or to think she's crazy. Not because I want to wheedle my way out of anything. But because it *has* to be denied. Because it's dangerous. And because maybe I *should* butt out and give them a chance. But if I admit that she could be right about Byron's feelings – and my own feelings – then it'll all break. Right now, right here. And it'll be my fault. And I don't want to break them up. I don't want to tear them apart so that I can have him, regardless of Molly's broken heart. I couldn't – wouldn't – do that. I have to shove my feelings down and bury them. Bury them alive and hope they will eventually die.

Molly snorts. 'And do you know what's really sad?' she continues, as if she's been holding all this in for a long time, like a balloon slowly filling with muddy water. She's going to burst and it's going to be messy. 'It's that all the while Byron's been in love with you, you've had a crush on Zach.'

'What? I don't even know him,' I mumble, my cheeks burning at being exposed 'How—'

'Don't deny it, Iris,' spits Molly. 'You had a big ol' crush on a YouTuber who you were never going to meet other than for a quick photo at a meet-and-greet. And then he vanishes.'

I shake my head, stunned that I'd been so obvious.

'It's always been you, Iris. For Byron.'

I glance at him, but he doesn't even look at me. He has the neck of his jumper pulled up over his mouth, as if he is trying to disappear.

'But you had this stupid fantasy that you were going to find Zach . . .'

'Molly, you're talking nonsense.'

'. . . and he'd fall madly in love with you for saving him and . . .'

'You don't even know what you're saying!'

'. . . you'd live happily ever after.'

'Just shut up!'

'But he's gone, Iris. And we're all stuck here, in this messed-up house, because of you. Because Iris has a crush on a ghost—'

Molly stops. Dead. Mouth open. Eyes on the doorway across the room. Heart thumping, I angle my torch but the beam gets eaten up by the darkness in the corridor beyond.

'Molly?'

She ignores me. Calling out, 'Hey. Wait!' she darts for the door and is gone.

'Molly? Molly!' Byron pauses and casts a backward glance to me, but his eyes are unable to hold mine. 'Molly, wait!' he says, turning away from me. And he tears after her.

I hate that everything just got totally messed up. I hate that there is so much I should have said to Byron, but I've always been afraid to put it into words in case it ruined our friendship. And I've left it all unsaid. And now it's. Too. Damn. Late. So instead, I open my mouth to call the others, but at the sound of a creak, I halt. I turn my torch to the source of the sound. The rocking chair gently rocks:

back, forth, back, forth. Slowing as if someone has just vacated it.

'What the—?' I don't get any further, as my hair is grabbed at the top of my head. So hard that I'm pulled off my feet.

28

MY CHEST HITS the bare floorboards with a thud, winding me, and my scream is lost somewhere in the back of my throat. I'm dragged across the floor with force. I drop the torch and the camera as my hands instinctively reach out to fight off my attacker. But I feel nothing – no one – there. Just my hair, pulled painfully taut.

I'm screaming, 'No! Stop! Please! Let me go. Help! Byron! Someone. HELP ME!' I dig my nails into the floorboards. I grasp a leg of the rocking chair, trailing it along the floor with me a little way, until my hand slips from the soft, damp wood.

'Please stop! Let me go! Arghhhh!'

I flail and struggle. I manage to raise my head a little. And in the light from my fallen torch, I can see that there is no one there. And yet my hair is stretched out in front of me, gripped by an unseen hand, and I am sliding along the floor. Fast. 'Stop! No no no, No. Please. No no no no no,' I scream. And then I realize that I'm being dragged towards the open mouth of the cupboard in the far corner. 'No – please!' I try to wrestle my hair free. But it's no use. I manage to hook one of my arms around the door frame and I lurch to a stop. Silence. Stillness. Just the sound of my ragged breath as I cling on. It's dark inside the cupboard. I can't see all the way to the end, but there's just enough light from the room behind me to see a low but deep crawl space in the eaves, its angles stretching down and right, and low wooden beams criss-crossing up to the rafters. I feel something icy in here with me. Cold. Dark. Evil. It tugs, lifting me upwards by my hair, off the floor a few centimetres. I bat my free hand in front of me but I connect with nothing but air and I'm still held tight. I yelp, pitching forward a little way as my arm slips, before coming to a jarring halt again as I grip the door frame with my fingers. I hold on, groaning with pain as my arm muscles strain against the force carrying me forwards and up. Hair rips. My fingers start to slip.

I lose my grip and, all in the space of my next scream, I'm pulled inside the cupboard, my hair is released and I hit the floor face first. Before I can even move – *SLAM!* – the door swings shut behind me, plunging me into total darkness.

'Hey!' I call. 'Hey, let me out!'

Nothing.

'Byron? Molly? Is anyone there?' I say, my chest tightening as the confined space closes in on me. It's stiflingly hot under the eaves. I'm disorientated and I wriggle and crawl round on the rough, dusty floorboards, my nose itching in the dust-mote smog I stir up. I'm not sure which way is the door and I hit my head on a beam as I sit up, and I feel around me, trying to find the door. I find it, and I push and pound on it hard, but it won't budge and I wonder what the hell just happened: what – who – dragged me in here? I realize that Byron and Molly have no idea where I am and I could be trapped in here for hours, days – will they ever find me? But surely they will find me, if I make enough noise. I bang and bang on the door and shout and scream, 'Help! Help! Can anyone hear me? Help me!' But no one comes, and it's so hot and stuffy, like there's no air. I can't breathe. It's all closing in on me. Constricting me. I pull my hoodie off to cool down, wincing as the fabric rips from where it had stuck to the dried blood from the deep scratches on my arm, and I wrap it around my waist. My heart pounds. I stop a moment when I hear the steady creaking of wood on wood start up from outside the cupboard. I know exactly what the sound is – the rocking chair, rocking back, forth, back, forth . . .

'Hello? Help! Help me!'

The rocking grows louder but no one comes to open the door.

Heart hammering, I think there must be another way out, so I turn and I crawl on my hands and knees, scared to try to stand, knowing there's not enough room for my full height, and afraid that I'll knock myself out on one of the low beams, and then no one will ever find me and I'll be locked in here forever, and I wonder if that's what happened to Zach and Lucas – did they get shut in somewhere and . . . it's too horrible to think . . . so I crawl and crawl, the hot air becoming thicker, the rough boards scraping my skin, and I must round a corner because suddenly there's some light. A window up ahead. Small and round and dirty, it doesn't let in much of the moonlight, just enough to see the outline of a shadowy figure standing in the corner. Small, like a child.

I halt. Paralysed. Sweat pools in the small of my back. For a moment it feels as if all the air is sucked out of the room. I can't breathe. I can't move. The shape shifts, as if taking a step towards me. And then I scream. I scream and scream, as I fall back and scramble on my elbows and butt, in what I'm praying is the direction of the door. Even though I know it's locked, I still, instinctively, head for the door. Maybe I can kick it open. I scramble back the way I came until the back of my head and my shoulders hit something solid. I grope behind me. Cold, crumbling brick. I feel along to my left, further, further, until my fingertips touch the wood of the door. And that's when I feel them: long thin ridges scored into the wood. I run my hand over the back of the door. Scratch marks? So many scratch marks. So deep.

Elizabeth's cupboard?

I wanted to find it. But not like this.

I push. I turn and kick. The door won't budge. I bang and shout and scream. 'Help! Get me out of here!' I pound on the wood with my clenched fists. All the while the rocking from outside grows frantic.

Anne?

'HELP!' I'll claw my way out if I have to.

But that didn't help Elizabeth.

'HELP! HELPHELPHELP!'

Scratch.

Scratch.

I gasp at the sound and turn, my back pressed against the door. I wipe sweat from my eyes. And I stare silently into the dark, eyes wide, searching for a shift in the shadows. Waiting for the figure to emerge from around the corner. Wanting to see and not wanting to see.

Scratch.

Scratch.

The sound is closer – right in front of me. All around me. I sit still and quiet. Maybe if I can't see it, it can't see me?

Scratch.

A whimpering escapes my lips. I clamp a hand over my mouth. My free hand brushes against something small, solid and cold on the floorboards and without knowing why or what it is, I close my fingers around it, squeezing tight.

Scratch.

At the sound – closer – I shut my eyes and grit my teeth and wait in the darkness for my fate.

Scratch.

In my next breath, the rocking stops and there's a

whoosh of air on the back of my neck, as the cupboard door swings open. Cold hands slide beneath my arms, gripping tight. For a moment, I wonder if Anne has got me, and I instinctively pull away, but feeling the smooth solidity of metal against my skin, as if from ringed fingers, I stop and call out, 'Byron!' He doesn't answer, but the rings, it has to be Byron. Before I have a chance to turn my head, his grip tightens and he hauls me backwards, out of the cupboard, before releasing me. Scrambling to my feet, I spin, expecting to see Byron.

But the room is empty.

Silent.

Still.

'Whaa . . . ?' Wild-haired and wide-eyed, my heart thumping, I flick my head every which way, not quite believing it's over, but too scared to run, as if I'm in a minefield and movement may trigger a blast. Remembering that I'm holding something I found in the cupboard, I uncurl my fingers, palm up, to reveal a silver skull ring. I stare at it, mouth open. *Lucas's ring?* Did he lose it inside the cupboard? Or did someone else place it there? With no time to think too hard on it, I shove the ring into my pocket. The beam of my torch is creating tall shadows of the rocking chair against the wall, still rocking oh so slightly. I dart towards the torch and swipe it up with a trembling hand, shining it erratically around the room and towards the open cupboard door, gasping at the sight of the scratch marks scored deep into the wood. Most are dulled with age, while others look paler. Fresher. *Lucas?* I expect Anne or Elizabeth to lurch from the darkness. Nothing. No one.

Just me.

'What the . . . ?' I shake my head in disbelief. I'm panting so hard I worry I'll hyperventilate. Someone pulled me out of that cupboard. So, where did they go? Grabbing my camera, I back up towards the door a couple of steps, torch beam swinging, before I turn and run.

I stop in the corridor, glancing left and right. 'Byron! Molly!' I have no idea which way they went. 'BYRON! MOLL!'

I choke back a sob, take a deep breath in and out, and I turn right.

What the hell happened back there?

I realize that the Canon has been recording the whole time. I stop around the next corner with my back to the wall and, with a shaky hand, I check the footage. Nothing, just a static shot of the floorboards and wall, while my screams can be heard, as I'm dragged away off-screen.

Recording, I raise the Canon so that I can see myself in the flip screen. My eyes are big and crazed. Mascara stains my cheeks in tracks. 'Something . . . just happened,' I say into the camera. I can hear the tremble in my voice. 'We didn't . . . get as far as . . . as doing a seance.' I stop at the sound of a creak and my head snaps to the right. 'Molly? Byron?' Nothing. I turn back to the camera. 'We . . . uh . . .' I begin, but out the corner of my eye, I catch sight of someone tall flit across the end of the corridor to the left.

'Byron?' I call, breathless with apprehension. 'By?'

Swinging the camera round to film ahead of me, I race along the corridor and around the corner, just in time to see someone disappearing around to the left.

'Byron. Wait,' I say, as I dart after him.

I turn the corner and come out on to the walkway around the central staircase, just in time to see a flash of a reflection in the window furthest to the left, before they disappear up the set of stairs to the second floor.

Not Byron.

I had only seen the reflection as if for the length of a camera flash. But I know exactly who I saw. I would recognize him anywhere.

Zach.

It was Zach.

29

I'M PARALYSED FOR a moment, the air knocked out of me. The image of Zach's face is emblazoned in my mind's eye. I remember the camera – have I picked it up on film? I go to the last recording, searching for the moment I'm back in the corridor. The shaky footage turns, and – there! – it catches the window at the end of the walkway. A reflection. Zach himself is out of shot, and I'm too far away for the face in the window to be anything other than a pale smudge, partially obscured by a mop of tousled hair. But I can make out the Z & L logo on the front of his black hoodie clearly enough. It's unmistakably him.

Zach.

Here.

Alive.

Zach is alive. It must have been him we've been hearing. Him who has been moving things. Zach's been here the whole time! He's been messing with us. But why? Why would he stay here? How could he have survived out here all this time? And where is Lucas? Is he alive too? Why would Zach mess with us, instead of just letting us know he's here? That he's OK. Especially if he's in any kind of trouble. And if it has been Zach this whole time, how does that explain the knife moving in an empty room? Or me being dragged across a room by my hair.

None of this makes any sense.

Just as if my curiosity is the bang of a starting pistol, I race around the walkway and I take the stairs two at a time in pursuit of him. An increasing feeling of dread invades me as I climb, remembering that this is the set of stairs that lead up to Anne's window. I don't want to go anywhere near it, but I have to catch up with Zach. I have to know why he never left.

I have to get him on camera.

This is it. This is the big one.

Bigger than I could ever have imagined.

He's alive!

It's so cold when I reach the top of the stairs that I can see a puff of my breath in the air before me and I pull my hoodie back on. I don't look round to the right, even though I feel someone there. Someone staring at me. I swing to the left, where the dust motes caught in my torch's beam whizz in a frenzy, as if someone has just passed through in a hurry.

'Zach?' I call as I round a corner. My cheeks flush and my body tingles with a mixture of fear and excitement, with a splash of awkward self-consciousness at the thought that Zach is here, just ahead of me.

Zach.

Here.

Oh my god.

My stomach flutters and my heart jitters.

Zach.

My inspiration. My hero. I think back to Molly telling Byron about my crush on him, and my cheeks burn.

'Zach?'

I catch a glimpse of his black-jeaned leg disappearing around the end of a corridor.

'Zach!'

I tear down corridors, calling his name. But no matter how fast I go, I can only catch glimpses of him ducking around the next corner.

Why doesn't he stop?

If he is alive, what does this mean? When he's made no attempt to let us know that he's here and that he's OK – what is he hiding? What is his intention?

But it's Zach. He's a good guy. I know he is. I know he wouldn't hurt us.

Why am I even thinking that he would want to hurt us?

My heads spins.

And then I stop as a chilling thought strikes me, knocking me off balance so that I have to grip a door frame.

What if Zach did something to Lucas . . . an accident or a prank gone wrong or something that he couldn't take back? Something that would look really bad. What if those last videos of him trying to find Lucas were to cover up the fact that he knows *exactly* where Lucas is. And *exactly* what happened to him. And what if he's been hiding out here, because he *can't* go back. And now we're here and . . . are we safe from him?

Has Lucas been trying to warn us from beyond the grave?

Those cold hands, with their ringed fingers, the ones that pulled me to safety from the cupboard – had that been Lucas?

What did Zach do?

But this is Zach! He couldn't . . . he wouldn't. But how do I know that? I don't know him. I only know a persona he put out on social media. I don't know the real Zach. Do any of us ever really know another person? What's beneath the surface. But even so, I can't believe he could do anything . . .

I hear a scraping sound coming from around the next corner. I have come too far to give up now. 'Zach?' I call as I edge towards the end of the corridor. I get there in time to see the blur of a booted foot disappear up a staircase to the right. I follow, filming everything. The staircase is empty when I get there. I charge up the steps two at a time. At the top, I find myself in the attic. It's creepy and dark up here, and the floorboards creak and wobble, giving that rocky, on-board-a-moving-ship sensation. I glance left and right. There's a corridor with doors on one side and a sloped ceiling on the other. It's tight and claustrophobic, and there's a chill to the air. I smell damp and dust and bird crap. I hear the scraping again, to the left, and I follow. I see him turn the next corner, and I run to catch up. As I round another corner, I see his reflection caught head-on in a small window at the end of the corridor.

I stop. My heart thumping and my mind reeling. I'm so stunned to see the reflection, to have confirmation that it really is him, that I forget I have a camera in my hand, until it's too late, and he's gone. But for one fleeting moment, I had seen Zach, so clear in the small square of black glass, and our eyes had met. And I'm sure . . . though I had to have been seeing things . . . but I'm certain that I had glimpsed a line of something thick and dark across his throat. Red blood oozing. But that would mean . . .

I'm breathing much too fast and my heart is hammering so hard that I start to see stars in the corners of my eyes, my head dizzy. I breathe, and I dart after him.

'Zach!'

'ZACH!'

When I turn the next corner, I realize he has taken me round in a circle. I'm back to the sloped ceilings at the top of the staircase. I see someone heading down the corridor, away from me. But it's not Zach. There's no sign of him. It's Molly. I call out to her, but she doesn't hear me, or if she does, she ignores me.

Is she still mad at me?

She turns at the steps that lead up to the roof itself. I'm about to follow when I hear a distant shout from below.

Byron.

The sound is sharp and urgent, and makes the breath catch in my throat.

'Molly, stay here, OK? I'll go see what's up with Byron, and I'll be back. Don't go anywhere until we get back. Stay on the roof. OK?'

But she's gone, and I hear the door click shut.

Leaving Molly heading up to the roof, I hurry down the stairs, following the sound of Byron's cries. As I get closer, I can hear that he's calling mine and Molly's names. Over and over, like he's been doing it for a while and his voice is raw.

'Byron!'

I run down corridors. 'Byron!' I twist and turn. The house seeming to want to devour me. 'Byron!'

'Iris?'

'Byron. Where are you, dude?'

'Iris!'

We almost collide as he tears around the next corner. His eyes widen at the sight of me and he stops, our bodies centimetres apart. So close. I can feel his heartbeat. Feel the heat off him. He stands before me, panting hard. His hair is damp with sweat, and he smooths his fringe out of his face with his fingers. If I raise myself on to my tiptoes, our lips will meet. There's an awkward tension between us – so much awkward tension in those few centimetres that separate us, like now he's found me he doesn't know what to do with me. Like we're no longer sure how to behave around each other. No longer sure what's allowed. What we want. It's all I can do not to go up on to my tiptoes.

'By?' The fear in his eyes as he stares at me makes me dizzy – Byron, unflappable, disbelieving Byron, afraid. I put a hand on his arm. 'What happened? Are you OK?'

'I couldn't find you,' he says, his words breathy. 'I thought you were right behind me.' He swallows. 'I felt you, right behind me, but . . . there was no one there. Not you. Not Molly.'

'Byron, I—'

'Where'd you go?'

'I didn't go anywhere. I never left the room, By. Something grabbed me. Dragged me across the room by my hair.'

He shakes his head. 'What?'

'Something pulled me into a cupboard and locked me inside. I only got out because . . . I think Lucas—'

'Iris, stop!'

'It's true. I swear.'

'Just stop lying.'

'I'm not! I think it was Anne. She pulled me right off my feet and into Elizabeth's cupboard. Lucas saved me. I think he died in that cupboard. Look,' I say, pulling the skull ring from my pocket and holding it up between my thumb and forefinger for Byron to see. 'This was inside. It's Lucas's. I recognize it from their videos. I think Anne dragged him in there and he was trapped inside. He must have lost this,' I say, raising the ring a little higher, 'while trying to claw his way out. Just like Elizabeth. There are scratches on the back of the door . . . Anne killed him, and I believe his spirit saved me from the same fate.'

'You tripped, Iris. That's all. You tripped and hit your head and—'

'No! Byron, listen to me. Something wanted me . . .' I pause for a beat. 'Do you get the feeling that the house is trying to split us up?'

For a moment, as I gaze into his wide eyes, which sparkle with fear and doubt, I think he's going to agree with me, that he's going to say, *Yes, this house is alive with evil intent and it wants to consume our souls and condemn us to an eternity of roaming its corridors and hallways*, but his eyes narrow and he shakes his head. 'It's a house, Iris, it's not capable of manipulation. It's just a house.'

There's my non-believing Byron. And while frustrating, his denial is almost a relief, and it gives me a glimmer of hope: there is still a chance that I've just gone completely and utterly mad and this is all in my imagination. Or else I have to admit that something just tried to kill me. But when Byron starts to believe . . .

All hope will be lost.

'No. No. There's something very wrong,' I say, because I don't have the luxury of Byron's certainty. 'The house is trying to split us up, and it's not the first time.' I stop for a beat, breathless with fear, before adding, 'Byron, I saw Zach.'

'What?'

'Zach. After I lost you guys, I saw someone. I followed them, thinking it was you, but look at this,' I say, finding the reflection in the window that I caught on video. 'There. See. It's Zach.'

I thrust the camera at Byron. He stares at the flip screen, squinting and tilting his head. 'Iris, it's just glare or a smudge or—'

'Don't! Don't do that.'

'What?'

'Try to come up with a rational explanation for something that is so obviously not rational. That. Is. Zach. Not glare. Not a smudge. Zach. Look, you can see the Z & L logo.'

Byron grips my shoulders and stares me right in the eyes. 'Iris, Zach is not here. You have to accept that Zach is gone.'

'No, he—'

'Iris! That can't be Zach in that reflection. It can't be.'

'Why, because it's not rational? Why can't you accept that not everything can be explained? That sometimes things are irrational. Ghosts exist, Byron.'

'Iris . . .'

'I saw him. Zach.'

'Iris, please—'

'No. You have to listen. At first, I thought he was really there. That he was alive. But then I followed him up to the attic and I saw his reflection in a window. Closer. Straight on. And . . .' I pause to let out a breath . . . 'his throat had been slit open.'

'Iris, come on. You've barely slept in two days,' says Byron. 'Maybe you've started hallucinating. Though I think it usually takes a few—'

'I'm not hallucinating. I saw him. I saw his reflection, right at the end of the corridor. And then he was gone.'

'So, did you get it on camera . . . the reflection?'

'No, I . . . I was too stunned to move. I . . .'

'Funny that.'

'No. It's true, By. It really happened. I saw him. His . . . his spirit or his energy or whatever you want to call it. I really did. And I ran to the end of the corridor where he would have turned into. But I saw Molly instead.'

'You saw Molly?'

'Yes.'

'Where is she? Is she OK?'

'Yeah. She's fine. She was heading towards the roof. That's when I heard you shouting. So, I said for her to wait for us up there, and then I came and found you. You were shouting so much, I thought something had happened to you. I was scared, Byron. If anything should happen to you . . .'

He stares at me, long and hard, and I can't quite read his expression: pain and confusion and hope and fear and regret. 'We should go up and get her,' he says after a moment, snapping out of his thoughts. 'And we need to figure out what we're going to do. It's too dark to safely go anywhere now. But we need to stay together, find somewhere secure for the rest of the night and head out at first light.'

I stare at him. 'But the seance . . .'

'It's over, Iris.'

'But I—'

'Stop! I've had enough of this ghost-hunting crap,' he says, defiance in his eyes. 'I've had enough of everything.'

He pushes past me, back the way I came, in the direction of the staircase to the attic. His last words ring in my ears: *I've had enough of everything.* And I wonder if I'm included in that *everything.*

'By . . .'

He doesn't turn around or even slow his pace. I trot to catch up with him, but I don't try to talk to him. Now's not the time, with nerves so frayed. But I can't believe that even after everything we have experienced in this house, after watching Zach and Lucas fall apart on-screen, after seeing footage of Zach's reflection in a window . . . he is still clinging to the hope that there is a rational explanation for everything. He is willing to believe anything – a smudge on the camera lens, glare, wood cooling, rats in the floorboards – because it's easier and more comfortable for him to believe than the supernatural existing.

By the time we reach the roof, it's empty. Molly isn't there. I stand by the ornate stone wall and look out across the landscape, touched silver by the moon. I can't see far, just the outlines of trees and bushes in the grounds below. I can't make out the woods in the dark. I wonder what it was that Zach saw at the edge of the woods that freaked him out so much, when he stood here the first time – or *who* he saw. Grace? One of the stolen children?

I shiver, and I think about how this weekend would have gone if we hadn't found Zach and Lucas's gear. If Thornhanger House had turned out to be just another regular creepy abandoned building. It would have been just another video with a few creaks and bangs in the dark. Me and Molly scaring ourselves, each of us politely wishing that the other wasn't here, while Byron calmly explains what he thinks is causing the candle to flicker: old buildings are draughty; or the camera to turn itself off: it's an old battery. We'd probably have dared ourselves on camera to go into the woods in the dark. Even Byron would freak out over that. Reason and logic can desert a person in the dark, dark woods.

But we did find Zach and Lucas's stuff, and this house has sucked us into whatever it was that sucked in Zach and Lucas. We may not have found their car, but I know that they never left this house. Neither of them.

'We have to do the seance, Byron. We have to know what happened to them.'

'No. My god, Iris. Enough is enough. We just have to find Molly and get out of here first thing,' he says, his features pale in the moonlight.

Neither of us move. I'm enjoying the night air on my skin and in my lungs: balmy but fresh. The thought of the dank air of the house makes me want to find Molly and run from this place right now, and never look back, despite the dark. Despite the secrets we would leave behind. To take our chances out in the hills and the moorland beyond. But something holds me here. Something even stronger now than the need to find out what happened to Zach and Lucas. I have the strangest feeling that the house won't let us go. Not easily. I don't know when the moment of no return happened. Was it the second we stepped foot over the threshold? Was it when we didn't leave when we found Zach and Lucas's stuff? Was it after we'd spent a night here? When we started watching the footage? I don't know, but I know that we've long since passed it. We've cursed ourselves. And I feel the clashing ripples of exhilaration and horror at that thought.

'Byron, please understand,' I say, shifting closer to him so that my body is as near to his as it can be without touching. I look into his eyes. 'This has gone too far now.'

'It went too far a long time ago.'

'No. What I mean is, we can't just leave. The house won't let us.'

'Iris, don't . . .'

'Don't you understand yet, By? We have to find out what happened to Zach and Lucas so that we can stop it from happening to us.'

30

'MOLLY!'

'Molly!'

I check my watch: 2.47 a.m. We've been searching for Molly for getting on for two hours. I'm not filming any of this. Instead, I have the camera and tripod in a bag, slung across my body. Just in case. My mobile is in my jeans back pocket, on the off-chance we find somewhere in this damn house with reception and we can call for help. My eyes burn with tiredness from a second night with no sleep, and my limbs are heavy, from pacing corridors for half the night. I'm beyond tired. I'm wired. Running off adrenaline. And even that is failing me.

'This is hopeless,' I say, leaning a hand on the range in the old kitchen. It is sticky, where decades worth of dust has settled in the grease and grime. I pull my hand away and wipe it on the leg of my jeans. 'Where is she?'

Byron shakes his head. 'I don't know. Where would she . . .' His voice cracks. He draws in a breath and covers his face with his hands. His shoulders slump.

I move towards him and wrap my arms around his waist, resting my forehead against his shoulder. We stand like that for a moment, me holding him. Until he suddenly pulls away, and without looking at me, he says, 'We should go back to the base camp. She might turn up there, and if we're not there, she might head off to look for us.' He turns and strides away. At the door, he pauses and without looking back he adds, 'And then we'll never find each other.'

I stand a moment, watching Byron disappear into the darkness of the corridor, with the old dresser casting its long shadow over me – as black and heavy as my regret – before heading after him. The crunch of my footsteps echoes off the cracked and grubby wall tiles.

I follow him silently through the twisting corridors to the L-shaped room that we use as a base camp, but stop just inside the doorway, fiddling with the strap of the camera bag, not sure how to say what needs to be said. 'Byron . . .'

'What?' he says, turning to look at me, his stare hollow. The room's fireplace is a black hole behind him.

Something has been biting and chewing on me while we searched, only I didn't want to put it into words. Because when you put things into words, they become real. But . . .

'Zach lost Lucas, remember? And now we've lost Molly, and—'

'Whoa. Hang on,' he says, putting a hand out to halt me. 'Iris. I'm going to ask you something, and I need you to give me an honest answer. The truth.'

'*OK*,' I say tentatively, wondering what he is about to say.

He lets out a breath and looks heavenward. He closes his eyes for a beat, before opening them and looking at me. 'I know that the channel and these videos are important to you.'

'Yeah. And? What are you getting at?'

'Did you have anything to do with Molly disappearing?' he blurts, as if trying to say it before he changes his mind, and he stares at me, his face pinched, like he's sucking on a lemon.

I can't speak for a moment, bile rising. I'm stung, as if from a punch to the face. How can he think something so awful of me? Knowing that he thinks I could do something to Molly throws me. It breaks something inside me. I shake my head, in disbelief, more than to convey my innocence. It's like being blamed for the car, only much worse. Much, much worse. 'You think I did something to her? That I have her bound and gagged somewhere?'

His eyes glisten with the tears that he's trying to hold in. 'It's just . . . it would be great for the video, right? Lucas goes missing. Molly goes missing . . .'

'Oh my god, Byron. Stop,' I say, backing up from him a step. 'Are you seriously suggesting that I've locked her up someplace to get a good video? How can you even think that? Byron, I would never—'

'The argument. You guys were really going for it. Did you follow Molly up to the roof . . . continue the argument . . . ? Did things get out of hand . . . ? Did you—?'

'Wait. Are you saying that you think I *hurt* Molly? Is that it?' I put a hand out to grab the door frame, needing to hold myself up. The room spins. My heart is beating like dice being rattled inside a shaker.

'How far would you go for a viral video, Iris?'

Is this how he sees me? Ruthless. Single-minded. Willing to do whatever it takes.

'No,' I say, shaking my head. 'You can't think that I'd . . .'

'Was it all you? The stuff moving. The car. Molly.'

'Byron. Stop. Christ. You've seen the footage. Something happened to Zach and Lucas here. You saw for yourself that a knife moved in a room covered by cameras. I was with you then, Byron. You must know that I had nothing to do with that. And you must know that I wouldn't hurt Molly. I wouldn't hurt anyone. Jesus! *You know me.* Just think about what you're saying. Think about what you've seen. What you've experienced. All the noises we've heard while we've been together. And for once in your life, open yourself up to the fact that something unexplained is happening here. Something beyond our comprehension. It's this house, By. This house is evil. It's full of vengeful spirits who want to hurt people the way that they've been hurt: Elizabeth. Anne. Edward. Grace. They are here. And maybe, just maybe, not all the spirits want to hurt us. Maybe Zach was trying to lead me to Molly to stop her from . . .'

'From what?'

'She was going to the roof. Why was she going to the roof?'

'Molly wouldn't,' he says, shaking his head. 'She wouldn't hurt herself.'

'Yet you're willing to believe that I hurt her,' I growl.

I could turn myself inside out with the frustration and hurt and shock that he'd think that I was capable of such a thing.

How can he? My Byron. How can he think that I could do something so awful?

He stares at me a moment, lips slightly parted. I'm waiting for him to say, *Of course I don't think that. That's crazy. I know you better than I know myself. You could never hurt anyone, Iris.* Instead, he shakes his head and says, 'Molly wouldn't. She wouldn't.'

'Yeah, and she wouldn't normally lose her shit either, Byron.' I spit the words as I glare at him, my stomach twisting, my cheeks burning. 'When have you ever seen Molly get mad at someone? It's not like her. It's this house. It's got into her head, like it did Zach and Lucas. It's got into all our heads. Earlier today, when I went outside for air, I had this crazy compulsion to go to the woods. That's where I was when you guys were packing up our stuff.'

'In the woods?'

'I never made it that far. I got scratched by some thorns and . . .' I stop and shake my head at the memory. 'I felt this . . . *rage*. But it wasn't my rage. And I . . .' I pause, thinking I'm not making much sense. 'Byron, I think the house made her—'

'Stop!'

'We have to consider—'

'Don't say it!'

I breathe in deeply. 'OK. But I think we should go and take a look. Outside,' I say. 'To see if . . .' I can't finish.

He stares at me, long and hard. I'm melting to mush beneath his red-hot glare.

'Oh god, Byron, what if she's hurt – how are we going to get her out? How are we going to get help?'

A ragged breath escapes his lips. 'Come on,' he says. And together we tear through the entrance hall, into the library, through the broken window, and out into the now-cool night.

31

WE WALK, SIDE by side, sweeping the ground with our torch beams.

'Molly?' I call. 'Molly? Molly!'

'MOLLY!'

'MOLLY!'

'If we find . . . *something* . . . how do I know you didn't . . .'

'What, push her?' I goad, stopping to glare at him.

'In the heat of the moment . . .'

'*Byron?*'

'Things get out of control. One shove in anger and—'

'You really would prefer to think that I'm to blame for everything – that I could shove someone off a roof – than just accept the existence of the supernatural. Why, Byron? *Why?*' I don't wait for a response, but push on ahead, shining my torch along the weed-infested ground. I trip as my foot gets caught in a tangled bush, and I right myself, keeping my head as high as I can manage.

In the dark, we stay close to the house. We search a small, cobweb-filled outhouse, which smells of coal and dust. We find the remains of a greenhouse. Glass smashed and its metal frame warped and rusting. Byron yelps as the ground swallows him, and I have to pull him from a sunken garden, so overgrown with weeds that we didn't see it coming, even with our torch beams. We dredge every bit of it, looking for Molly.

We widen our search, in case Molly has simply stormed off somewhere and is hiding out. Twigs snap underfoot and undergrowth swooshes at our legs as we wind our way through the trees, until we're back at the chapel. I swing my torch up to illuminate the vestibule door as we emerge from the cool, dank, dark wood that surrounds it. The arched door is closed. I try to remember if we closed it after we left but I can't. As I twist the iron handle and push, the door creaks even louder in the quiet stillness of the night. I go inside first, training my torch beam on the inner door, which is also closed. I'm pretty sure we left this one open, but, again, I'm not certain. It's a heavy door, so it could easily have closed by itself. My stomach swirls and my heart thumps at the thought of the shadows beneath the door earlier. Shadows that had looked like feet walking off to the right. It's too dark on the other side of the door now to see anything other than a strip of deep black.

We pass through the inner door and into the chapel,

treading slowly and carefully so as not to make too much noise, not wanting to scare Molly, if she is here, and, equally, not wanting to stir anything else into action. But as we shine our torch beams around the room, we see it's just as empty as it was the last time we were here.

Even so, I tentatively call out 'Molly?' as we edge along the aisle towards the altar. My voice echoes off the cold stone walls. 'Moll?'

Nothing.

With a sigh, I turn and start to make my way back to the door. It's then that my torch beam catches something I hadn't noticed when we were here before in daylight: in the far left-hand corner – my left as I'm facing the way out, so to the right of the vestibule on the way in – it looks as if the wood panelling doesn't actually reach all the way to the stone wall. I edge a little closer so that my torch beam can reach better, and I see more wood panelling behind the wall, as though you can go behind it.

'By,' I whisper, my heart racing and my mouth dry. 'Look.' I nod with my head for him to follow my torch beam. 'You see it? A gap. In the wall.'

'Oh my god, I can't believe we missed that.'

As I move towards it, Byron flings out a hand and grabs my arm. Quietly, he says, 'Iris, we don't know what's back there. Or who.'

'Exactly. That's why we have to take a look.'

As I pull away from him, I hear him hiss, 'Be careful, for god's sake,' and we both creep towards the mysterious gap in the wall, moving stealthily.

I pause at the opening, Byron pressed close beside me. If it were daylight, I'd be able to use my camera's flip screen to see around the edge, but it's dark, so all I'd see would be blackness. Tentatively, I strain my neck to peer around the other side, keeping my torch beam angled low to give a little light but trying to avoid signalling our approach to anyone or anything inside. I see a small, narrow wooden staircase, which runs up the inside of the false wall. I carefully shift my torch beam upwards a little, but I can't see anything beyond the top of the stairs. All remains still.

I glance back at Byron. 'We have to go up,' I say. 'We have to check everywhere.'

He nods resignedly, but he must be thinking exactly what I'm thinking: those shadowy feet we saw beneath the door the first time we were here had moved in this direction.

There's not room for us to walk side by side, so Byron goes first, the old steps creaking way more than either of us would like. I take a steadying breath and follow. Almost at the top, I see Byron pause. He goes down on to his hands and knees on the steps and, keeping himself low, he stetches his neck to peer around the top of the stairs to the left. I wait and watch, my ears straining for any sounds, my palms sweating. My mouth dry. Still on his hands and knees, Byron slowly crawls up the steps, until he is at the very top, where he draws himself to his feet, torch beam trained ahead of him, round to the left.

'Holy crap,' he says.

'What? What is it?' I hiss. 'Is there anyone there?'

'No. But . . .'

'But what? What can you see?' I clamber up the rest of the stairs, joining him.

'Oh shit.'

As my torch beam joins Byron's, the small, windowless secret room that we now find ourselves in is fully illuminated. It's probably not much bigger than our bathroom back home and runs the width and breadth of the vestibule below it. There's a single mattress in one corner, with rumpled, dirty sheets in a tangled mess and one stained, crumpled pillow. A small, low table sits in the opposite corner, with a few centimetres between it and the mattress. Its surface is littered with empty food and drink cans, and candles burnt down to varying heights. Carrier bags full of lord knows what are piled up here and there. Strewn across the limited floor space are items of filthy clothing, sticks and leaves. Some of the sticks and leaves have been woven into bundles and shapes, along with black feathers, dried flowers and what look and smell like dried herbs of some sort, and have been hung from the rafters. By far the worst items scattered around the room are the bones. *Bones*. Though they are small and clearly animal bones. But that doesn't make it any less creepy. As I take it all in, I have to cover my nose with the back of my hand against the ingrained smell: acrid and stale and suffocating.

Someone *is* living here.

Byron doesn't say it with his words – *I told you so* – but he says it with the look he shoots me.

I edge forwards a little way and kick at a piece of clothing with the toe of my Converse. The stiff, stained, worn fabric opens out to reveal a long plaid skirt – a woman? Or does the skirt belong to one of the house's victims?

'We need to go, right now,' says Byron. 'Before they come back.'

I don't argue. I let him grab my arm and pull me to the stairs. With every step down, I hold my breath, fully expecting someone to appear at the bottom of the staircase, carving knife in hand, blocking our way, and ready to hack us to pieces. Just like they probably did to Zach and Lucas. To Molly?

Oh god, no, no, no.

But we make it down the stairs and around the corner and out the door into the vestibule and then out – OUT OUT – into the dark night air, where we run for the cover of the woods. We run on, deeper into the woods, feet snagging on undergrowth, with only what little moonlight breaks through the trees to guide us. Not far from the house, Byron slows and stops. I stop too, both of us panting hard. I double over with my hands on my knees to get my breath.

'Christ! There's someone here,' I say to Byron, and I'm still waiting for him to say *I told you so*, but he doesn't.

'They must have been playing with us the whole time,' he says, in not much more than a whisper, as he wipes his sweat-damp fringe from his face. 'Molly's stuff being messed up, the footsteps, noises we've heard. My mum's car. They must have taken the battery.'

I straighten up and lean back against a tree trunk to support my trembling legs. 'Yes, to a point. But think about it,' I say, keeping my own voice low, my eyes darting between the trees, as we have no idea where the 'someone' is right now, 'we can't pin *all* the activity on them, By. No matter how much you want to. The knife, for example. There was no one in that room. No way they could have got in without being filmed. And I know you don't believe me, but I've seen things that are definitely not human. Zach's ghost, that pale face in the window . . . I was dragged across the room by my hair and locked in a cupboard, for Christ's sake. Those. Things. Happened.'

Byron lets out a groan, as if he doesn't want to go there again, and he goes down on to his haunches, his hands in prayer position in front of his mouth.

'Who do you think it is?' I ask, sliding down so that I'm sitting on my haunches too, with my back against the tree, level with Byron. We both have our torches off, to keep ourselves hidden, but I can see him well enough in the moonlight. His skin is pale and his eyes glisten with tears.

He lowers his hands and fixes his wild eyes on mine. 'Some nutcase who murdered Zach and Lucas and now they're after us.'

I squeeze my eyes shut for a beat. Opening them, I say, 'Do you think it could be someone with a connection to the house?'

'What d'you mean? Like who?'

I think of the women's clothing. 'Grace?'

'*Grace*?'

'The housemistress. The one who's thought to have come back here after the school closed down and who was supposed to have stolen children to appease Charlotte Turner's ghost.'

'Yeah. But she killed herself, didn't she? Jumped off the roof.'

'But she might not have,' I say, things starting to make sense – at least to me. 'It's possible that bit of the story has been mistold over the years. The timeline could add up, if she was a youngish housemistress in the 1970s. She could still be alive today. Though she'd be in her seventies or eighties by now.'

'Why her?' asks Byron with a shrug.

'Because,' I begin, 'she stole children to feed souls to Charlotte, right? What if she's still stealing souls to . . . I don't know . . . feed to the house. To stop it from claiming her.'

'Oh god, Iris,' says Byron, as he stands.

I rise to my feet. Byron is shaking his head in disbelief, but I don't let that stop me. I really think I'm on to something. 'No, listen. Throughout its history, this house has tried to take as many souls as it can. Maybe something Violet did when she killed Lord Thornhanger, Emma and herself put a curse on the house, maybe she *did* use dark magic for the murder, and the house became hungry. Or maybe this land has always been cursed. I don't know.'

'Iris . . .'

'But this house. It wants souls. And maybe its appetite has increased over the years, especially now it's been empty for so long, so it doesn't let anyone else go. Apart from Grace herself, because she lures people here or prevents anyone unlucky enough to show up on their own accord from leaving, thus feeding the house. So, in return, it lets her live.'

'Iris—'

'And if that's the case,' I continue, ignoring Byron, 'then I don't think we're necessarily in any danger from Grace,' I say, with a small shake of my head. 'We're already here. She'll just try to keep us here until the house gets us. Which probably explains the car battery going missing. But—'

'Oh. My. God. Stop!' snaps Byron. I do, and I stand looking at him, my mouth open, with my next word left hanging. 'Iris, you are delusional.'

'No, I don't think—'

'Stop,' he says, calmer this time, but no less commanding. 'No more of this haunting BS, OK? There is someone else here. And what we need to focus on is where this nutjob is right now and whether they have Molly. Or if they've . . . if they've . . . If this psycho has done anything to her . . .'

'Oh Byron,' I say as he hangs his head, and I take a step towards him.

He takes a step back, the rebuff making my cheeks burn. After a beat, he says, 'Look, let's just go back to the house and figure out what to do next.' Looking me in the eye, he adds, 'But if anything has happened to Molly, one way or another, it's on you.'

We walk in silence, until we reach the broken window. Byron pauses, turning to me. 'You know what?' he begins, one hand on the window ledge. 'You want to know why I'm a such a hardened non-believer? Why I can't just accept that the supernatural exists . . . even to make Molly happy?'

'Why?' I say, my voice not much more than a broken whisper.

'Because if we live in a world where ghosts exist – where not everything can be explained by science – then it makes the world an even more unpredictable place than it already is. It means there's even more to worry about. More uncertainty. More thoughts going round and round and round inside my head and making me doubt my decisions and forcing me to try to predict outcomes that I have no control over. Trying to read other people's minds; trying to work out what they're thinking. What they want. And then getting it all so bloody wrong anyway.'

'By.' I take a step towards him.

'Don't,' he says, hand out. 'I really don't want anything from you right now.'

He turns and climbs through the window. I move to follow, but I stop. I'll give him a second. We'll only argue more if I go after him now. I lean back against the cold stone, utterly deflated and beaten. Damp soaks through my hoodie, the chill making its way into my bones. Slipping down on to my haunches, I put my head in my hands.

Where *is* Molly?

Has the house done something to her?

Or does some psycho have her?

No. She will turn up. She has to. This house is so big, she probably took a wrong turn and she's conducting her own seance, totally unaware that Byron and I are worried. And that Byron condemned me for her murder. Or maybe she's cooling off after our row. Maybe she's trying to figure out what she wants. Where she and Byron go from here. Where she and I go. Where Byron and I go. There's probably so much stuff going on inside her head right now that she just wants to be alone. She'll be found when she wants to be found.

But what if she fell from the roof and crawled off, hurt, into the grounds. What if she is dying, just out of sight?

What if someone has her?

Stop.

She's fine.

She'll turn up.

I lean against the side of the house and shine my torch out ahead of me. If she's somewhere in the overgrown grounds, injured, I don't know if we'll ever find her. Not in the dark. *Stop. Just stop. She's fine.* The beam of light doesn't go far, but I can see sporadic bushes and trees. Trees that slowly begin to cluster and that eventually form the distant haunted woods. I shiver when I think of those woods – all those missing children. Anne, dead. Her face twisted with fright.

Breath catches at the back of my throat and fear grazes my insides as I wonder if the woods might try to lure me again. But even more terrifying is that I'm aware of a ripple of excitement building at the thought. I almost want to feel that tug. To lose myself.

But I feel nothing. Nothing other than relief and disappointment. And maybe, just maybe the faintest tickle of a longing—

I sweep the torch to the left, at the sound of a rustle, breaking the spell. I almost have a heart attack when I spot a pair of eyes reflected in the light: a fox, frozen for a moment, suddenly shoots off in the direction of the woods. Feeling vulnerable out here and not wanting to leave Byron on his own, I stand and climb through the window after him, calling out 'Byron!' as I edge my way through the library. 'By . . .'

As I emerge into the entrance hall, I stop – dead – attracted by the light from a torch, which rests on the landing of the central staircase. Byron is a dark shape beside it, half in the light. I sweep my torch beam up, not understanding at first what I'm seeing. Byron is standing in front of the mirror, staring at his reflection. Transfixed.

'By?'

I notice that he has my knife gripped in one hand.

Time stops in a drawn-in breath. An image of Elizabeth's father, cutting his own throat while staring at his reflection, flashes in my mind's eye. I remember Zach, that moment I saw his reflection in the attic window, blood oozing from his slit throat.

Byron.

'BYRON!'

I run towards him.

32

I TAKE THE stairs two – maybe even three – at a time. I'm not even aware of what my feet are doing. I just have to get to Byron. I'm powerless as I watch him raise the knife. *No no no.* I'm screaming at him to stop. To please stop. To put the knife down. To stop. For god's sake. Stop. Don't do it! STOP! But my words have all the effectiveness of a watering can against a forest fire.

He holds the knife to the flesh of his throat.

'BYRON!'

At the top of the stairs, I catch a glimpse of desperate sorrow in his eyes in the mirror as he stares at his own reflection, so deep. So lost.

I'm not even aware that I've dropped my torch, until I hear the repetitive smashing thuds as it rolls down each step in my wake. And I scream, 'NONONONONO!' until I'm raw, as I throw myself at him.

Coming at him from behind on his right side, I instinctively grasp his knife arm just above the wrist, and I push the knife forwards and out, away from his flesh. I fear that if he puts up a struggle, I won't be strong enough to stop him from turning the knife on himself or on me. But I don't care about myself, just him, and, thankfully, he offers no resistance. I hold his knife arm out to the side, panting, while I try to prise his fingers from the handle with my free hand. But his grip is too tight. I groan from the effort.

'Byron!' I say, shaking his arm. 'By!'

The look of hopeless despair in his eyes switches to wide-eyed horror and panic, as he snaps out of whatever had gripped him. His eyes find mine in the mirror. We're held there for a moment, before he glances down at the knife, still clenched in his fist; my hand around his wrist.

'What the . . . ?'

'Please drop the knife, Byron.'

Glancing from me and back down to the knife, he lets it go, like it's red-hot. It clatters to the floor, while he stares at the palm of his hand.

I release his wrist and put the palm of my hand against his right cheek, turning him around and directing his gaze to mine. 'Byron. Oh my god, By. You scared me. Jesus. Are you OK? What happened? Do you remember?'

'I . . .' His eyes are wild, and his face is creased with fear and confusion, like someone waking from a nightmare, their head still foggy and thick with dreams.

'Byron, you had the knife at your throat,' I say. I'm so

angry that he'd do something so stupid, even though I'm sure that something had compelled him to do it, just like something had compelled me to go towards the woods. Something old and deep and dark and angry. 'Byron, please say something,' I say, when he stares at me, open-mouthed. I'm gripped by the sudden urge to hit him for scaring me so much, even though I know it wasn't him. 'Do you remember anything?'

'I . . . Jesus . . . It's like . . . I could see myself doing it,' he says. 'The knife in my hand, walking up here, staring into the mirror, lifting the knife. Wanting to stop the pain. Oh my god, Iris. The pain. The sorrow. The heartbreak. I was drowning in it. But I don't know where it came from. And I . . . I know it sounds crazy, but I just needed it to *stop* so that I could rest. And I thought . . . Agh . . . I just wanted to rest. But I don't remember why. I couldn't stop myself. I . . .'

A tear rolls down his cheek.

'It's OK.' I fling my arms around him. His arms go around me. Tight. 'It's not you. It's this house. It's trying to destroy all of us. It's infecting us.' We stand there, clinging on to each other. Holding each other up. I feel him trembling, and his shoulders shaking with sobs.

'I'm so sorry, Byron,' I say into his shoulder. 'I'm so sorry for everything.' My cheeks are sticky with tears. They soak into Byron's jumper, but he doesn't appear to notice or care. He places a hand on the back of my head and holds me to him. 'I know it's my fault we're stuck here. I should have listened to you and Molly when we first got here. You were right. We should have gone straight to the police. And now it's too late. We're stuck here. Because of me.' I shudder as a sob wracks my body.

'Shhhh,' he says, as he strokes the back of my head, his turn to comfort me. Even though I don't deserve it.

'I've messed . . . everything up,' I say between sobs. 'We've lost . . . lost Molly.' My voice cracks. 'And you hate me.'

'I don't hate you,' he says, pulling away from me and gripping my shoulders. His eyes are red-rimmed, his cheeks tear-stained, and there's a look of something else, something beneath the fear and the horror, something I can't quite make out. Something that unsettles me. 'I could never hate you, Iris. I . . .' He pauses and bites his lower lip, his eyes fixed on mine. Looking deeper. Deeper. 'Molly was right. It's always been you. It always will be. I'm in love with you.'

Despite my fear, my heart fizzes and swells as if it's a full bottle of Coke that someone has dropped a whole packet of Mentos into. 'By,' I begin, my voice catching. 'I love you. You have to know that. I love you. I just . . . I never felt—'

He shakes his head. 'It's OK, Iris,' he says, cutting me off. 'It doesn't matter. You never felt the same way about me. I know. I always knew. And it's OK. But I never stopped hoping.' He shakes his head. 'Idiot that I am.'

'No, By, it's not what I—'

'Shit . . .' A drop of blood falls from his left nostril on to the front of his jumper, and my words are left unsaid.

Another drop. And another. He instinctively puts a hand to his nose. Blood trickles over his fingers, then it pours. 'What the . . . ?'

'Christ,' I say. 'Oh my god.'

He has both hands cupped beneath his nose, as bright red blood flows from both nostrils. It oozes between his fingers and drips on to the bare floorboards. And I think how this house wants his blood. If not from his throat, then from his nose.

I'm frozen for a moment, the shock of so much blood.

'Iris?' He looks at me pleadingly, pale, wide-eyed and helpless.

'Here,' I say, as I hurriedly pull off my hooded top, taking the camera bag off with it. I discard the bag at my feet, and as I push Byron's hands away so that I can place my top under his nose, I hear spilt blood splash to the floor.

He helps me hold the hoodie in place, while I pinch the bridge of his nose, trying to stop the flow. This is what we have to do when May gets nosebleeds. Though hers are light and easily stemmed. Not like this.

'Are you OK?' I say to him. 'Do you feel light-headed?' I wonder how he can lose so much blood but still be on his feet.

'I'm OK,' he says, his words nasal and muffled by blood and by the hoodie, all bunched up beneath his nose. I can feel the warm, sticky blood oozing through the fabric. 'I think it's easing a . . .' His words trail off, and we both turn to stare down the staircase at the sound of slow, purposeful footsteps from somewhere below.

'What the . . . ?'

The footsteps grow louder. And, with a chill, I wonder if it is whoever is living in the chapel. But then I remember something that Molly said, after I told her about me feeling suddenly nauseous: that it is a sign of a spirit being present. Nausea or headaches or . . . nosebleeds. I hadn't believed her then. But now . . .

Byron lets go of my hoodie, and I lower it. His face is sticky and red, and dark, drying blood has started to crust his nostrils, but the flow has, thankfully, eased to a dribble, which he dabs at with the sleeve of his jumper. I throw the sodden hoodie down. Slinging the camera bag over my shoulder, I pick up Byron's torch and move to the very edge of the landing to get a better look downstairs.

'Look. There,' says Byron, pointing in the direction of the library, as a shadow flits across the pool of moonlight outside the doorway. Only way in. Only way out. We're trapped. I'm aware of Byron drawing up beside me. His warmth. His solidity. His fingers – sticky with blood – slipping between mine. But I can't take my eyes off the doorway as I wait to see who – what – will come through.

'Molly?' Her name comes out as no more than a hopeful, croaked whisper. I turn to Byron. 'Do you think . . . ?'

'Iris, I don't think that's Molly,' he says, wiping dried blood from his cheek with the back of a hand.

He's already pulling me back and up the staircase, where it branches to the left.

'How do you . . . Shouldn't we just . . .'

'I just know. OK? It's *not* Molly. You were right. It's

this house. It's evil. It's always been the house, Iris.'

I pull him to a stop, and I stare into his eyes. It's then I realize what that look is, the one I couldn't work out before. The look that is so alien on his face.

Belief.

Byron the Non-believer believes in this house and its ghosts.

The weight of that realization threatens to topple me all the way down the stairs. But I cling to Byron's hand and, at the sound of quickening footsteps, we turn and race up the stairs.

33

'WHERE ARE WE going?' I say, with a glance over my shoulder. I see nothing following us, but I know it doesn't mean that nothing is.

'We're going to find Molly then hide until it's light and we can get out of here. Or at least keep moving so they can't find us.'

I wonder who the 'they' are. Grace, alive and wanting to exchange our souls for her own safety? Or one of the house's ghosts? Elizabeth's father? Had he possessed Byron? Had he possessed Zach? Forced him to slit his own throat? Is that what happened to Zach? But, if so, what about his body? Where is it? Why isn't it on the landing, in front of the mirror? Was he able to crawl away and hide somewhere while he bled to death? Was his body dragged off by a hungry wild animal? Did Grace move it? And what other spirits are in this house with us . . .

Elizabeth, Violet, Lord Thornhanger? The stolen children? Anne? Did she lock Lucas in Elizabeth's cupboard? What happened to Molly? Did someone possess her? Force her into . . . Oh god. No no no. This can't be happening.

What have I done?

'We have to do something,' I say, pulling Byron to a stop.

'What? What can we do? Iris, this place . . . it's . . . it's evil,' he says, his eyes wide. Crazed. That look, it chills me to my bones. I don't think I will ever be able to forget that look in his eyes.

'Help the spirits trapped inside this house to pass over. That's what we can do,' I say, resolutely. I cast nervous glances over my shoulder as I talk. 'So that they can find peace. So that this *house* can be at peace.'

'Do you even know how?' he asks. Blood smears Byron's cheeks and crusts around his left nostril. His brow is creased, his mouth set in a line.

'I've seen a YouTube video,' I say with a weak smile.

He snorts, humourlessly.

'Please, Byron. If the house hasn't already . . . If Molly's still . . . It's our best bet to get her back. It's got to be worth a try,' I say, grasping his arm. 'Maybe then the house will let us go.'

Apprehension coils itself around my heart and my lungs, squeezing tighter, tighter, tighter, as Byron and I clasp hands around the candles. The orange glow lights his face from beneath, casting shadows on his features. Features so familiar, but that I have never seen like this. Twisted and pale with belief and terror. Eyes haunted. The camera is set up so that Byron and myself are in shot and, wanting to ward off the dark a little more, I left the torch on, positioning it by the wall behind me. It throws a little light on the old, raggedy toys beneath the window, making their shadows shoot off at an angle.

'If there is anyone here, in this house with us, please follow the light of our candles,' I begin, holding eye contact with Byron. 'Let the light draw you to us. Know that we only want to help you, and to listen to you. To help any lost souls trapped in this house to pass over into the light. To where your loved ones are waiting for you. To let you and this house be at peace. If there is anyone here who would—' I stop, my head flicking towards the door to the corridor, which stands half-open. 'Did you hear that?' I say. 'Please tell me you heard that.'

'A scraping?'

I nod. I swallow, as I stare into the darkness beyond the door, waiting for something to form from the shadows, straining my ears and my eyes. My heart pounding.

Nothing.

I let out the breath I've been holding and, turning back, I continue. 'If there is anyone . . . anyone here with us, we welcome you with open hearts and open minds and good intentions.' My eyes dart around the gloomy room as I pause for a beat. Watching. Listening. 'If you are stuck, let us guide you—'

'A footstep?' says Byron, his eyes wide.

I nod; a small, barely detectable movement. 'From just outside the door, I think.' I release a steadying breath and draw in another.

I'm so very aware that there is no way out of this room other than through that door.

'Please, come forward. We mean you no harm. No disrespect. Feel safe to communicate with us. Anne. Elizabeth. Edward. Charlotte. Zach. Violet—'

Bang!

We both flinch. The sound had come from above us. I glance to the ceiling, but I see nothing, other than cracked plaster and the remains of an ornate ceiling rose. Byron's grip on my hands tightens.

'Violet, is that you?' says Byron. His voice trembles, and I'm drowning in the gravity of his belief. 'Give us a sign to let us know. Make a sound.' Silence. 'Knock something. Or make the candles flicker. Move one of the toys.'

My eyes shift to the left, watching for any movement among the old toys: the horse rocking or the pram rolling. A message scrawled on the blackboard by a ghostly hand.

Nothing.

'Lucas, are you here?' I ask, remembering that we had success with him during the first seance.

Silence.

'Molly?' I say, my voice a tight whisper. 'Molly, are you—'

There's a sharp thud as something – a stone or a small piece of rubble perhaps – comes flying from the shadows at the end of the room and lands somewhere behind the camera, making both Byron and me jump.

'Jesus! Where did that come from?' asks Byron.

I shake my head. I can't speak for a moment, and I wonder if the camera will have picked it up.

Molly? Is it Molly? Could it be . . .

No. No. No.

'Molly,' I try again, my throat tight. 'Molly, is that you?'

Silence.

'Violet, are you here with us?'

'Do you feel that?' asks Byron.

'What?'

'A temperature drop. I can feel it getting colder.'

'I'm not sure. But I feel like there's someone here with us. A presence. I can feel . . .' I glance over my shoulder, convinced that someone is behind me. Looking over me. How I'd felt downstairs in the base camp, that first night, when I couldn't sleep. Just as if someone is looming over me . . . 'I can feel someone.'

No one there.

'Violet, did you . . . did you awaken something . . . something in this house?' I continue, stumbling over my words as my lips tremble, and my eyes flit around the room. 'Did Grace die here? Make a sound if Grace fell from the roof and died.'

Silence.

'Is this house hungry?' asks Byron.

Tap.

'Does . . . does Thornhanger House want our souls?'

Tap.

'Is there a way to escape—'

Crack!

Again, something is thrown across the room, this time hitting the tripod. I hear whatever it is rolling off along the floorboards.

'Christ! What was . . .' I stop when I hear a steady, sharp *thud* . . . *thud* . . . *thud* . . . *thud* . . . coming from the end of the room. Byron lets go of my hands, picks up a candle and turns, arm extended to shine its light behind him.

'What the . . . ?'

In the glow, we watch as a marble topples from the jar, hitting the surface of the dresser with a small *thud*, where it rolls off the edge and on to the floorboards with a cracking *thud*. Another follows.

Thud.

Thud.

'How . . .' My words trail off.

I gasp.

Byron turns back to me. 'What? What is it?' he asks.

'I feel someone's breath on the top of my head,' I say, slowly. Steadily. 'Cold. Icy.' A rush of adrenaline makes me break out in goosebumps, and the hair all over my body stands on end. I swallow. 'There's someone behind me.' I whip round. Nothing there. Nothing that I can see. When I turn back, Byron has set the candle down and is holding the camera in his hands. He's watching back some footage.

'What is it, By?' I say, noting his drawn features. His wide eyes. His gaping mouth.

'By?'

Little rocks of dread fill me up as he turns the camera so that the flip screen is facing me. There's a landslide in my stomach as I take the camera from him. I watch the footage that we have just recorded, my eyes big. My mouth dry. Blood rushes in my ears. And I let out a gasp of breath at the sight of a shadow cast over me, as if someone is standing behind me, caught in the torchlight.

I can't move. My lips part but I can't speak. My eyes flick up to Byron. He's staring past me. His eyeline raised.

'Can . . . can you see it?'

Without looking at me, he shakes his head.

I feel like a mouse that is afraid to move in case it should alert the cat to its presence. I remain where I am, too scared to look over my shoulder. I can feel them, whoever it is behind me, cold and dark, like a bad dream lingering in the waking world. Remembering how I have felt a presence behind me so many times, I wonder if someone has been following me ever since we arrived at Thornhanger House.

Slowly, I lean across and place the camera back on the tripod to continue. To see this through. Byron puts his hand on my arm.

'Iris. We've got to go.'

'But we can't stop now. We have to end this.'

'The whispering – can't you hear it?'

I shake my head. 'We can help—'

'We can't help!' he snaps at me. 'No one can help.'

'But . . .'

'Iris, get up.' Byron is on his feet. He picks up the torch, before grasping one of my hands. 'We've got to go.'

'But what about Molly?' Byron's hollow expression chills me. 'Do you think she's—'

At the sound of smashing glass, I let out a scream. My head snaps to the end of the room, where the jar has toppled and marbles thud and crash and clink and rattle as they roll and scatter across the floor.

'Iris!'

My head snaps back to Byron.

I thought I could do it. I thought I could help. That I could stop this. Put it right. All of it. But it's too much. Too ingrained. Decades and decades of hurt and anger and fear and heartbreak and hate and loss.

Letting Byron pull me up, I glance back to where the shadow had been. I see nothing.

'GO!' Byron yells, startling me into action.

My gaze flicks to him. 'Wait!' I say. 'The camera.'

'Leave it!' he growls, as he tugs me towards the door.

'No way,' I say, freeing myself of his grip.

'Iris!'

I swipe up the camera. We've risked so much for this, there's no way I'm leaving evidence behind.

'Come on, Iris!'

Careful not to slip on the marbles that have spread across the floor, I follow Byron out of the room.

*

We tear down corridors. We twist and turn, the camera recording, and I can't help the feeling that we're going deeper into the house. Like it's tricking us. It doesn't want us to leave. I have no idea if anything is pursuing us. I can only hear the pounding of our booted feet on bare floorboards, the thumping of my heart and the whoosh of air past my ears. But I can't imagine it is going to let us get away so easily. I yelp as I take a corner too sharply and I hit my elbow against the hard edge of the wall. I swipe hair out of my eyes so that I can see. In the flash of the torch beam, I think I catch a glimpse of someone standing at the end of a corridor. Someone slight in frame. Someone claimed by the house. *Molly?* My breath catches. But I don't stop. I don't look back. I hear a faint cry – a gasp for help – from somewhere deep in the house. Byron must hear it, too, as he flicks a side-glance at me. He shakes his head, his expression grave. A warning not to stop. Not to listen. Not to believe it. To keep running. Running. Running. Down the central staircase, Byron stops in front of the mirror.

'Byron!' I grip his arm and drag him away. He snaps out of whatever momentarily grasped his mind, and we fly down the rest of the stairs.

'Our stuff,' I say, halting as we reach the entrance hall.

'Leave it!'

Byron grabs my forearm.

'But Zach and Lucas's cameras. The evidence . . .'

I'm about to pull away from Byron, not willing to leave such valuable evidence, when I see a shift in the shadows in the base-camp room through the partially open door. Backing up a step, I hear slow footsteps. Growing louder. Faster. Coming this way. Towards the doorway. Part of me wants to wait to see who – what – comes through that door. Like the gravitational pull of a black hole. I so want to see over the event horizon, but to do so will be deadly.

But the things I will see.

The things I will learn.

'Iris, come on!'

I feel Byron tug on my arm. I don't resist. I turn and we run together, through the library to the broken window. Byron grips the window frame and hauls himself up and out. His feet crunch on concrete as he drops down on the other side. He waits while I scramble up on to the windowsill. One leg through, I lose my balance and Byron grasps my elbow for support as I slide the other leg through, and I hold on to the rotting window frame as I lower myself down, and—

'No! My camera.' It slips from my hand. I whip round and swipe for it as it topples back, over the windowsill. I miss and it hits the floorboards on the other side of the window with a sickening crack. I go to climb up, but Byron grips my arm, pulling me back.

'Leave it.'

'I can't. I . . . Everything on it. The proof.'

'It's not worth it.'

'But . . .' The footage on that camera will go viral. Us finding Zach and Lucas's belongings, that shadow looming over me during the seance, Zach's reflection in the window, my bag moving . . . it's all proof that Zach and Lucas were here and that ghosts exist. This is going to blow up the internet. If I leave the camera, after everything we have gone through to get the footage, after everything we have lost, it will all be for nothing. Absolutely nothing.

I pull away from Byron and heave myself up.

'Iris! Iris, come down.'

I stop when I hear a sound from back inside the house: footsteps. Shadows shift across the threshold of the open door to the hallway. I glance from the camera – just out of reach on the other side of the window – to the doorway, where the shadows grow longer. The footsteps grow louder. It will only take me a second to get in, grab the camera and get out.

Louder.

'Iris. Don't!'

As the shadows grow longer still, something in my gut warns me that if I take one step back inside Thornhanger House, I won't make it out alive. Feet on the ground, I feel my back pocket – my mobile. I can at least get one more video on my phone camera of our escape. I pull it out and, pressing record, I hold my phone out in front of me, filming the dark, shifting shadows in the library as I back up from the window.

Leaving my Canon to the ghosts, I turn from Thornhanger House and slip my hand into Byron's. We break into a run, but a short way from the house, I stop, pulling Byron in towards me. My stomach fizzes with longing and regret. I'm not entirely sure the house has finished with us, and I can't risk leaving this unsaid any longer.

'By. What I tried to tell you earlier . . .'

He looks at me. 'Not now. We—'

'Stop. Just listen. I have to get this out. I should have had the courage to tell you this long ago: the reason I never let anything happen between us isn't because I never felt *the same*, it's because I never felt *good enough*. For you.'

'What?'

'I worried that it – us – would be another thing for me to fail at and I would ruin our friendship. Because I'm useless at everything. And I'd lose you for good. So, I let my stupid crush on Zach get in the way of my feelings for you. Because it was safer. But it's always been you, By. Always.'

I stop and look into his eyes imploringly, scared of what comes next – of what he will say. His eyes flit left and right, searching mine, his mouth hangs slightly open but no words come out. And I worry that he's not going to say anything at all. My insides swirl and my breath catches, and I just want him to say something. Anything. Then, unsure which one of us leans in first, our lips touch and we kiss. And it's absolutely everything all at once: every wonderful and silly and awkward and funny and comforting and painful and loving and exciting and terrifying and heartbreaking moment we've shared throughout our lives together, right up to this point in time. I don't want it to end. When we do break apart, I'm breathless and I'm hit with a sense of loss, and I want to kiss him again. Because it's EVERYTHING. Instead, I stare into his eyes, which glisten with tears, and he has this stupid half grin on his face, kept in check by the crazy, scary situation we're in. I forget I'm still filming on my phone, and I fling my arms around him and he does the same and we embrace. We hold each other. So tight. Both of us crying. Tears of joy and sadness and fear and regret.

'I love you, Iris,' he says.

'I love you, Byron,' I say.

As we pull apart, Byron boops me on the nose, and he smiles wistfully at me.

'You're an idiot,' he says.

'I know,' I say.

And, hand in hand, we run.

34

IT'S STILL A little dark, only just dawn. Dew from the long grasses soaks my jeans, and the air chills my bare arms. We tear through the undergrowth of the once- grand grounds, the beam of Byron's torch cutting erratically through the semi-darkness, while I film our escape. I trip over a bush, stumble over tree roots. 'I've got you, Iris,' says Byron, not letting go of my hand. My jeans whoosh through tall grasses and weeds. Feet pound the dry earth. My hair is like streamers in the wind behind me.

We run.

Away from the house and its ghosts.

We run on. The sun is rising, but, as the trees around us draw closer and closer, we're shadowed from the silvery light. It gets darker and darker. Colder and colder. Twigs snap under foot. Feet sink into soft mulch. Branches scratch. I stumble over something. I glance back to see the half-smashed face of a porcelain doll, staring up at me through some tangled weeds with its one dead eye. And it's then that I realize with a thud where we are.

We're in the woods.

Where they are the thickest.

We must have become disorientated somehow. I thought we were running towards the gates and the tumbledown wall. With no choice, I run on, knowing that we will eventually come out the other side, to the stream that marks the boundary of Thornhanger House, and the meadow. Where Elizabeth's mother died.

Somewhere along the way, our fingers have slipped from each other, and I have taken the lead, filming ahead of me. I wonder if Byron has registered yet that we are running through the woods where Grace brought the stolen children. Where Anne died of fright.

The sooner we're out, the better.

Beams of sunlight break through the trees, giving me some comfort that we're heading away from that horrible house and its dark secrets. We'll cross the stream and trek through the meadow and we'll find a road, and we'll get home. As soon as we get a phone signal, I'll call my dad. My lovely, larger-than-life dad, with his big, infectious laugh, will drive up here to pick us up. And take us home. I'll let him know where we are and he'll jump right in the car and come and get us.

Our respective families think we're in the Lake District – about twenty miles away – in case my parents spoke to Byron's parents. We told them all we were camping in the

Lake District. We were going to own up to Thornhanger House afterwards, like it wasn't planned and we just stumbled upon it.

Molly.

The thought of her hits me like a cannonball to the chest – how are we going to explain what happened to Molly? *We* don't even know what happened to her. Not really. How can we begin to explain? I choke back a sob at the thought of Molly's grandmother. There will be a police investigation. There will be questions to answer. There will be disbelief. We'll tell them about Thornhanger House. Police officers will search the building. They will find the cameras. All of them. They will watch the footage.

They won't want to believe.

But they'll have to believe.

Won't they?

With a jolt that almost causes me to trip over a tree root, it registers that we didn't actually capture anything concrete on film. Not one thing. Not to anyone who wasn't there. We can't prove no one was in the room when my bag shook or when the knife was thrown; that one of us wasn't hiding in a blind spot. No one will believe that the shadow that fell across me during the last seance wasn't Molly standing behind me. They'll think that glimpse of Zach in the window is nothing but glare. Without all that footage being edited into a narrative, all anyone will see is some kids freaking themselves out in a big old house in the middle of nowhere.

Who is going to believe us?

It really was all for nothing.

But I push that thought from my mind for now, and I focus on escape. I spot the stream up ahead.

At last!

Leaping over a fallen log, I run on, my phone held out in front of me, filming, Byron at my heels. I can't see him, but I can sense him – feel his presence – as we tear through the wood. Tears mark tracks down my cheeks. Sweat mixes with the tears, stinging my eyes and blurring my vision. I wipe at the sweat and tears with my fingers. My heart races in time with my footfalls. The trees start to thin, and the light pours in around me.

We've done it.

We've escaped.

We've escaped Thornhanger House and its ghosts.

I splash through the stream, my battered Converse getting drenched by the icy, clear water, while my feet crunch on the stones and gravel, stirring up clouds of mud. But I don't even care about my cold, wet feet. We're out. Across the line. I feel lighter with the sense of relief. The meadow is so beautiful, with long grasses and flowers in white and yellow and blue and pink. Morning dew soaks my already-wet jeans even more. It's only now, in this lush meadow, that I realize how dank and lifeless Thornhanger House and its grounds had been.

I slow my pace, safely over the boundary, and I flip the view on my phone camera so that my red, sweaty, wild-eyed face fills the screen. My breath ragged, I say, 'This is crazy, you guys. I don't even know where to begin. I'll keep this short and make another video when we've had a chance to get our shit together, but . . . we've proved the paranormal exists! I . . . uh . . . I can't even think straight right now, but we found proof of what happened to Zach and Lucas. We know where they went and what happened to them, and we'll reveal all in our next update, when we've had a chance to process. It's unbelievable. But it all happened, one hundred per cent. We . . . ugh . . .' I lose my words a moment as a lump catches in my throat and I wipe a tear from my cheek with my free hand. 'We don't know where Molly is. We think – I don't even know how to say this – we think the house got her. Just like it did Zach and Lucas. Uh . . .' I wipe at the tears that are flowing freely now. 'Byron and I barely made it out.' I glance around for him, a grin on my face pushing through my tears, ready to fling my arms around him. *We're free!*

But he's not there.

35

BYRON CAN'T BE far. I don't remember us getting separated. He was right there. Right behind me. I felt him. I heard him. He probably just tripped over. He'll be here in a minute, I reason. Turning back to my phone, I say, 'That's it for now. I'll record another update with more info as soon as I can.' And I press stop.

Exiting the camera screen, I notice I have a signal. A SIGNAL. My heart flips, and I don't believe it at first. 'Oh my god. Yes!' I say. I can phone my dad. The police . . . And then I get an idea: with a signal, I can upload what I recorded as we ran from Thornhanger House to the YouTube channel. YouTube first, and then the phone calls. My stomach fizzes as I think what an amazing teaser the footage will make, drumming up some interest before we can record a full video about our experience: *Our Weekend of Horror at Thornhanger House – What*

Exactly Happened to Zach and Lucas. It'll go viral, for sure.

And if the police can recover our cameras . . .

What will happen when police swarm this place – how will the house react?

Upload complete, I'm about to call my dad when I realize Byron still hasn't shown up. I pause with my thumb hovering above the green phone icon, a chill settling in my stomach. How long has it been? I'd been so focused on the video and the upload that I hadn't noticed he's still not here.

My heart stops.

'Byron?'

I don't understand. He was right behind me. I stand with my hands on my hips and scan the edge of the wood.

'Byron!'

There's no response. I wonder what could be keeping him. Trying to ignore the rising prickles of panic inside me, I call again, 'Byron?'

I peer through the trees, into the gloom. I see nothing, not even a flash of the torch beam. I hear nothing but the morning song of the birds and the gentle rushing of the stream.

'Byron!'

Delaying the phone call just a moment longer, I need to know that Byron's OK. *Of course he is!* I stride through the long grass and flowers, back towards the stream's bank. But I fall. Over what, I'm not sure. And I'm tumbling and the world is spinning and I'm not sure which way is up and which is down. It's like when I got caught in a big wave in the sea as a little kid. It picked me up and it threw me about and I went over and over; my head was sucked below the surface of the water, and I couldn't see or breathe and I thought I would drown, until the wave spat me out. I'm tumbling now, over and over, and I hear a crack, followed by a sharp, sudden pain in my neck. I wonder what it is – is it me, have I broken something? The pain is fleeting. It must have been a fallen branch snapping beneath me.

And then I'm on my feet in the meadow. But it's like someone has turned the contrast down. It's still sunny, but everything is muted, and I can't feel the warmth of the sun on my skin, but I'm not cold either, and I can't make out the yellow flowers from the blue ones, which is strange, and disorientating and confusing.

In a daze, I carry on towards the stream.

'Byron?'

'Byron!'

'BYRON!'

Each call more desperate than the last.

'BY—'

There! I hear him call. It's distant and distorted, but it's him. Unmistakably him. I release a held breath. He's in the wood. He can't be far behind me.

'Byron! Over here! BYRON!'

I splash back into the stream. I keep calling his name, over and over, hoping my voice will lead him to me. But when I hear his cry again, I'm not sure if it's any closer.

'BYRON!'

I try calling my dad, but I don't hear it ring on the other end. Just static. I try Mum. Poppy. Amba. I call 999. Again, nothing but the hiss and crackle of static. *What's going on?* I can't feel the icy water of the stream. I can't feel anything. And although I'm in the stream, I can't make it to the other side. Like trying to join the same poles of two magnets, the bank on the other side of the stream seems to be pushing me away. But that's crazy. It makes no sense at all.

'BYRON!'

I hear a distraught, almost angry cry, definitely closer this time. I know it's Byron. But I can't see him.

'Byron!'

Shadows shift deep inside the wood. 'Byron?' I hold my breath, squinting into the gloom. Movement between the trees catches my eye and – yes – I spot him marching through the undergrowth, towards the stream.

'Byron! Over here. I'm here!' I call and wave my hands above my head to get his attention, relief flooding me. But the relief is short-lived when he doesn't break his stride. 'Byron! *By*?' I go still. He doesn't see me, even though I'm just across the stream. He doesn't hear me, no matter how loud I call his name. 'BYRON!'

A few metres from the edge of the wood, on the opposite bank, he stops. His features are twisted and red with rage. I gasp as his steely eyes settle on me. No, not on me, but right through me, like I'm not even here.

'By? *Byron*?' I say, my voice cracking with fear and

uncertainty. 'Byron, please. I'm here. See me. *Please*.' He doesn't respond. I can only watch as his eyes grow suddenly wide and his mouth gapes open, silently at first, and then he screams. A piercing, unnatural, blood-chilling scream. I put my hands over my ears but the sound cuts through me, before stopping so abruptly that I think I must have lost my hearing. Byron drops heavily to the ground.

'BYRON!' I scream, but he doesn't move. He's nothing but a lump in the shadows.

'BYRON! BYRON! BYRON!'

I try and try and try to cross the stream, exhausting myself with the effort. I try to get back over the property line to reach him. To see if he's OK. But Thornhanger House will no longer let me in.

EPILOGUE

'WHAT'S UP, GUYS! It's Iris, Molly and Byron here.'

'Hi, guys.' Molly leans in for a close-up and sticks out her tongue. 'What's up!'

'Yo.' Byron makes a peace sign to the camera. 'We're *baaaaack*.' He spreads his arms wide as he grins to the camera, leaning over the others and taking up most of the frame.

Iris jostles Byron playfully from where she sits between him and Molly on her neatly made bed, so that she is, again, centre stage. 'So, we're coming to you today with this teaser trailer for our up-and-coming *Hunting for Zach and Lucas* video. As regular viewers of our channel and of Zach and Lucas's channel will know, they went missing last Halloween. And we've been searching for them ever since.'

'As well as visiting some creepy locations and making

some cool vids along the way,' says Molly.

'But now . . . pause for a drum roll –' the sound of Byron playing a drumbeat on Iris's knee – 'we think we've tracked them down.'

'Dun dun duuun!'

'And,' continues Iris, 'this weekend—'

'For the *whole* weekend!' Molly cuts in.

'We're going to be shooting somewhere pretty special.'

'So, keep an eye out for the video, guys – coming your way soon!' says Byron. 'It's going to be awwwwesome,' he adds, with more than a hint of irony to his voice, as if he doesn't believe it's going to be awesome at all.

'It *is* going to be awesome,' says Molly, with a sitting-down shoulder-roll dance move.

'Yeah, we're pretty excited about this one,' says Iris, pushing a rebellious curl from her face. '*Annnnd*, just to up the pressure . . . we think it's the One. Lucky number thirteen.'

'*You* think this is the one, Iris,' says Byron. 'We're just along for the ride.'

'Thanks for putting a downer on things, By.'

'It's called being realistic,' he says, before sticking his tongue out at Iris. 'And I'm just doing ma job, ma'am. Keeping it real.'

'Yeah, well. Whatever, dude. This is going to be one epic video that you, our lovely viewers, will NOT want to miss. We've discovered some seriously creepy info about our. Top. Secret. Location. So, *whatever* happens, this next video is going to be our best ever!'

'Make sure you tune in, guys! For epic fun times,' Byron adds, irony creeping back into his voice.

'And make sure you subscribe for all our latest updates,' says Molly, with a sweet-as-pie smile.

'Like and subscribe! And we'll see you next week,' says Iris, pointing at the camera with a finger-gun.

She is about to sign off, but Byron cuts in, 'You know, most teenagers play video games or go out and party or hang on the weekends, but we have sleepovers in creepy-as-[bleep] abandoned buildings.'

'You live for it, Byron,' says Iris, nudging him in the side. Byron playfully pinches Iris, and the pair laugh and wrestle on the bed, while Molly stares at them from the side, her eyes slightly narrowed, while she chews on the cuff of her sweatshirt. But as she remembers the camera, she brightens into a smile.

As she and Byron continue to play-fight, Iris says to camera, 'Like and subscribe, and we'll see you soon!'

A close-up of Iris's palm fills the screen as she reaches forwards and turns the camera off. The screen goes black.

COMING SOON – The next Hunting for Zach and Lucas video: THIS TIME IT'S THE ONE!!!

102,769 views • 5 June

Channel Fear

54,845 subscribers

Lolly Pop 9 days ago

Good luck, guys. I look forward to seeing the video! 

JakeBaker 9 days ago

"This time it's the one" Not going to hold my breath lol

K_ate_R 9 days ago

Give it uuuuuuuuup!!!

Rachel L 8 days ago

Hey. Where you guys going? Sounds awesome!

Matty 7 days ago

Let me guess... they weren't there...

The gloomy interior of a large dank room can be seen, shot through a smashed window. Tall bookshelves line a couple of the walls but other than that, the vast space is bare. Abandoned. It's hard to make much out as the camera moves backwards, but the long shadows that fall into the room through a doorway towards the far-left corner appear to shift and grow longer, as if someone is about to emerge at any moment.

As the camera swings round, there is a glimpse of Byron, and then another shift and all that can be seen in frame is the overgrown grounds, lit by a torch beam in the dawn. The camera shows a jerk of forward motion, before it stops and swings to the right to catch Byron at the edge of the frame as he appears to be drawn closer to the person behind the camera. The footage sweeps downwards to show a shot of the tangle of weeds and long grass and one Converse-clad foot, going in and out of frame as the footage shakes.

Off camera, Iris's voice says: 'By. What I tried to tell

you earlier . . .'

Byron: 'Not now. We—'

Iris: 'Stop. Just listen. I have to get this out. I should have had the courage to tell you this long ago: the reason I never let anything happen between us isn't because I never felt *the same*, it's because I never felt *good enough*. For you.'

Byron: 'What?'

Iris: 'I worried that it – us – would be another thing for me to fail at and I would ruin our friendship. Because I'm useless at everything. And I'd lose you for good. So, I let my stupid crush on Zach get in the way of my feelings for you. Because it was safer. But it's always been you, By. Always.'

There's a pause of a few beats and then the footage rocks forward just slightly, before shakily swinging up and around, revealing a brief glimpse of Byron, his eyes glistening, a tight half-grin on his lips. It settles to show what's behind Byron, back towards the grounds at the front of the house, the footage at an angle.

Caught in the distance, unnoticed by Iris and Byron, is Molly. Half shrouded by the soft shadows of dawn, she's statue-still as she stares towards Iris and Byron, as if taking in the betrayal. Eyes wide and wet with tears that flow and cut streaks down her dirty cheeks. Mouth hanging open. She's holding what looks to be a car battery.

From off-screen, Byron says: 'I love you, Iris.'

Iris: 'I love you, Byron.'

The footage draws back to show Byron in frame as Iris

points the camera at him, though Molly can still be seen in the background, still unnoticed. With a wistful smile, Byron reaches out a hand that disappears behind the camera.

Byron: 'You're an idiot.'

Iris: 'I know.'

As she watches, Molly's features darken. She shakes her head slowly. Measuredly. In a way that is most un-Molly-like. Slowly, she backs away one step. Two steps. Gripping the car battery in front of her like a prize, she turns from her friend and boyfriend and strides in the direction of the main gate and Byron's mum's car.

Leaving Iris and Byron to Thornhanger House . . .

OUR ESCAPE FROM HORROR HOUSE! We know what happened to Zach and Lucas teaser video!!!

212,466 views • 7 June

Channel Fear

54,845 subscribers

Andrea_Wilson 7 days ago

WFT is this?!

Emmy K 7 days ago

Guys. Is this a joke? I mean, it's pretty messed up if this is a joke. How do you think Zach and Lucas's families would feel watching this?

Summer Day 7 days ago

OMG! I can't believe they're missing 🙁 They're actually missing. Just like Zach and Lucas!!!

Jay J 6 days ago

FFS! Fake!!! This is just a publicity stunt. They're not missing. It's just been a few days

Luna_girl03 5 days ago

Where r u guys? Hope ur OK. I love ur vids. This one is sooo creepy! Really had me going for a bit what with all the missing rumours. And when Molly goes off after seeing Iris and Byron confessing their love but they don't know they've been seen! 😦😦 The drama 😲 And the whole 'We don't know where Molly is...' speech at the end – so clever! Glad ur getting lots of views and subs now ❤️ More of this found-footage/short-movie style content, pleeeeease. It really works!

> **Sara Marie** 3 days ago
>
> Yeah, I don't think this is fiction. I'm thinking this is real...?

Lost boy129 5 days ago

Did you really find Zach and Lucas or was it the abominable snow-man?!!! 😆

Fred a bear 5 days ago

Did u find Elvis?

Sara Marie 3 days ago

OMG!!! This is serious. They're missing! I can't believe some of you are treating this like a joke! Some of these comments... ☹️

Cute Cat 2 days ago

You guys are coming back, right?

Jess Long 1 day ago

Guys! Are you out there? Post an update. We need to know you're OK.

Acknowledgements

Writing *Channel Fear* has been such an incredible experience. Not just because I've been able to spend so much time thinking about dark and spooky things but because I've got to work with some amazing and inspiring people, all of whom have made this book so much better than I could have wished for.

A world of thanks to my editor, Kesia Lupo. It's been such a joy to work with you. Thank you for believing in Iris, Molly and Byron and in me as an author. Your brilliant edits have honed this book and made my dream come true. I owe you so much gratitude. A huge thank you to Barry Cunningham and all the wonderful folks at Chicken House: Rachel Hickman, Elinor Bagenal, Rachel Leyshon, Esther Waller, Laura Myers, Jazz Bartlett Love, Olivia Jeggo and Emily Groom-Collis. It's a pleasure to work with you on this fabulous journey, and I feel so lucky to have had this opportunity. You really are the best team ever!

None of this would have happened if it weren't for my amazing agent, Lydia Silver. Thanks for believing in me and for your guidance and patience over the years. You have brought so much to this story with your fantastic ideas and insights. I can't thank you enough.

Thanks also to Andrew Davis for the stunning cover

design. And to my eagle-eyed copy-editor, Fraser Crichton, thank you for saving me from certain embarrassment. (I'll never write draft when I mean draught again!)

To my wonderful sons, Tom and Dexter. You never cease to amaze and inspire me with how awesome and talented you both are. I'm so proud of you. Dexter, thank you for introducing me to the world of YouTube ghost-hunters. Thornhanger House would not exist without you.

A special thank you goes to the urban explorers and ghost-hunters of YouTube who spend nights in haunted and abandoned buildings so that I don't have to – who am I kidding, I'd love to. Please send invites! In particular, thanks to Exploring With Josh, Exploring with Fighters, and Sam and Colby. Book research has never been so much fun (I wasn't just binge-watching YouTube videos while eating snacks, I was working hard, I promise!). Extra-special thanks go to the brilliant Elton Castee, Corey Scherer and all of the wonderful OVERNIGHT/TFIL team. Guys, thank you for the inspiration. *Channel Fear* began as a nugget of an idea while binging your TFIL videos several years ago, and I've been a massive fan and avid viewer ever since.

Finally, to everyone who has chosen this book, I thank you so much. It means the world to me, and I hope you enjoyed reading it as much as I enjoyed writing it.

TRY ANOTHER GREAT BOOK FROM CHICKEN HOUSE

THE LOOP by BEN OLIVER

Luka Kane will die in the Loop, a prison controlled by artificial intelligence. Delays to his execution are granted if he submits to medical experiments, but escape is made impossible by the detonator sewn into his heart.

On Luka's sixteenth birthday, the monotony of life in the Loop alters: the government-issued rain stops falling and rumours of outside unrest start to spread.

This might be his one chance to escape – and to stop the deletion of humankind . . .

A terrifying and sinister look into the future that will leave your jaw on the floor.

KASS MORGAN, AUTHOR OF *THE 100*

Paperback, ISBN 978-1-912626-55-7, £8.99 • ebook, ISBN 978-1-912626-61-8, £8.99